Wind and the Rocs

by
Gary Halleen

This novel is dedicated to my beautiful wife, Pamela, as well as my children, grandchildren, brother, sister, and father. Many of you will notice I used variations of your names in my story. I hope you don't mind. Pam, you especially read every page multiple times, gave me ideas, and were more supportive than I could have imagined. This book is for you, because it never would have happened without you.

You were all so helpful as I put my story into words. I can't express how much I appreciate your reading my story and giving me feedback. You encouraged me to take a story I've been telling people for the past 15 years and make it real. Thank you, and I love you all!

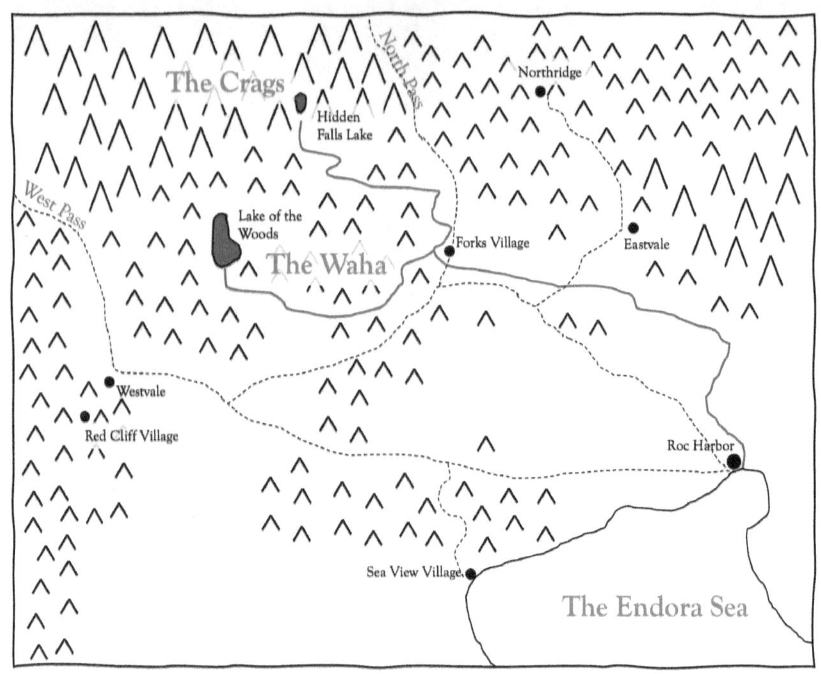

Map of the Cragwoods

Northern Isles
Loma City
The Northern Channel
Gollbourg
Daener City
Loma
The Great Sea
The Crags
Hidden Falls Lake
The Waha
Lake of the Woods
North Pass
West Pass
Forks Village
Newbridge
Eastwick
Westville
Red Cliff Village
Ice Harbor
Sea View Village
The Endora Sea

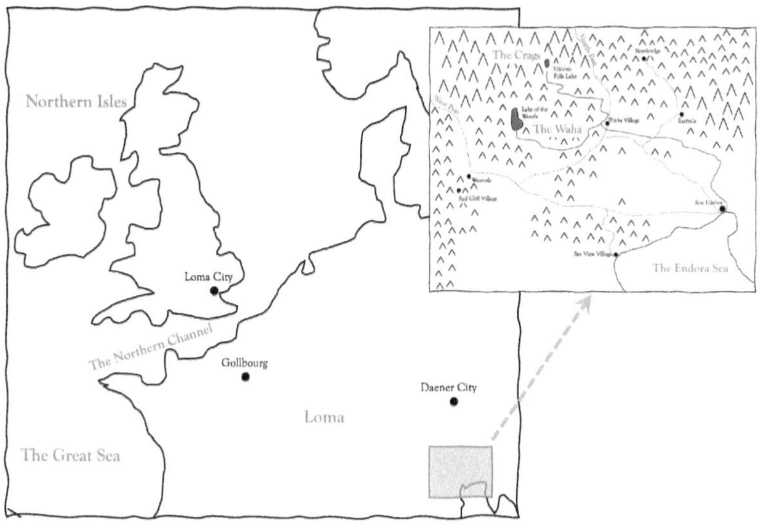

Map of Loma

Part I

1
Life in the Cragwoods
The Roc

The huge grey bird sat atop his perch, high in the crags, overlooking a lush, green forest. The sun was just rising in the east – peeking over the tips of the mountains, and waking up the forest below. He spread his wings and gave them a brief shake to knock the dewy moisture from his feathers. His stomach grumbled as he looked at each wing, and admired their shape and breadth. Fully 20 feet long, each wing was perfectly colored. He was one of the largest rocs in the crags, and the soft, greyish white of the wing bottoms blended in well against a cloudy sky, as there commonly was in the land surrounding the mountains. The tops of his wings were mostly grey with patches of light brown.

A few minutes later, and the sun was shining on his back. It was going to be warm and sunny today. Hunting would be a bit of a challenge. He wouldn't want to spook any game by flying openly over the clearings. Today he'd need to be stealthy. On overcast days, he'd hunt from high up, just below the clouds, and let his wings blend into the clouds, trusting his sharp eyes to spy his meal in a clearing, or drinking from a creek. Today was sunny with no clouds. He'd skim just over the treetops, watching, listening, and smelling – and hoping – to surprise an animal in a clearing. He didn't like being hungry.

He stood and spread his wings. Then, looking towards a clearing in the distance – maybe 60 or so miles away – he leaned forward, pushing hard with his powerful legs, and then beat down hard with his wings as he fell from the crag. In just a second or so, he felt the updraft catch his enormous wings, and he soared.

The great roc beat his wings to pick up speed, and banked to the right, heading toward the small high-mountain lakes. From a distance, he looked much like a very large eagle. Up close, one could see the differences. Besides wingspan, his body was proportionately larger. His legs were very meaty and strong, with large, sharp talons.

He might get lucky, and find a mountain goat or sheep in the open, or maybe even one of the tasty red stags, catching a drink in a lake. He kept an eye towards the smaller cliffs near some of the lakes, watching for wood rocs – a smaller, more agile, roc. Wood rocs were too small to pose much of a danger to him, but they liked to attack anything intruding in their space, and could take large bites if he didn't see them first. The only time they were a real danger was if two or three attacked at the same time.

As he flew over the small lakes, all he saw were small morsels. Not even worth the energy of catching them. Just some fish near the surface, and a small lynx crouching near the water waiting for one of the fish to venture too close. A single wood roc screeched at him and gave a short chase before giving up. He looked with scorn at the smaller bird. He banked slightly to the left and headed to the clearing. This particular clearing was a new favorite of the roc.

Several years ago, lightning struck some of the large, leafy trees during a storm, causing a forest fire, which burned hot and destroyed many of the tall trees. It left behind a large clearing over a mile long where the fire followed a large stream through a rocky canyon. He'd often find deer, or sometimes large cats, too focused on feeding or drinking to be watching the sky.

It took over an hour before he got close to the clearing. Along the way, he passed a few other older, smaller, clearings, but hadn't found his breakfast yet. He dropped lower, until his great size was skimming just above the trees. He smelled meat ahead, and readied his talons. Just a couple hundred yards before the clearing, he startled some two-legged prey. The two humans went diving from the tops of one of the trees into the branches below. Disappointing! He hadn't expected to see them, and wasn't able to grab either of them before they darted away. That was too bad. Humans made a tasty change to his diet, and it had been a while since his last taste of one.

He forgot about the humans as he swept along the edge of the clearing and spied a large elk munching on some berries in the clearing below. It was looking down at the bushes and didn't notice the big bird speed by. The roc flew past and then circled back to the clearing. He beat his wings a few times to pick up extra speed, and dropped to the forest floor, almost 200 feet below the tree tops, aiming right for the elk. The unfortunate animal looked up just in time to realize his fate and take two ineffective leaps towards the trees before the roc's sharp talons seized the elk, pulling him from the ground, up into the air. It was a large elk, with a full rack of antlers. What a prize! The roc would have a full belly today.

His wings beat hard to pull the elk far into the air. The elk struggled for a few minutes, but its breathing and muscle spasms would stop before they made it back to the crags.

A Close Call in the Trees

Two boys, both in their mid-teens, climbed the stairs alongside the tree trunk into the upper branches of the canopy. Up here, 200 feet or so above the ground, the branches were much smaller than the huge branches below, where most of the houses were built. This high up, wind moved the branches quite a bit. However, light filtered through the leaves and it was great for gardening. Along the branches were garden boxes used to grow much of the food and medicine used throughout the village of Westvale. It was early morning – just after sunrise – and the gardeners hadn't climbed the stairs yet to tend to their plants.

The weather was supposed to be sunny and hot today, which meant the ripplefruit would be extra sweet, and the boys intended to get as many as they could before others arrived. Ripplefruit was always good. On a normal day, they were fist-sized and tangy-sweet, with a flavor like peach combined with watermelon. However, on hot sunny days, they produced a lot more sugary nectar, swelling to about half again as large in just minutes, and becoming almost addictively sweet. The vines grew in the very top of the canopy, with their roots parasitically attaching to the limbs of the ironwood trees. If the boys got there before the gardeners, they'd be able to actually watch them swell in size when direct sunlight was on them. They could eat a couple themselves, and then bring a few more back down to share with friends. Once the gardeners arrived, they'd be chased off. Ripplefruit were a favorite ingredient in wines the village sold to neighboring regions.

The easiest way to the top of the canopy was to follow the steep stairs as high as possible, and then climb a knotted rope to the roc platform. At the top of each village was a special platform for riders to land their rocs. These wooden decks varied in size from as small as 10-12 feet, to as large as 150 feet. Westvale's platform was one of the largest, and served as host for activities when many riders were in the village at the same time. A rope ladder was rolled up on the platform, and could be dropped onto the highest stairway landing from above. If the ladder wasn't already rolled down, someone needed to shimmy up the knotted rope and release the ladder. The elders liked the ladder to be put away when not in use, as that supposedly prevented youths from climbing onto the platform.

As they reached the highest landing, Caes looked at his best friend, and said, "Well, Jory, you wanna drop the ladder?" Neither liked volunteering to climb the 30-foot long rope to the platform.

"Oh, no, Caes! You suckered me into climbing last time. It's your turn." Jory affectionately punched his buddy in the arm. Jory was 15, but looked older. He had long, dark brown hair, pulled into a ponytail, and was wearing shorts and a leather sleeveless shirt. He was lean and tall, but muscular for his age.

"Hm. I was hoping you forgot," said Caes. He grinned at his friend. "Fine. Don't shake the rope on me."

Caes, also 15, but looking a bit younger, scratched his head through his short blonde hair, and grabbed the rope. He climbed rapidly up, and when he was about half-way, Jory grabbed the rope and started swinging it around.

"Knock it off, Jory! I'm gonna kick your butt!"

"Yeah, I know. You always say that, but I'm still waiting," Jory shouted back.

When Caes reached the top, he pulled himself up onto the platform, and released the rolled-up rope ladder. The end of it hit the landing in front of Jory, who wrapped the loose ends around the hooks in the landing, and then climbed rapidly to the top.

Both boys knelt at the edge of the platform and searched the skies for a few minutes, hiding beneath the branches of the trees. The sky was blue, with not a cloud to be seen. The sun was just over the top of the distant Crag Peak Mountains. They saw a few small birds flying around, and off in the distance, it looked like some rocs were flying, but there were none in the immediate area.

"Okay, let's go," Jory said, patting Caes on the back. Hunched over, they both ran along the edge of the platform, all the way to the opposite side. Even though the sky looked clear, they didn't want to tempt a passing roc by walking straight across the center of the platform, away from shelter.

When they got there, they saw that none of the ripplefruit were growing close to the platform. The closest cluster was a good eight or ten feet away, wrapped around some high branches. It looked like the gardeners had already harvested the fruit up here. If they wanted some for themselves, they were going to need to climb off the platform into the treetops.

"Oh great," said Caes. "Did you bring a rope?"

"Yeah," said Jory, as he pulled a thin coil of rope from his waist pouch. "Here, you're smaller than me. You go get them."

Oh great, thought Caes. He knew Jory was right. The branches this high were pretty small. He and Jory were probably both too heavy, but Caes was lighter than Jory, and he was too stubborn to give in and suggest they give up, and go back down. He took the rope from his friend, and tightened a loop in the end of it, wrapping it around his chest, and testing it to make sure it wouldn't slip.

"I guess I've gotta," he said. "Are you going to hold your end, or tie it to something?"

"Let's tie it," said Jory, and he dropped to his knees to tie the other end of the rope around a support beam for the platform. He pulled the slack out, measuring it in his arms. "It looks like it's about 15 feet or so."

"Alright," said Caes. He squatted on his heels, and scanned the skies again, slowly looking in a full circle. Jory did the same. After a minute, he shrugged, and said, "Well, here goes."

He swung his arms, and dove out to grab the nearest branch. He got ahold of it, and held on while the branch bobbed and swung back and forth from this weight. Man, if his parents saw him now, he'd be dead! He was dangling in the top of a tree, high above the ground, hoping the branch and rope were both strong enough to hold him. Caes swung his leg over the branch and started crawling to the next branch, willing himself to be lighter.

When he reached the cluster of fruit, he took his knife from its sheath and started cutting the first yellow ball of ripplefruit from the vine. When it came free, he tossed it to his friend, and started cutting the next. There were about ten of the fruits here. He was glad they were all close together because he didn't want to try climbing to the next cluster.

As he reached down to start cutting the final fruit from the vine, he looked up to say something to Jory, and then forgot everything, including what he was doing. Straight in front of him, just a few feet above the trees, was a huge Great Roc barreling down on them both!

"Watch out!" he screamed, and dove into the trees. He missed the branch he reached for, and fell, jerking to a stop when the rope reached the end of its slack. He dangled 15 feet below the platform.

Jory threw himself flat onto the deck, as he craned his head around to see what Caes was yelling about. All he got a chance to see was a huge shape speed over him, talons grabbing air close to where he'd just recently been kneeling. He scurried forward, and dropped over the edge of the platform, hanging onto the edge with his hands. He pulled himself up so his chin lifted above the edge, and looked all around. The roc didn't swing back around for a second pass.

"Caes, you alright?" he yelled.

"I think so," he heard in response. Below him, Caes was kicking his feet, trying to swing himself towards a branch. He finally got his feet wrapped around it. "Was there a rider on him?"

"I don't think so. It looked like a wild one", said Jory. "I think he was hunting. Oh man, he barely missed me! This sucks. I think I peed myself."

Caes started laughing. "Oh yeah, you're a big tough hunter! Oh man, my ribs hurt.   Do you think you can pull me up? I feel like a bruised wind chime."

Jory answered, "Yeah, just a minute, okay? I'm still shaking."

A couple minutes later, with Jory pulling on the rope, he swung his leg up over the edge, and pulled himself back on top of the platform. He stayed low, and then slowly scanned the sky again. It looked clear, so he stood up and scanned it again. His legs were shaking bad, and he felt the urge throw up. He'd nearly been breakfast for a hungry giant bird.

"That stupid bird made me lose my knife," Caes said. "It fell when I jumped. Cut me loose, okay? I need to get to the ground and find my knife before my dad sees it's missing." Jory took out his own knife, and cut the rope free from both the platform and his friend. Then he coiled the rope up, and the two of them grabbed the fruit that were now scattered around the platform. They shoved them into a bag they brought with them, and then ran back around the edge of the platform to where the ladder led back down to safety. Caes climbed down the ladder and untied it from the landing, and waited while his friend secured the ladder on top and slid down the knotted rope.

When they were both on the landing, they both started chuckling, then laughing so hard that both had to sit and wait for their laughing to subside.

"No more excitement today, right?" said Caes. His friend punched him in the shoulder, smiling, as the two of them started back down the stairs to the village. This was going to be a great story to tell their friends!

The Rangers

Catscratch looked up at Ben, his apprentice, who was high up in a tree. Ben, painted a camouflage pattern of browns and greens, and wearing filthy leather pants and shirt, leather boots, and carrying a longbow over his shoulder, looked down at Catscratch, who was dressed very similar to him, except the older ranger was carrying a spear, and had a short sword strapped to his back.

"What did you see?", Catscratch signed to Ben.

"Birds just flew up behind us a hundred yards away", Ben replied, in the sign language. *"I think something is stalking us."*

Catscratch grumbled. He wasn't looking forward to climbing, but maybe they should sit up in the tree and wait for a while. *"Alright. I'll climb up and sit for a bit. Maybe see what's following us."*

He climbed up into the tree about 20 feet, and found comfortable branches to sit on. Ben climbed down from his higher perch and joined him. They sat quietly. Catscratch reached into his hip bag and pulled out some dried fruit. He quietly chewed his snack.

Ten minutes later, a grey tiger crept below the tree, sniffing the air. Ben and Catscratch watched the large cat below them. Ben raised his eyebrows as he looked at the old ranger, silently asking if he should do anything.

The ranger signed *"let her go"* to Ben. Most people in the village
didn't care for feline meat. Animals tended to taste like what
they ate. Grey tigers fed on just about any meat they could find,
including human, as well as leftover kill they happened upon.
While the hide would be nice, he didn't want to kill something
he wouldn't want to eat.

After the tiger finally moved away from the tree, and wandered
back into the forest, they waited another 20 minutes to give the
tiger time to, hopefully, find something else to stalk.

The two climbed down the tree, took note of the tiger's tracks,
and continued towards their destination. Today they were
headed for the Canyon Creek burn clearing. It wasn't in the
same direction as the tiger was headed, but they'd remain
vigilant, regardless.

The burn clearing wasn't too far from them, or from Westvale.
Lately, it was a good hunting ground. With luck, Ben would be
able to bag a nice deer this morning. Unless they had to hide
again from the tiger or one of the other denizens of the forest,
they should be there within the next 15 minutes or so. They
should have plenty of time to hunt, and make it back to
Westvale before dark. Otherwise, they'd have to find or build
shelter for the night.

They walked along a game trail for a bit, and then Catscratch
climbed up onto a boulder to look around. The old ranger
pulled off his floppy hat, and scratched what remained of his
grey hair. He looked to the east and saw the sun peeking over
the crags. It looked to be a very nice day. He was looking
forward to retiring soon, and sleeping every night in the
comfort of his home in the village rather than wedging himself
into a nook in a tree, or hiding in a hole or other makeshift
shelter. The tree he and Ben slept in last night left a crook in his
back that made it hard to walk fast today.

Once he retired, maybe he'd even consider moving to Roc Harbor and live in a real house on the ground. Probably not, though. He'd been here in the vale for so many years, it would be hard to move back to civilization.

Cragwoods, the forests in this part of Loma, were dangerous for anyone. They were home to several fearsome plants and animals. Some were obviously dangerous, like the shadow cat, wild rocs, grizzly bears, and of course, the grey tiger they'd just seen. Others were less obvious, but equally deadly, like the crawling mantrap vine. The vine had beautiful large flowers and a fruit that strongly resembled the ripplefruit that usually grew higher in the trees. The mantrap vine's roots were very shallow, and pulled free from the ground so the vine could crawl across the ground and grab unsuspecting creatures or people.

Few had the skills to survive, solo, on the ground. Many people had succumbed to animal attacks, or been entangled by the mantrap vine and eaten by the carnivorous plant.

Catscratch had been training Ben for the past two years, and couldn't help feeling proud of him. He was a good student. He paid attention, was thoughtful, and nearly ready to take the Ranger's Ordeal, a life-or-death test of skills to see if he was competent to take a ranger's name for himself. During the Ranger's Ordeal, the apprentices were taken, alone, several miles into the forest with only a few survival items: a knife, bow and arrows, flint and steel, and of course, their rangers' flute, which was known as a picco. They had to survive by themselves for an entire week without calling for help. At the end of the week, in order to take on a ranger's name, they had to return with sufficient game to contribute to the celebratory dinner and naming ceremony.

In most years, the naming ceremony and dinner were cause for party. However, frequently, it was a sad affair. Surviving the Ordeal was always an iffy thing. There were many times when students didn't live through the week.

Rangers filled an important role throughout the Cragwoods. With only one real city - Roc Harbor - the Cragwoods was a rough, mountainous, forest filled with dangerous terrain and creatures. There were several villages scattered through the woods. Mostly, these were built vertically in the trees. While various tree species – fir, pine, maple, oak, and more – grew throughout the region, groves of ironwood trees were largest, and the favorite for housing the villages. These trees were sturdy, and grew very large. The tops of these trees regularly rose to over 200 feet. Ironwood trees looked much like very large versions of maples, with branches growing both up into the sky as well as horizontal on large limbs. In addition to their size, ironwoods were different in that they didn't lose all their leaves in the fall and winter. Instead, as new leaves grew, older ones would drop, which meant the trees stayed green and full throughout the year. Homes were built on the largest branches and along the trunk, with wooden or rope paths connecting the homes together.

An untrained person on the ground, alone, could quickly become a meal for any of the creatures found throughout the region. When someone needed to be on the ground, they would use a ranger as an escort to keep them safe. Rangers also spent much of their time hunting for game to keep the villages fed. Lastly, trading wagons going between the villages and Roc Harbor also needed escorts.

Catscratch had trained a number of students over the years, and had decided Ben would be his last. The kid was good. He was seventeen years old, and the short, stocky youth could walk quieter than most rangers. He was quite efficient with his bow, and provided more meat to the village than Catscratch did, himself. He communicated well, too. Sometimes the two of them wouldn't speak a single word to each other for hours at a time, but they could carry out whole conversations with sign language - using hand and finger gestures, the picco, or just body language.

The picco was a short, thin musical instrument about 4 inches long, with holes and a mouthpiece. Each ranger, or ranger apprentice, carried a picco with them in a pocket or around their neck on a string. It had a flute-like tone that carried long distances. Over the centuries, a complete musical language had been created. Rangers used it to communicate when hand signals or talking didn't work. The same language was used by the Roc Riders, who had their own flutes. A riders' flute had two lengths, while the rangers' picco was fixed in length. When collapsed to their shortest length, a riders' flute produced a sound too high for humans to hear, but perfect for calling rocs. Extended, they sounded nearly the same as a picco. Riders and Rangers could communicate from the air to the ground, or vice versa. For example, an injured ranger could call a passing rider and ask the rider to rescue the ranger.

Ben was fluent with his picco, just as he was good in other ranger tasks.

Yes, he was nearly ready for the Ordeal.

Catscratch signed Ben, *"You lead for a bit. I'll follow you."*

Ben nodded and walked ahead of him. Soon, they reached the clearing. As they got to the edge, Ben signed, "*Stop and watch*". Both of them crawled into some bushes and watched the clearing. They spotted a mountain lion in the distance, taking a drink from the creek. Ben said, "*Let's go right. Stay away from the lion*".

The ranger answered, "*Fine. I'll follow*".

They continued along the edge of the clearing until they came to the small canyon. Ben spotted fresh sign on the ground. "*Elk. Very fresh. Moving this direction. Looks like a bull*".

"*Let's get him*", said Catscratch.

"*I'll climb the cliff and look for him*", said Ben. He slung his bow over his shoulder and climbed up the cliff face. Catscratch sat among some bushes and looked around, scanning the ground and sky, while also keeping an eye on Ben. He leaned over and picked a handful of huckleberries from a nearby bush and popped them into his mouth.

Looking up, he saw Ben had reached the top of the cliff. Ben signaled, "*I see the elk. 400 yards away*". He pointed in the direction of the elk. Catscratch saw Ben silently mouth some words, and felt a brief tingle of magic. Ben must be getting a closer look.

In a moment, Ben signaled, "*Nice one. He's a five point*". This referred to the number of points on the elk's antlers. A five point meant his rack had five points on each side of his antlers. This was a large, mature elk. "*I'm coming down now*".

The old hunter nodded, and thought the younger hunter's distance vision spell was a handy ability to have. He seemed to be able to cast it easily, and without distracting himself from other tasks. He also seemed to be able to cast it as often as he desired. Catscratch was sure it would be a nice asset for a ranger to possess. His own gifts weren't as directly helpful to his occupation. Although, he had to admit, he loved his ability to magically heat his food, or himself, when needed. As well, his gift allowed him to make his own dried fruit!

Once Ben reached the ground, the two hunters continued moving silently towards the elk. As they got closer, they were careful to keep their scent away from the elk. It had found a nice grove of berries, and was feeding on them.

Catscratch signed, "*Go ahead. I'll wait here for you*". The two of them were 100 yards from the elk now.

Ben nodded, *okay*, and nocked an arrow as he silently crept ahead.

When Ben got within 40 yards, he dropped to a knee, and readied for a shot on the elk. It was turned away from him, and he didn't have a good shot yet. All he needed was for the elk to turn either left or right, and he could get a nice heart shot.

Ben took a quick look around him to make sure the grey tiger hadn't crept up on him again. He didn't think he had, because Catscratch would have warned him, but it was good to be safe. Seeing nothing following him, he turned back to the elk, and saw that it was turning to the left. Perfect! The elk looked around, like he felt like he was watched. Ben lowered himself just slightly and waited. The angle still wasn't quite right.

The elk turned a bit more, and now the shot was perfect. Ben
raised slightly, and pulled the bow string back to his ear as he
sighted in on the heart of the elk. Right as he was relaxing his
finger to shoot, the elk spun his head around, looking right over
Ben's head, and leaped forward. Ben's arrow was in the air, but
it bounced off a rock where the elk was supposed to be. He
swore as he grabbed another arrow and watched as a huge
great roc came directly over his head and seized the elk with his
strong, sharp, talons. Next thing he knew, the bird and elk were
both hundreds of feet in the air, and disappearing rapidly.

Crap!

Oh well. Back to the hunt to find something else.

2
Crislan

Brun Updraft stood on the wooden platform, high in the canopy of trees, his hands on his hips, as he looked at each of the four boys sitting before him in a semi-circle. Brun was a short, stocky man of about 50, with his brown hair mostly grey now. He had a short well-trimmed beard that was also grey. The boys, all in their mid-to-late teens, were chatting quietly as they watched the four large birds attached to the platform on the opposite side from them. Each boy were wearing leather pants and jackets, just as Brun was. The platform was large, well over 100 feet wide.

Brun cleared his throat, and said, "All right guys. Listen up."

He waited a moment while the boys stopped talking and watched him instead of the rocs.

"Today, you're going to take turns with these birds. These aren't the easy, well-trained birds you're used to. These are all young and barely trained. As far as you're concerned, they're completely untrained. Is that clear?"

He looked slowly at each boy. "You're each going to rope a bird and pretend this is the Trials. Any questions?"

One of the boys, a dark haired teen, named Jatt, raised his hand. "Brun, does this mean we're all ready for the Trials?"

"No, it doesn't", Brun replied. "One or two of you are probably ready. The rest are getting close, but not quite there yet."

"Am I ready?", Jatt pressed.

"I haven't decided yet. What do you think?", asked Brun. "If you're ready, I'll let you know after today. Okay. Crislan, you're first. Pick your bird."

Crislan smiled and got to his feet. He was a tall seventeen year-old with medium length blonde hair and a fit body. He grabbed his riding pack and slipped it over his shoulders, and snapped the belt into place. He reached down and took his rope into his hand, and looked towards the rocs. After a few seconds, he took a step in their direction.

Midway across the platform, he stopped and picked up a saddle from the floor.

The teen looked confident as he lightly tossed the loop of rope in his hand, spinning it in a slow circle. He seemed confident as he walked slowly across the wooden platform toward the giant birds. Four great rocs were on the platform, here near Red Cliff Village. Three of them were huge, and one just slightly smaller. Two of the biggest birds were mottled colored, and another of the large ones was black. The smaller one was brown. Each bird had a thick rope tied to its left leg. The other end was anchored through a hole in the wooden decking.

Crislan glanced to the left at the high mountains in the distance, and then at the safety rider gliding in circles above them. Another safety rider sat on his bird near the far edge of the platform.

The teens talked softly amongst themselves, as they all tried to guess which bird Crislan was going to pick this time.

"Go for the black one, Cris!" yelled Jatt. Crislan glanced over at his friend and smiled.

"Quiet, Jatt!", Brun called out. "Quiet, all of you! Remember, during the Trials you won't have trained rocs. They'll be wild, and they'll gut you if you give them half a chance. Concentrate! Lose focus and lose an arm, or your life. Jatt, for yelling, you're carrying water jugs tonight. Pick a buddy to share the fun."

Brun Updraft was a gruff, tough, master. He was a strict coach, and demanded discipline. The group quieted immediately. Carrying water meant Jatt would spend the evening lugging several heavy jugs of water up into the aerie from the stream below. Brun heard groans coming from the boys, and then they all became quiet. None of them wanted to 'share the fun'.

Everyone knew Crislan was an excellent rider. Today was probably his final training flight. As long as today went well, he'd be participating in the Rider's Trials. If he succeeded in the Trials, he'd become a rider, and join his father in the ranks of this elite group who soared above the green, tree-borne countryside, to travel the world.

 "Now, which bird will it be, Cris?" asked Brun, softly.

"The brown, sir", replied Crislan.

"Okay, take it slow now. He's a smaller one, and a bit on the wild side. I figure he's about a quarter wood."

Crislan hunched over slightly and slowly approached the brown roc. Even if it was a bit smaller than the other three birds, it was still taller than he was. Its wingspan must be close to fifteen feet on each wing. If he lost focus, it could easily snap his arm with its beak or grab him with its talons. Up until this week, all the birds had been older and well trained. The birds today were younger, and only partially trained. They were more unpredictable and spooked easily. A fully-grown great roc was large enough to carry away a draft horse. A younger one like this could still carry a grown man with ease.

When he was close, he set the saddle down, and eased closer. He had to get close enough to the big bird to throw the rope over its head, and hold its head down long enough to fasten a breaking harness. Then, place the saddle on its back and cinch it tight. Lastly, pull loose the rope anchoring leg to the platform, scoot up onto its back, and hang on tight. He had to take the roc into the air long enough to gain control of it, and guide it through a set of maneuvers for at least 5 minutes, and then land safely again on the platform.

Crislan remembered how this seemed like a lot when he'd first become a rider student. Now, it was a simple set of maneuvers, assuming the roc didn't try to eat him first.

A wood roc was a smaller species than the larger great roc. You would think the smaller bird would be easier to control, but it was really the opposite. The smaller wood rocs were downright vicious, faster than a cat, and stronger than they looked. They were mostly unbreakable, too. They were just too wily to hang on to. It was a common practice, though, for breeders to try to hatch birds with some woody in them because they'd make better fighting birds. Crislan wanted this brown because it would be good practice for the Trials, when all the birds were unbroken.

As he approached the bird, it backed up half a step. Crislan tossed the loop towards its head, but the bird lunged at his stomach, and the rope missed. He jumped back, and turned to let the beak miss him.

He smiled a bit. He loved the challenge. He stared into the bird's eyes and whispered softly. The spell he used was a simple calming cantrip that would hopefully relax the bird.

He coiled the rope again, and waited a few moments to see if the bird calmed at all. It seemed to relax a bit, so he stepped forward to toss it again. This time, the rope slid neatly over its head, and Crislan pulled down hard on the rope, forcing the roc's head low. Then he stepped on the rope as he tied a quick slipknot around the bird's leg. Having its neck and leg tied together was frustrating to the bird, and kept it distracted while he hurried to fasten a harness around its neck. A few seconds later, and the harness was on.

Crislan grinned. This was going well! He hooked the saddle with his foot and pulled it close. Reaching down, he grabbed it and set it on the roc's back. The bird was getting agitated again, so he whispered the calming cantrip again. Finally securing the saddle, he climbed onto its back. The roc wasn't happy and twisted around to try and reach Crislan with its beak. Crislan tugged on the opposite rein to pull the head back forward, and then reached down and tugged the two ropes free from the roc's leg.

The roc let loose a screech, took two quick steps, and launched straight into the air. Crislan held onto the harness tightly as the bird flew up and veered to the left, before diving and spinning to the right, hoping to throw the boy from its back. Crislan dug his boots into the sides of the bird.

Down below, he heard Jatt yell, "Hang on!"

In a matter of seconds, they were far above the thick canopy of trees. From the corner of his eyes, he could see the two safety riders. Their job was to catch him if he fell off his bird - not that it was likely to happen. Crislan was arguably the best of all the students, and he'd been training for two years already. Riding came natural to him, just like it had to his father, and generations of others in his family before that.

The bird flew higher. Rocs were very fast. In level flight, they could reach speeds of 60mph, although they normally flew a bit slower. They could dive much faster, and that's what the brown roc did now. It tucked its wings and dove into a steep dive towards the trees. Crislan's stomach went into his throat. He pulled back on the reins, pulling the head back, and forcing the big bird to put his wings back out and level out. When the bird leveled out for a couple seconds, he mouthed the calming spell again. Rocs were too big for such a simple spell to have much effect or last long, but it helped slightly, and the bird slowed, and seemed to relax just a bit.

Now, it was time to take control. He pulled the reins to the left, and the roc began to turn. Good! He pulled down and to the left some more, and the roc dropped some altitude and circled back towards the platform. After a couple more minutes of gently turning left and right, he decided it was time to take the roc through the mandatory maneuvers.

Crislan reached into his shirt and pulled out the string holding his riders' flute. With the flute in its longest position, he put it to his mouth and played *"Ready to test"* for Brun and the others to hear. The musical language was required when flying, at least if you cared about others understanding you. With the wind and distances involved, talking or even yelling would be ineffective. The musical notes, and the words and phrases they described, were very valuable. The same flute, collapsed to the shortest position, played notes far too high for a human to hear, but were ideal for calling a roc.

Below him, Brun used his own flute to reply, *"Circle to the left, and then circle to the right."*

He began taking the roc through the mandatory maneuvers. First, he made a full circle to the left, followed by a full circle to the right.

Brun played, *"Good! Now skim the platform."*
Crislan turned the big bird towards the platform, and dove to a few feet above it, and glided past Brun and the three boys watching him. As he gained altitude on the far side, the roc suddenly pulled its wings and barrel-rolled. Crislan nearly fell, but was able to hook his feet and stay in the saddle. He got the bird back in level flight and looked back at the platform. His heart was pounding. That caught him off guard!

Brun played, *"Nice save. Try the skim again."*

Crislan put the bird into a banking left turn until he was lined up on the platform again, and pulled it down into a shallow dive and skimmed the platform about two feet above it. This time, when he gained altitude, the bird behaved.

"Now climb high, and spiral to land."

Crislan pulled up on the reins, and the large bird climbed steeply until he was high enough that the platform could be covered with his thumb, when his arm was fully extended. After this, he flew directly over the platform and pulled back until the big bird nearly stopped. Then he began the slow spiral down to the platform, pulling back on the reins, and landed gently on the wood.

Nearly perfect flight! He held the bird still while one of the Riders tied an anchor rope to its foot, and then slid off the bird onto the platform.

"Nice job, Crislan!" Jatt shouted.

Brun glared at Jatt, and then turned back to Crislan. "It was a nice job, Crislan", he said. "Do that at the Trials, and you'll be a rider." The stocky man grinned and slapped him on the back, and then walked to the remaining students. "Okay, who's next?"

3
Magic Lessons

Caes and Jory sat on a branch on the fourth level of a big ironwood tree, enjoying the fruit of their escapades earlier. This particular branch wasn't used to support any homes yet, and was hidden back behind some large clusters of leaves and branches. The boys considered this their secret hideout. It was three trees west of the roc platform, and a couple levels higher than most of the older homes. With as large as the ironwood trees were, this put them a couple hundred yards away. Both of them had a partially eaten ripplefruit, and were working to finish off the rest before an adult came along to ask where it came from. While it wasn't exactly *wrong* to be eating them, it wasn't considered okay that they'd plucked them from the place they'd been. However, if no one saw, then no one could complain to their parents.

"What are you doing today?", asked Jory. "Well, once you finish eating, anyway?"

"I've got lessons with Maeve. What about you?"

"Writing with mom", said Jory. "I don't understand why she cares so much about stupid letters and stuff. When I get picked by the riders or the rangers, I won't need to know how to write dumb letters."

Both of the boys were about the age when they'd be selected for their career training. Right now, at 15, they were learning the basics that would be needed with nearly every occupation. There was a lot of prestige in becoming a rider or ranger, but there were a lot of other career choices. Most boys and girls had dreams of riding rocs or of fighting lions and tigers and shadow cats, but the reality was most were picked for more mundane jobs. There were needs for a lot of careers throughout the Cragwoods. These ranged from gardeners to healers; from weapons makers to seamstresses; from blacksmiths to home builders.

In a few short months, each trade's master would look at the letters of applications from potential students, and compare them against the needs they had. They'd put together a list of the students they were interested in, and send invitations to the kids and their families. While Jory might be selected to be a rider, or a ranger, there was also a good chance he'd become home builder or smith or something else.

Caes was almost certainly going to be selected as a Rider. His family had a long history as riders. Riders took surnames related to the air or weather. His surname was Wind. He didn't remember who originally chose that name, but it was a great grandparent or maybe great, great, grandparent. They had a long history in the occupation, and it would most likely continue with Caes.

Caes tossed the seed pod from the ripplefruit into the air and wiped his hands on his pants. "Well, I need to get going. Last week I was late to my lesson and Maeve threatened to make me scrub her floors. If I'm late again, she'll make me do it for sure!"

He stood up and waved goodbye to Jory. Then, he headed down the wooden stairs to the third level. From there, he'd make his way north to the big oak tree about half a mile away. There were paths in the trees most of the way, and a couple rope bridges in the only places the paths hadn't grown or been built yet.

Most people in Westvale built homes in big ironwoods, but Maeve had picked a big oak tree. Most of the villagers avoided smaller trees. While the oak was big for an oak, it was tiny when compared to the ironwoods. The house sat about 30 feet above the ground, and was painted a shade of violet. Few homes in Westvale were painted, but for some reason Maeve liked it that way. When Caes made it across the rope bridge from an ironwood tree to Maeve's oak tree, he stopped and shook the bell hanging from the end of the bridge. After a moment, the door to her house opened, and the magician looked out at Caes.

"You're a few minutes early this time, young man", she said.

Maeve was a pretty, petite woman. She had brown hair with a little grey mixed in, and looked like she was in her 40s. Caes wasn't sure of her age, and knew better than to ask.

"Yeah, well…" Caes always felt a little intimidated by the magic user. "I didn't want to clean your floors."

Maeve smiled and said, "Come on in."

Inside, the house was cluttered. Purple flowers, cups, and other miscellaneous items were everywhere. Obviously, she liked the color.

They walked into a back room which happened to be neat and clean, and without purple.
"Take a seat, Caes", she said.

He sat down in one of two chairs, and Maeve sat in the other. Between them was a small table. It was the same room he'd been sitting in once a week for the past several months. If today was like most days, they would visit for a while, and then he'd learn – or at least try to learn – a new cantrip. A cantrip was a weak spell that was quick to cast with little effort. It also didn't do a whole lot of interesting things, but it was fun either way. In the past months, he'd learned a handful of them. For example, he'd learned how to blow a feather across the table. That was his first cantrip. It seemed cool at the time, but now he didn't see any use for it, at all. Another time, he'd found he could use a cantrip to make a glass ball glow with light – only to learn later that it was a magic glass ball in the first place. His cantrip just triggered its embedded spell. Kind of lame.

Last week, he'd learned the same calming cantrip both his mother and brother knew. That one was cool.

Maeve said, "Today I want to give you a test, Caes. You've learned a few cantrips, but I want to know if you have a stronger ability towards a certain color of magic."

Caes looked at her and shook his head. "I don't know what you mean, Maeve. What's the color of magic?"

She stood up and walked into the other room, and came back with a couple cups of water. She reached onto a shelf and took down a jar with tea in it. She scooped some of the leaves into two tea holders and dropped them into the two cups.

"So far, we've learned simple spells, but pretty weak ones that nearly anyone can learn if they try hard enough. We call them cantrips. As spells get more powerful, fewer and fewer people can cast them." She held her hand above her cup and moved it around slowly in the air above the cup, and whispered some words that were hard to hear. Steam began to rise above her cup. After a few seconds, she picked up her cup and took a sip.

"See", she said. "I just used a cantrip to heat my water. I have magical gifts that span a few colors. Think of the colors as an ability to easily work with certain types of magic. Red is fire magic. I can heat the water in my cup easily with it. I can also do this."

She turned and looked at the fireplace along the wall. There were a few logs piled in it. She pointed a finger at the logs and made an odd grunting type of noise that Caes realized were words. The logs suddenly burst into flames.

"I heated the water with a simple cantrip. I lit the fireplace with a red spell." Then, she held her hand in front of her, with the palm up. She spoke another grunting set of words and a flame appeared in her hand. "That's another red spell."

With a wave of her hand, both the fireplace and the flame in her hand disappeared. There was a slight smell of burnt hair in the air.

"My gifts are mostly red. I can also use a bit of brown magic, but not as easily. Brown lets me perform animal magic. The calming cantrip you and your brother know is like that. Only, brown spells are quite a bit more powerful than a cantrip. Are you following me in this?"

This whole idea of magic having colors was new to Caes. He supposed it made a little sense, but it kind of made his head hurt thinking about it. "Yes, I think I'm understanding... Does everyone learn this?"

"No, not everyone does. Most people know they have a gift and can use some cantrips. But they don't learn about colors. You're learning cantrips quicker than most others, so I want to know if you can do more than that. Okay?"

"Yeah", said Caes.

"Okay, good", she said. "What we're going to do today is see if you have any ability to do more than cast cantrips. I'm going to say some words that you may or may not be able to understand. If you understand something, let me know. That'll be the first indication you might have a gift. I know it sounds silly, but you can think of a color as a language as well. Words and sentences will sound like gibberish if you aren't capable of using a color. I can understand most colors only because I've studied for a long time."

She took a sip of her tea. Then she looked at his, shrugged, and heated his up as well. "I forgot you don't know how to do that."

"Now, listen carefully…" and she proceeded to say a bunch of words he couldn't understand.

The next hour went like that. There were a few sentences he could understand, but Maeve didn't tell him what any of it meant.

At the end of the hour, Maeve got up and took two books from a shelf. She carried them to the table and set one of them in front of Caes. "This is a book of brown magic. I suspect you might be able to read it. Open it and see what it says."

Caes opened the cover to the first page. "Okay. Yeah, I can read this. What's the big deal?"

"That's what I thought", she said. "Here. Try this one now." She set the other book down in front of him.

He opened the second book. The pages were covered with unintelligible words. "This looks like a different language. I can't read it."

"That book is red magic. You didn't understand the red magic words I spoke either." She paused for a moment. "Without training, a person with a gift towards a color will be able to understand the words, whether written or spoken. You might not be able to cast the spells yet, but you'll understand them. If you don't have the gift, it'll just be nonsense to you. Later, with training, it's possible to learn how to read or speak the other colors, but not necessarily cast their spells."

"So, are you saying I can be a magician?", Caes asked.

"You seem to have the potential, if you choose to follow that path. If you don't, you'll still have the ability to learn cantrips, but brown ones will be easier and more effective for you than any other colors. Does that make sense to you?"

"I think so", said Caes. "How many colors are there?"

"Ten is the general understanding, although I think there are likely more. Only about six are common", Maeve replied.

"What about Crislan? Did he take this test, too?"

"He did. He was gifted with green, mixed with a little brown. He got the green gift from your mother's side", said Maeve.

"He didn't want to be a magician, though, did he?", said Caes.

"No", she laughed. "Riding is far too important to him."

"Yeah, he's really good at it", said Caes. "He's going to be the best rider in the world. And I'm going to be almost as good when I start riding." A big grin was on his face.

"That doesn't surprise me", she said. "If you change your mind, write a letter of request, and I'll find a brown teacher for you. You could be pretty good at brown magic if you try hard enough." She stopped and watched his face.

"Okay, let's get started on more brown cantrips. For the first, we'll need to be outside. I'm going to try to teach you 'Call Birds'. Brown magic can sometimes let you communicate with animals. Small birds are pretty open to it for beginners. Let's find a quiet space outside and see if you can get a bird to land on your arm." She stood and headed for the door. Caes pushed his chair back, and followed her.

4
Carrying Water

Later in the day, after training was done, all of the riders and students flew back to the aerie to care for their rocs - all except the two students tasked with carrying water, anyway. Jatt and Crislan took tree paths as far as they could, and then needed to climb all the way to the ground. Jatt kicked the rolled-up rope ladder at the final level so it dangled in the dirt below. They were still quite a ways from the aerie, but at the edge of the grove of ironwood trees that made up Westvale. The aerie was about two miles west of Westvale and about three miles north of Red Cliff Village. It served both villages. Trails wound through the forest, connecting the aerie with the two villages, but it was unsafe for individuals to walk them without the protection of rangers.

"Why did you have to pick me?" grumbled Crislan.

Jatt replied, "Well, how many times do you have left? Brun said you're ready for the Trials. And really, who else would I want to share the pain with?"

"Yeah, well, that doesn't mean I want to carry water all the way up to the aerie."

Jatt grinned and climbed down the ladder.

As they climbed down the rope ladder to the ground, they nodded at two rangers sitting on a log.

"Hi Rangers", called Crislan. Then he saw his younger brother sitting across the small clearing on another log. "Hey Caes, what are you doing?"

The first ranger, a young guy named Bonk, waved a hand at Crislan. He was in his early 20s, with a scar on his forehead. He'd smacked his face on a rock during the Ordeal last year, and had been called Bonk ever since. The other ranger was a girl about the same age, with dark reddish brown hair. Her name was Lucky. Crislan was pretty sure all of the rangers knew the meaning behind her name, but no one else did. Crislan had had a crush on her for the past couple of years, but Lucky didn't seem to notice. She gave a short nod in Crislan's direction.

It was common for rangers to be given new names upon successful completion of the Ranger Ordeal. There didn't seem to be any rhyme or reason to the names given. While he knew how Bonk got his name, he wasn't sure on most of the others. Crislan supposed Lucky must have nearly died during her Ordeal. Or, maybe she'd gotten lucky when killing a predator. Or maybe she got lucky and didn't have a lion kill her instead. Someday he might have a chance to ask her. At least, if she ever did anything besides nodding to him.

"Rangers Bonk and Lucky are going to escort you guys," said Caes. "I heard you had a great flight today!"

"Yeah, the whole day was great until my idiot friend here picked me to help him carry water", said Crislan.

Only rangers were allowed on the ground without a ranger for protection. In these forests, there were a lot of very dangerous animals. Bonk smiled and chuckled quietly. Rangers were trained to survive in the dangerous terrain, and were often assigned duty protecting others who needed to come out of the trees or off the cliff. Both rangers had bows in their laps, and swords on their hips.

"Are you two going to help us carry the water?", asked Jatt, looking at the rangers.

"Ha! You're a funny one.", said Bonk. "Who's going to protect you from the shadow cats when our arms are full?"

"Yeah, it was worth a try", said Jatt, as he shrugged and started down the trail. Lucky walked next to him. Crislan, Caes, and Bonk watched them round a corner.

Crislan looked at Caes, and asked, "What do you think, little brother? Do you want some exercise? Maybe carry some water up the hill?"

Caes smiled, and stood. "Sure!" Caes loved being around his brother. He looked up to Crislan like only a younger brother can. As far as Caes was concerned, Crislan was the coolest, strongest, smartest brother anywhere. They were about two years apart in age. Caes would do just about anything for his older brother. The three started down the trail. In a few minutes, they caught up to Jatt and Lucky.

"Hey Cris, did you really ride a woody today?", asked Caes.

His brother replied, "It wasn't a real wood roc, but yeah, it was part woody. It was no big deal."

Jatt said, "It was crazy! I thought Crislan was going to be thrown off. Brun chewed him out for picking that bird."

"I figure, if he doesn't want me to pick a woody, he shouldn't put one on the platform", said Crislan.

Several minutes later, they arrived at the stairs leading up a cliff face to the aerie. There was a creek near the bottom and a storage shed next to it. The stairs went up for as far as one could see. They'd heard there were about 500 steps zigzagging up the cliff. About every 100 steps there was a bench to rest on. Jatt opened the door to the shed and pulled out a stack of buckets. He handed two each to Crislan and Caes, and kept two for himself. They carried the buckets to the stream and filled them with cool water. Once the buckets were filled, the three boys started climbing the stairs to the aerie.

Carrying water was one of Brun's favorite punishments – among a seemingly never-ending list of creative tasks. He liked to make the students carry water to build their strength and endurance on the long, steep, climb. Taking breaks at the benches was against his rules, and if he caught you resting, he'd get even more creative in making you regret doing it. For most of the climb, you couldn't see the ground or the top of the cliff. The boys didn't know how Brun always knew when someone took a break, but they weren't going to chance it.

There were a series of pipes and pumps that provided water to the aerie, so the buckets they carried wasn't necessary. But, Brun liked to keep the students in shape, and on any given day, there were boys and girls carrying buckets of water up the hill throughout the day.

At the top of the climb was a trough of water. The three boys dumped their buckets in, and then started back down the hill. Brun's rules stated "The aerie needs 12 buckets of water each day." That meant at least one more trip up the hill. If Caes hadn't joined them, it would have meant three trips up instead of just two.

Half an hour later, the three dumped their final buckets into the trough. The sun hadn't gone completely behind the trees yet, but it was starting to cool off. The breeze up here at the aerie was nice. The three boys sat down in the shade to catch their breath and wait for their sweat to dry.

Caes hadn't been at the aerie for quite a while. The place was exciting for him. He looked around at it. The aerie was situated on a flat area. It was at the top of a cliff, but with other cliffs rising even higher on each side. The area by the edge of the cliff was big enough for a couple of rocs to take off or land at the same time. This flat area was probably 75 feet across. There was a wooden rail fence near the edge to keep people from falling off. On the far side of the flat area was a large building against a cliff face. It had big doors. The doors were big enough for a roc to walk through if its wings were folded back. This building was where injured rocs could be treated.

On the left and right sides were doorways carved into the rock of the cliffs. Behind the doors were various rooms for riders to stay in, have meetings, and more. The center area, called the Courtyard, had a thatched roof. Community meetings were often held here, although it was a difficult hike and climb to get here from either Westvale or Red Cliff Village. Often, people would catch rides on a roc or in a carriage carried beneath one. Scattered about the cliffs were small ledges the big birds used for their nests. When a rider landed at the aerie, he or she would climb off their bird, remove the harness and saddle, and release the bird. It would either fly to its nest or would go find food.

Brun walked up as they sat. "Well, waddya know? You got a shadow today, Crislan." He nodded at Caes, and said. "Good evening, son. I 'spose you want a ride home, huh?" said the old master rider. "I guess you all deserve it today, even if you did get noisy and obnoxious today, Jatt." He paused to look at Jatt for a moment.

He turned to look at Crislan again. "Good job today, Crislan, with that woody. Just don't do something dumb like that in the Trials. Don't show off! Just pick a bird and break it. No one cares whether you pick a hard roc or an easy one. Just do it, and don't get hurt." He looked Crislan in the eyes until the boy looked away. Then he looked at Jatt.

"Good job with your bird, too, Jatt," he said. "I think you're ready for the Trials, as well." One thing about Brun – he might be gruff, but he also was good with praise when a student did well. "Now, see if you can find a rider or three to fly you all back home. Crislan, Jatt, go stay with your folks tonight. I'm sure they'll want to visit with you after your rides today. I'll see you tomorrow."

Jatt beamed with happiness and gave Crislan a high-five.

"Alright!" said Caes. "Thanks, Brun!" The three of them hurried over to where some riders were sitting around a fire in the courtyard, talking. After a couple minutes, they'd gotten three of the riders to agree to a ride.

5
CC

Crislan and Caes climbed down the tree from the platform to their parents' home, near the bottom level of homes. Their father, Jerod Wind, was a veteran rider, and the village leader of Westvale. As such, and because their lineage of riders was so long, their family had first choice of available houses. The homes lower on the tree were more stable, and didn't move as much when the wind blew.

Jatt's family lived a few levels higher. Both his parents were riders, but his father had been injured a few months ago, and wasn't riding until he healed. In the meantime, he worked in the aerie, helping to care for the birds.

Jerod still flew regularly, but was also required to deal with village issues. He had to fly to Roc Harbor frequently to deal with trade issues and political things. Their mother, Ella was a gardener. She had strong green gifts, making her very good at plant manipulation. Ella sometimes worked in the garden boxes at the highest levels of the trees, and sometimes on other levels, using her gifts to strengthen the paths through the trees, or encourage the trees to grow new paths.

The two boys walked through the door, and saw their parents softly talking in the living room. Both were drinking tea. They looked up when the boys came in.

"Hi CC", their mother said. She smiled at them both. Both boys
hated the nickname their mom loved to use to refer to both of
them together, but they'd long ago given up trying to get her to
stop using it. Whenever they tried to get her to stop, she just
laughed and used it even more often. Their mom was beautiful,
with long blonde hair, and a smile that could improve anyone's
mood. She was taller than most women, and almost tall enough
to look directly into her husband's eyes.
Their father was strong, and just slightly taller than his wife. He
had short, dark hair with hints of grey.

"How was your day, boys?", their father asked.

"It was good", said Caes. "I rode on a roc from the aerie!
What's for dinner?"

"My final Trials rehearsal was today", said Crislan. "It was
pretty good. The bird surprised me, and almost threw me once.
But, I hooked my feet and stayed on." He paused for a minute,
and then continued, "Brun was happy with the ride. Have the
riders decided on where we're holding the Trials?"

"Yes," their father said. "Eastvale was supposed to host it, but
their platform isn't finished yet, so we've decided to hold it
here, instead. The students from Eastvale and Northridge will
be coming next weekend. Your mother and I were just
discussing that. There are going to be 6 or 8 students
participating."

"What are you doing between now and the Trials?", his mother
asked.

"Brun wants me to practice carrying cargo boxes", said Crislan.

Cargo boxes were large freight boxes, and usually had skids or wheels attached. They were loaded with whatever needed to be transported, and a rider and roc would land on or beside it. The box would be attached via straps to a freight saddle, and the roc would leap into the air, jerking the box along with it until airborne. It looked scary to people on the ground or in the trees. But, with an experienced roc and rider, it was a lot scarier to watch than it really was. On small cargo boxes, there was sometimes a wooden bar mounted on the top so a roc could slowly glide to it and snatch the box in its claws without even stopping.

There were a couple of ways to get cargo into and out of the Cragwoods. With very heavy loads, like ore and other rocks, or large tree trunks, the only good way was to load onto a cargo wagon with a team of horses or oxen and slowly pull it along the roads, accompanied by a group of rangers for protection. This was slow, dangerous, and subject to inclement weather. The Cragwoods had a lot of rain, and the dirt roads through the woods could get nasty in a hurry.

For other loads, the preferred transportation was with a roc. The cargo was loaded into cargo boxes, or even nets if the cargo allowed, and flown to Roc Harbor. While the trip was nearly 300 miles (one way), a large roc could make the trip in a day – sometimes two days if the load were heavy enough and the roc needed to stop and rest several times. The largest of the great rocs could carry a large draft horse in weight. That meant over 2,000 pounds of cargo. Most boxes were loaded much lighter than that. When cargo was transported by roc, the trip was relatively quick and safe.

Moving people was similar in both respects. Wagons were often used, especially for new people moving to the villages from Roc Harbor or even the more distant Daener City. A wagon with a family aboard would make the trip from Roc Harbor in two to four weeks, depending on weather conditions.

If the family could afford the luxury, a carriage carried by a roc would make the same trip in a single day. Residents of the various villages could normally catch rides for little or no money, especially if they had goods or skills to trade with. A single passenger would often ride behind the roc's rider in a double saddle, and not need a carriage. In this case, the roc could pour on the speed and make the trip in a matter of a 4 hours or so. The air was chilly when flying up high, though, and the rider and passenger both needed to be properly dressed in riding leathers. Even in the summer, when air temperatures reached into the 90s on the surface, the air up in the sky might drop into the 40s or even colder.

Young riders weren't typically allowed to carry carriages until they amassed enough experience. Most young riders also weren't allowed to carry cargo boxes or nets, but if they showed sufficient promise, they might start early. Crislan being told to practice with cargo boxes was a clear indication of what his trainers felt about his abilities.

"That's good, son", Jerod said. "I'm looking forward to your becoming a rider. I don't carry cargo much anymore, but it would be fun to fly with you as a partner and not just as my son."

"Brun told us there are usually two riders whenever you have cargo to carry. Is that right?", asked Crislan.

"Yes, usually", said Jerod. "For cargo and carriages, both, we like to have two in case there are problems. Sometimes we don't have two riders available, though, but we like to have two whenever we can."

6
Roc Harbor

It had been about a week since Crislan's practice ride. This morning, both boys were eating breakfast when their father came into the room carrying a cup of coffee.

"Good morning!" he said.

"Hi dad" the two brothers said in unison.

"What are your plans for the day?" asked their father.

Caes was busy chewing, so Crislan answered first. "As soon as I finish eating, I'm heading up to the aerie to work with the cargo team. Brun doesn't want me in his regular class this week."

Caes said, "Today's another day with Maeve."

"I'm heading to Roc Harbor with an empty carriage. Do you boys want to go with me? We'll be there for a day or so, and then I'll fly the mayor's family here to watch the Trials next weekend. Cris, we can ask Brun to let you take a roc, and fly beside me, and think of it as additional training. Caes, you can either ride in the carriage, or behind me. Whichever you'd prefer."

"Sure, dad! That sounds fun.", said Crislan.

Caes responded, "Awesome! Can I ride behind Crislan?"

"No, you can't. You can ride behind me. Or if you'd prefer, you can ride in the carriage with your mother."

Jerod took a breakfast roll from the plate on the table, and took a bite, chewing it slowly and finally finishing it. He washed it down with some coffee. He looked at Caes, and said, "Do your riding leathers still fit? You're growing again."

His son looked down at his pants and noticed the pants were riding up his leg. "Uh... Maybe they still fit."

"If they're too short, or too tight, you can wear my old pair. They'll be baggy, but will keep you warm. If you don't like how they fit, you can ride in the carriage."

"Thank you, dad. I don't want to ride like a land walker." Caes was convinced he was going to be the next great roc rider, right after his brother. A rider would never want to sit in a carriage!

"Okay," his father said. "I'm heading to the aerie now to get things ready. I'll speak with Brun when I get there and clear things with him. Caes, you should head to Maeve's place and tell her you'll be gone today. Be up on the platform by 10. Crislan and I will meet you there to pick you up."

"You said mom's going with us?" asked Caes.

"Yes, she's going. She's fixing a broken garden box right now, but she'll be on the platform when you get there.

"Oh... your mom said there might be a dance tomorrow in Roc Harbor. Make sure you both take some nice clothes. I don't know if we'll be at the dance, but your mom will probably push for it."

"Okay, dad", Crislan said. Caes just nodded his head.

At mid-morning, Caes was already on the platform, sitting under a newly-constructed shade cover, eating a ripplefruit when he saw his mother climb onto the platform. The cover did double duty, as it also protected people sitting under it from the talons of a passing wild roc.

"Did you save any of that for me?" his mother asked.

"No, sorry!" Caes replied.

"That's okay, I was just teasing anyway", she said. "Your leather pants look a bit baggy. Are those your dad's?"

"Yeah. Mine were too small and dad let me use his old ones", Caes answered.

Ella was wearing her leather riding clothes, as well. She sat down next to Caes, under the shelter. He looked at his mother and wondered where they'd both ride. He'd assumed his mother would ride in the carriage, but that didn't make sense if she was wearing her leather.

Before he could ask about it, a screech sounded from above, and two rocs – one with a large carriage beneath it – circled down to the platform. The one with the carriage – his father's roc – slowed to almost a hover, and the carriage skids bumped onto the platform. His roc beat its wings hard and came to a landing just in front of it. The other roc – with Crislan riding – landed next to it. His father slid off his bird and walked over to the covered area.

Caes was about to ask his parents about the riding situation when his father beat him to it.

"It looks like you plan on riding the roc rather than inside the carriage, Ella." He paused, and then continued, "You can ride behind me. I guess Crislan can carry Caes. If he's been carrying cargo boxes, he can probably handle his brother without a problem."

Wow! Caes was very excited. He'd ridden as a passenger several times, but never behind his big brother. He reached down and grabbed his mother's travel bag, as well as his own, and carried them both to the carriage. He opened the storage bay door and set them inside.

His father took two rider's backpacks from a strap on his saddle and handed both to Caes. "Here, help your mom put one on, and then strap the other on your back." The packs were heavier than expected. They sloshed like the bladders were full of water. That made sense. It would be 5 hours, or more, in the air. They'd get thirsty. A flexible hose was affixed to the side of each pack, which made it easy to suck some water in when needed.

When they were ready to go, Jerod laced his hands together and made a step for Ella out of them. She put her left foot in his hands, and gracefully stepped up into the rear seat of the passenger saddle. She grabbed the safety strap and wrapped it around her waist and tied it. Jerod reached up and grabbed the saddle horn and pulled himself into his own seat.

Caes walked over to Crislan's bird. His brother leaned to the left and held his arm out. Caes grabbed it, and Crislan pulled firmly, allowing him to pull himself up into his own seat behind Crislan. He reached to his right, and grabbed his safety strap. Once it was securely tied around his waist, he tapped his brother and said, "Alright, I'm all set!"

His dad looked up in the sky and slowly looked all the way
around to make sure other birds weren't flying overhead. In his
left hand was his riders' flute. It was collapsed into the short
position. He ran his hand over the feathers in the roc's neck and
gave a gentle pat. He brought the flute to his lips and played a
note or several. Caes and the others couldn't hear anything
coming from the flute, but both knew the rocs could hear it.
The giant bird shook its wings, and leapt into the air, with the
wings beating rapidly. The straps attached to the carriage lost
all their slack, and the carriage jerked into motion, sliding across
the platform for six or eight feet before lifting into the air.
It was awesome to watch his dad and the bird lift something
that large into the air.

When his dad's roc was circling higher, his brother similarly
played something with his own flute, and their bird leapt into
the air as well. In just a few moments, they'd passed the
heavier-laden bird, and circled around to give their father time
to get speed going.

As they came into position behind their father, they heard his
flute playing, *"Crislan, can you find the way to Roc Harbor?"*

"Yes I can", Crislan replied with his own flute.

"Then take the lead", their father answered.

With that, the family made their way to the big city of Roc
Harbor.

They made the flight uneventfully. The trip took about 7 hours.
They'd stopped a couple times for bio breaks. Once alongside a
very pretty river with whitewater rapids, and the other time in a
high-mountain meadow. On the second stop, his father had
disconnected the carriage from his roc. Both rocs had taken off
on their own, leaving the four of them alone in the meadow.
The big birds were getting hungry, and 45 minutes or so later,
they returned to the family.

When they took off again, it only took a couple hours before
they left the heavily forested area, and saw farms and then the
buildings of the city. Caes hadn't been here for several years.
After living in the village, and wandering through trees, it
didn't look natural to see buildings on the ground, and people
walking on streets.

By now, his father was in the lead. He was a regular visitor to
the city. As senior rider at Westvale, he was obligated to attend
important meetings with other senior riders from other villages
and the mayor and city council of Roc Harbor. Together they
made up the governing council of the entire Cragwoods.

Caes saw a large square, surrounded by short buildings. His
father was headed right towards it. As he was descending
toward the square, Jerod played a message with his flute, *"Two
riders, with guests, from Westvale."*

"Welcome to Roc Harbor, riders!" came a reply from the ground.

Both rocs landed in the square. A group of uniformed
attendants came out of the buildings and met the Wind family.
The attendants detached the heavy straps from the carriage,
while Jerod unhooked the other ends from the saddle. By the
time they'd put the straps away, another attendant had
appeared with two large draft horses. They waited 100 yards
away from the rocs. Jerod and Crislan removed the saddles
from the big birds, as well as the harnesses.

"They ate just a couple hours ago", Jerod said to one of the attendants. "Your horses are safe."

"Thank you, sir. I am Evvik. Where are you planning to keep your rocs?"

"If your roc house is free, that's probably best. If it's full, then I'll just release them."

"Oh, the house is currently empty. We actually have three of the houses now, and none are occupied today.", Evvik replied. "You can pick any of those three to the left."

"Perfect. Crislan, throw a lead over your bird, and let's take them to their shelter. Honey, I'll meet you and Caes at the guesthouse."

Crislan and Jerod both looped leads over their roc's necks and they walked them across the square and through large barn-style doors of the first building. Caes and his mother walked the opposite direction to some slightly taller buildings. Evvik walked with them. "Will you be wanting one room or two, my lady?"

Ella replied, "We can get by with either. If there's plenty of room, I'm sure the boys would like their own room."

"No problem", Evvik responded. "We have several available. Do you need transportation to anywhere in town?"

"Can you have a carriage brought to the guesthouse in about an hour? We'll be paying a visit to the mayor. He's expecting us for dinner."

"Certainly, my lady", he said.

They entered the guesthouse and located two rooms close together. Ella chose one for her and her husband, and the other for their boys.

"You might want to bathe and change before dinner, Caes. When Crislan gets there, tell him to do the same. Meet us outside at 6:30. The mayor's house isn't far, but we don't want to be late." With that, she walked inside her room and shut the door.

A few minutes before 7:00, the carriage rolled up in front of the mayor's home. It was an elegant carriage, with the outside painted with a mural of a great roc. As it came to a stop at the home, staff came out to the driveway and met them.

"Sir," said one of the staff, "the mayor is in the sitting room. I'll show you the way."

"Don't bother", said Jerod. "I've been here before. We know the way."

He led the other three inside the front door, and walked through house to the sitting room. The door was shut, but Jerod wasn't about to knock and wait for 'permission' to enter. He was a senior rider, and the mayor was, well, just the mayor. He would be polite, but it was important to always remind him who held power in the Cragwoods. He turned the knob and opened the door. Inside the room was a nicely decorated sitting area. There were leather chairs and an immaculate fireplace with a nice fire burning in it. The mayor, dressed in his formal wear, complete with a cape, was sitting in an easy chair. His wife was sitting in a chair just to his right, with an end table between them. Both were sipping glasses of white wine.

Mayor Halvorson was an older man, with a grey, balding head of hair and clean shaven. His wife, Melony, was quite a bit younger and very beautiful. Her hair was long and red with loose curls. She was wearing a long floral dress.

"Ah, Rider Wind!", said the mayor. "I'm so glad you could find time to meet us here. I trust you had a pleasant ride?"

"Of course, Ryan. And how are you doing? Melony, it's nice to see you.", said Jerod. "You've both met my lovely wife, Ella. I'd like to introduce you to my sons, Crislan and Caes."

The two boys offered their hands. After a brief shake, the mayor said, "What a great looking family! Dinner will be served in the formal dining room in about 30 minutes. We have time for a drink and some friendly banter beforehand." He waved his arm at the other chairs and sofa in the room. The four Wind family members found seats. A servant entered and took drink orders. Ella ordered a glass of wine. Jerod chose a whisky, neat. The two boys each asked for ripplefruit juice, or whatever other juice was available. Apple juice was served to them.

Over drinks, the Mayor Halvorson, Melony, Jerod and Ella engaged in small talk. They talked about the weather, the state of the wine business in the Cragwoods, and the latest trends in women's' fashion in Roc Harbor, as well as the other large cities throughout Loma, which was the larger continent Cragwoods was on.

After several minutes of small talk, the mayor brought up a different subject.

"So, Rider Wind," the mayor started rather formally, "my daughter and her good friend wish to submit a letter to the riders. I'm worried it's too much for them, but they're both adamant about it. They want to leave the city, and pursue a career as riders."

He paused for a minute, and then continued, "Would it be asking too much to hope you'd be supportive of their request? They've never been outside of the city, and I explained to them it's an entirely different lifestyle in the villages than in Roc Harbor. Umm… I'm sorry. I'm rambling. Would the riders even consider a city girl, I mean, two city girls? If it helps, they're so very stubborn. I mean, in a good way. They're determined. Yes, that's the word I was hunting for."

Melony interjected, "Rider Wind, is this a crazy idea? We've been trying to get our daughter to go into politics, and maybe follow in her father's footsteps, but, well, she's just not interested. When we told her we were going to watch the Trials, she got so excited! Do girls ever become riders?"

Jerod chuckled, and leaned back in his seat. "Ryan, of course there are… I'm sorry, Ryan and Melony, yes there are women riders. We don't place any limits on the sex of the riders, just so long as they're proficient and work hard. Of the 20 riders we have now at Red Cliff aerie – that's the aerie that supports both Westvale and Red Cliff Village – I think six of them are women. It's not about their sex, but is more about their level of interest and how hard they work at it."

"Of course", said Ella. She reached over and took Melony's hand in her own. "Are you asking Jerod to sponsor your daughter? I'm positive he'd be willing to do that." She looked at her husband, who looked her in the eyes and realized his wife had seen to the heart of the topic.

Jerod said, "Oh yes. Yes. I'd be happy to meet your daughter and her friend. And I'd be happy to submit their letter to the riders. As long as they seem determined, I'll sign on to be their sponsor. That doesn't guarantee they're selected but it should give them a better shot at it."

The mayor smiled, and said, "Thank you, very much, Rider Wind! You have no idea how relieved I would be for you to sponsor and watch over them as they go through training."

"Of course, Ryan. And please call me Jerod when we're in private", said Jerod.

About that time, a servant came in and announced dinner was ready if everyone would please follow him into the dining room.

The Halvorsons and Winds walked into the dining room. The table was set for seven people. As they took their seats, a teen girl came into the room, walked to the mayor and his wife and took the seat next to her mother. She was about 15 or 16 years old, with red hair matching her mother's.

"Ah, Rider Wind and Ella, this is my daughter. Pienna, this is Jerod Wind and his lovely wife, Ella. And, these are their sons, Crislan and Caes. Rider Wind is the senior rider from Westvale. Crislan has just about completed his training and will be taking the Rider's Trials next week when we're there."

Pienna stood and shook Jerod's and then Ella's hands. "I'm pleased to meet you both. Hi Crislan and Caes." She took her seat again. Crislan's eyes stayed on her for a minute. She saw him looking and smiled in return.

Of course, thought Caes. Girls always liked his brother.

Shortly after they were all seated – the adults on one end of the table, and the teens at the other end – servants began bringing food and drinks into the room. First came bottles of wine. Caes noticed some of it was ripplefruit wine, from Westvale. Next came a bowl of salad and another bowl of mixed fruits and vegetables. He saw ripplefruit, huckleberry, strawberry, and apple in it, mixed with cucumber slices, celery chunks, and cherry tomatoes.

As they were all dishing the salad and fruit into their plates, another servant brought in a plate with baked sweet potatoes. Afterwards, another brought in a plate with salmon filets and large grilled shrimp. The smell was amazing. Ocean fish was rare in Westvale. They sometimes had river fish, but things like salmon and shrimp weren't usually available.

Talk at dinner, with the adults anyway, was about things like city finances, the status of shipments from other regions in Loma, the quality of wine, mead, and beer from the various villages, and of course, rumors. It was all pretty boring to the three teens. They had their own conversation at the other end of the table.

"Pienna, what's it like growing up here in Roc Harbor?", said Caes. "Does it seem odd to live in houses on the ground, and walk around on the streets?"

Pienna giggled, and said, "That's funny! Where else would we live or walk?"

"Well, we live in tree houses in Westvale. I mean, in the villages, everyone lives in tree houses. It feels strange to be here in this house. It doesn't move with the wind, at all!"

Pienna said, "You think our houses are strange because they're on the ground, but we think your houses are strange, up in the trees."

"Caes", said Crislan, "it's not strange to Pienna because that's the only way she's ever lived."

"That's right. You know, Crislan, my friends call me Pi." She smiled at Crislan.

"Thanks, Pi. You can call me Cris if you want", said Crislan.

Pienna said, "I'm going with my parents to watch the Trials. This will be my first time in one of the villages. Is it really as dangerous as people say?"

"It can be if you walk around on the ground," said Crislan. "If you stay off the ground, you know, up in the trees, it's very safe. Just don't climb all the way to the top. It's a long way down, so you don't want to fall – and sometimes wild rocs look for food in the treetops. The most dangerous creatures are on the ground, though."

"How do you go from one house to another if you don't go to the ground?"

Caes interjected, "There are paths all over the place. Branches grow wide, and flat on the top, so it's easy to walk on. Where there aren't wide branches, people have built boardwalks and rope bridges. I can go from my house to all of my friends' houses and never leave the trees."

"Yeah, Caes is right. If the branches don't make paths where you want to go, there are usually bridges – sometimes wooden and sometimes rope – that take you somewhere", said Crislan. "Your dad said you were thinking about writing a letter to be a rider…"

"Oh yeah, it's boring here. I think your rocs are amazing!
They're so majestic! It would be so exciting to ride them. My
friend – I call her Ronni but her name is Saffron – wants to be a
rider also. We're both writing our letters", said Pi. "Ronni and
I have been friends all our lives."

She paused for a moment. "Am I rambling?"

Crislan laughed. "Just a little, but it's okay. I think it's cute."

Caes rolled his eyes.

Dinner ended, and the Wind family made their way back to the
guesthouse. When they got there, the boys went to their room.
Caes poked fun at his big brother about how he kept looking at
Pi, and how he called her cute.

Crislan just shrugged it off and suggested Caes was jealous.

"I'm not jealous. It's just funny how girls always like you", said
Caes.

"She's cute! I love her red curly hair", said Crislan. "I'm going
to take her to the dance after the Trials. She just doesn't know it
yet. I'll ask her to go before we fly home."

"Isn't she a little young for you?" asked Caes.

"No way!" said Crislan. "She's only a couple years younger.
Hey, I wonder what Ronni looks like."

"Really? You haven't even danced with her yet, and you're
talking about her friend?"

"Ha!" said Crislan, "You ARE jealous!"

Caes grabbed the pillow from his bed and smacked Crislan in
the head with it. Crislan laughed and tackled Caes. They both
fell to the floor, laughing and wrestling. Crislan was bigger and
stronger, but Caes was coming into his own. They wrestled for
a few minutes before Crislan pushed himself away. The two
boys looked at each other and smiled.

Crislan stood up and started to walk away, when Caes threw
his pillow at the back of Crislan's head. The wrestling started
over again. This time, they rolled into an end-table and
knocked it over. That ended the wrestling. Luckily nothing
broke. Their parents wouldn't be happy if they broke things.
There was a banging on the door. Crislan hurried to open it.
Their father was on the other side.

"You two sound like bears fighting. Are you about done?"

"We're good, dad", said Crislan. "Just some wrestling."

"Uh huh. That's what I thought. Remember, this is a
guesthouse. Don't break anything!" said Jerod.

"Crislan thinks Pi is cute!" said Caes.

Crislan grabbed a pillow and threatened to throw it at Caes.
Then they both started laughing. "Now you know how the
wrestling got started, dad!"

Jerod chuckled, and said, "Alright, settle down and relax. It's
going to be dark soon. Have you figured out how to turn on the
lights?"

"I figured there were candles or something", said Crislan.

"No. They've got lightstones here. Let me show you." He walked across the room and picked up a glass globe with a stone set in the center of it, and carried it back to the boys. "See this? This is a lightstone in the middle. The glass part is just decorative." He set the globe on one of the end-tables.

"Now watch. These are set to respond to a spark cantrip. If you don't know one of those, you can just tap it three times on the top." He tapped the globe three times and it started glowing. "Put your finger on the side and move it up, and the light gets brighter. Down, and it gets dim. Pretty fancy, huh!"

"That's neat!", said Caes. "Hey dad, I've got a question for you... Why didn't mom become a rider?"

"I was wondering when you'd ask", said Jerod. "Your mother is quite talented at plant magic. She wanted to pursue that instead of riding. You've seen how she can make plants do incredible things, like widening walking paths in the trees, or having the trees build their own handrails. Not many people can do that."

"Maeve was telling me about colors of magic, and that there's different abilities people have. Is that what you mean?", said Caes.

Jerod answered, "Yes, exactly. Your mom has what are known as 'talents' rather than simply 'gifts'. That means she can cast more powerful spells than the cantrips most of us use. Her talents are strong enough she might have been able to become an adept – what most people think of as a magician. She just needs more training. Whenever the two of us come to Roc Harbor, she spends a few hours with a magician here, and learns a little more."

"Why didn't she study to become a magician when she was younger?" Crislan asked.

"Funny you should ask, Crislan", his father said. "You happened. When she was pregnant with you, she no longer wanted to study full-time."

"Where is mom right now?" Caes asked.

"She's in our room getting ready for bed", his father said. "You should think about doing the same. Tomorrow, your mom is going to spend the morning with the magician. His name is Jamis. While she's gone, the three of us are going to take care of some shopping. Caes, you need some new leather riding gear. You look sloppy wearing my old ones. Crislan, you need some new boots. Yours are looking ratty. Your mom gave me a list of a few things she needs. Then, we'll go visit a friend of mine for an hour or so. When your mom gets back from her lesson, we'll get the Halvorsons loaded up in the carriage and fly home. It'll be a long day, so get a good night's sleep."

"Okay dad", both boys said.

"Good night, sons", said Jerod. Then he walked out and shut the door.

The next morning, Caes and Crislan awoke early and made their way to the dining room, where an assortment of meats, fruits, and juice was waiting for them. They filled their plates and started eating. As they were eating, their mother and father entered, and took seats at the table.

"Hi mom!" said Caes.

"Good morning", said Crislan.

"Hi CC! How are you two doing this morning?", said their mother.

"Please don't say that in public, mom. It's embarrassing", said Crislan.

"It's fine", she said. "Don't worry about it."

"Dad said you're meeting with a magician today?" said Crislan.

"Yes, I'll be back in three hours or so. Maybe four. As soon as I finish eating and drinking a cup of coffee, I'll take off. His shop isn't far from here. It'll only take 5 minutes or so to walk there."

"We'll walk you there if you want", said Crislan.

"Thank you, but that's okay", Ella said. "You all need to get to the leather shop early enough to hopefully get any adjustments made to what you buy."

The family made small talk for the next fifteen minutes, and then they all got up and prepared to leave.

"Crislan, would you go check on the rocs before we leave?" their dad asked. "Make sure there's some meat for them to eat?"

"Sure, I'll check, dad, but I saw a couple sheep taken into the roc house when Caes and I got here", said Crislan.

"Thanks, son", said Jerod.

Ella gave her husband a brief kiss, and squeezed his hand. Then, she headed to the door and her walk to the magician's shop.

Crislan headed out the door towards the roc house. Caes and his father went to their rooms to make sure everything was packed for their flight later that day. Then, they headed out the front door of the guesthouse and met Crislan. The three of them headed down the street towards the main part of town.

7
Random's Revenge

Jerod and his sons walked for about 15 minutes and arrived in a commercial area of Roc Harbor. They'd walked first through a residential area with very nice houses. There were large yards and servant's buildings at most of them. Their father explained, as they walked, that this part of Roc Harbor was where most of the wealthy families lived, as well as the city officials. He explained that most of the citizens lived on the other side of the city – away from the wealthy neighborhood. All of the homes they saw were huge compared to the home they had in the trees in Westvale. Some of the houses even had walls and gates around the property.

They made a couple of turns on different street corners, and arrived at a shop called Corwin's Leather. There were several craft shops on that block. Caes noticed a blacksmith, a furniture shop, and a fletcher right next to each other. He also saw another shop he didn't recognize, a few buildings down. The sign out front said 'Tinker'.

"What's a tinker, dad?" he asked.

His dad looked around and saw the shop. "That's a shop where magical items are made - things like the lightstones you had in your room."

"Oh really? Can we go there and see?" asked Caes.

"We probably won't have time, but maybe. If not, we might stop there next time we're here", said their father.

Jerod walked to the door of Corwin's and opened it. His sons followed him through.

Inside was a tall blonde man with a long shaggy beard. He was hammering on something behind a counter. When the three walked into the room, he looked up, and set his hammer down. A grin appeared on his face.

"Well look who fell off a roc in my part of the world!" he said. "Jerod, it's been a long time!" He walked around the counter, and grabbed Jerod in a bear hug, and lifted his feet off the ground. "What are you doing here, my friend?"

"Hi Corwin, I hope you're doing well", Jerod said.

"Better than I deserve, my friend. How is life in Westvale?"

The two men talked for a few minutes and shared information about their families. Jerod waved his hand in the direction of his sons. "Corwin, these are my boys. The taller one is Crislan. He's taking the Riders Trials in a few days. The other is Caes. He's fifteen and submitting his letter to the riders. I expect he'll start training soon." He paused a moment while the boys each shook Corwin's hand.

He continued, "Boys, this is Corwin Stormcloud. We go back a long ways. He grew up in Westvale and was a rider for many years."

"It's just Corwin now, Jerod", Corwin said. "I'm not a rider anymore."

"You rode with honor for many years, my friend. You only retired when you were injured. As far as I'm concerned, you're still Stormcloud", said Jerod.

"I appreciate your saying that, Jerod, but that's not what the rules say", said Corwin.

Jerod said, "When you retired, I was just another rider, Corwin. I'm senior rider now. If I say you're Stormcloud, then that's that. When I get back home, I'll put it in writing, and have the other riders vote on it. It'll happen."

"Well, I appreciate that", said Corwin. "If it happens, I'll owe you. Just ask."

Jerod turned and looked at the boys. "Do you two remember learning about the Battle of the Crags? Cragwoods was invaded by an army from Eastlund, through the northern pass. The rangers and riders teamed up to repel them, and our forces were taking heavy losses. We don't have a standing army, you know. I'd taken arrows through my left arm and leg. My roc was killed, and I was trying to get to safety and avoid the invaders. If it wasn't for Corwin, they probably would've gotten me, and my body would still be there. But, Corwin managed to find me and carry me back from the battle so I could heal."

"Wow! I never heard that!" said Crislan.

"Yeah, that's right", said Corwin. Your dad is embellishing it a bit, but that's close enough. I retired about eight or nine years ago when I took a fall from my bird, and got hung up in a tree for a bit. I'd thrown my net when I fell, and that was good. I didn't fall all the way to the ground, but a branch hit me wrong and snapped my leg. It was taking forever to heal, and I decided to retire and move here.

"I miss it sometimes… usually when someone like your dad shows up and stirs all the old memories."

"It's good to see you're doing well, Corwin", Jerod said.

There was a brief pause by everyone.

"What can I do for you guys?" asked Corwin.

"Caes, here, needs new riding gear. He outgrew his last outfit and he's wearing one of my old ones, but it hangs on him pretty loose."

"That's pretty easy to do", Corwin said. "I've got several partial pieces here and should be able to fit them if you give me an hour or so." He walked to a small platform in the corner, and Caes noticed he limped when he walked. "Hop up on this platform and let me take some measurements, young man."

"I need some new boots for Crislan also, Corwin. Where do you recommend?" asked Jerod.

"About a block down the street, on the right side, is a good cobbler. He keeps some good inventory, so maybe you can find something in stock. It's called 'Stompers' for some weird reason. Tell him I sent you."

As Corwin finished taking measurements, he said, "Why don't you leave me for a couple hours and I'll see if I can get this gear sized for you. Are you stopping by Random's while you're here?"

Jerod answered, "Probably. If we have time after stopping at Stompers."

"What is Random's?" asked Crislan.

"Just another friend's place", said Jerod. He gave Corwin a hug, patted him on the shoulder, and headed to the door. "Thanks again, my old friend!"

"Don't mention it", said Corwin. "Leave me alone to work!"

Jerod and the boys walked down the street to Stompers. They walked inside and found an elderly man working on the sole of a shoe on a workbench. "Good morning, visitors", the man said.

"Good morning, cobbler", said their father. "Corwin suggested we come here and see about some riding boots for Crislan here", and he waved his hand towards his son.

"Certainly", said the cobbler. He grabbed a measuring stick on the wall and motioned for Crislan to take a seat in a chair. "Let's measure your feet, lad, and see what I have that might fit."

As luck had it, Stompers had three different boots that fit perfectly. The leather on one of the pairs was exceptionally soft and supple. Crislan asked about them.

"Ah, yes, that's made from shadow cat hide. It's naturally waterproof, and makes movement very silent. Notice the darker leather on them. They're not cheap, though! Those are about the same price as the other two, together. Actually, maybe as much as three of the others – if I had that many, anyway." He chuckled and looked at Jerod with a question in his eyes.

The cobbler wrote a number on a piece of paper and handed it to Jerod, who looked at the paper and shook his head. "That's quite a bit", said Jerod. "Can you give me a discount? Crislan is taking the Rider Trials in a few days."

"Hm… I don't normally do that, but… well… let me see. Corwin sent you, huh? Oh, shoot, how about 25% off?"

"That's a deal", said Jerod. "It's a pleasure doing business with you." He pulled a pouch from his belt and dug out some coins and handed them to the older man.

"Why don't you see if you have some boots that would fit Caes, here, also?" said Jerod.

"Sure, sure!", said the cobbler.

About 10 minutes later, the three left the cobbler's shop with boots. Crislan had his shadow cat boots, and Caes had a pair of deerskin boots. Jerod pointed at the intersection half a block down, and said, "We have time. Let's go to Random's and get something to eat."

The two boys followed their dad. As they walked down the street, Caes said, "Hey dad, when we were at Corwin's earlier… He said something about throwing a net. What's that mean?" Jerod answered, "All riders carry a small pouch on their hip. I'm sure you've seen it, right?"

"Yeah", said Caes.

"We keep a thin rope net in it. One end is attached to the pouch – and to our waist as well – and the other end is weighted to make it easy to throw. If you are thrown from your roc, you grab the net and throw it if there are trees under you. The net snags the branches and keeps you from falling all the way to the ground", said Jerod.

Crislan added, "You'll learn all about it when you start rider training. They took us all up on a tall tree with a small platform on it. We had to take turns standing on the platform with the net in our hands, and then jump off and throw it. It's scary but fun at the same time. You have to cross your legs to hold them together when you jump so a branch doesn't get you in the gonads!"

"That's crazy!" said Caes. "How many times did you have to do that?"

"I don't know. I guess we did it about ten times. At first, we jumped three times on the same day. And then sometimes they decide everyone needs a refresher and you do it again on different days. The trickiest part is grabbing the rope the right way. There's a thick heavy part of the rope that's packed on top of the pouch. You grab it and chuck it as hard as you can." He laughed and said, "I remember Jatt peed himself the first time he had to jump off that platform. It's pretty scary!"

Caes pictured himself jumping off a platform and throwing the net. The thought of it made his knees tremble a bit. They walked quietly the rest of the way to Random's.

After about three blocks, they arrived at a building with a covered patio in the front and a door sitting at the back of the patio. A sign hung over the door. 'Random's Revenge' was painted on it in bright blue letters.

"Watch your coin purses, boys", their father said.

"What?" said Crislan, as he shoved his purse inside his pants. "Are there thieves here?"

His father laughed. "Not that I know of, but the owner, Random, is a character. He's likely to charm the money right out of your purse anyway."

They walked through the door and into a half-full inn. Caes wasn't sure if it would be classified as a restaurant or tavern, but seemed to have a bar as well as tables for patrons to sit at.

An ugly man with tattoos all over his arms and face was tending bar. Caes whispered to his dad, "Is that Random?"

"No, it's not. That's just the bartender. I don't remember his name", Jerod answered. He found an empty table and sat in one of the chairs. Caes and Crislan took their seats.

A blonde woman came over to them. "What do you want to drink, guys?"

Jerod answered for them all. "Just some water for now. Is Random around?"

"Water? Sure. I'll bring you some. Random is upstairs in his office. Should I grab him? What should I tell him?"

"Water is good", said Jerod. "And maybe a menu, if there's more than one thing on it."

"Not much on the menu this early, but I can get you some stew and bread. Or, if you want to wait a bit, I can have the cook put some ribs on a platter. They should be almost done by now", she said. "What about Random?"

Jerod said, "Just tell him Jerod is here. He'll know me."

"Sure thing." And she walked away.

She brought a pitcher of water and three glasses, and asked, "Did you decide on food?"

"I think the stew and bread sounds good, ma'am", said Jerod.

She nodded and walked away. A few minutes later, a short, thin man with a weasel-like face came up. He had a short black beard. "Jerod! Oh man, I haven't seen you in forever!"

"Pull up a seat, you little weasel", said their father. "Watch your purses boys. The thief is here!"

Caes wasn't sure if his dad was joking, but supposed he probably was.

Random was laughing. "Who are these two strapping boys?"

"Random, these are my boys. Crislan and Caes. Boys, say hi to my oldest friend in the world."

"Pleasure to meet you both!", Random said. "I think I saw you last maybe twelve years ago. You were both only about yay high", and he held his hand a couple feet above the floor.

"Hi, Mr. Random", said Caes.

"Ha! It's just Random, but thanks for the 'Mister'." Random grinned wide as he looked form one face to the other. "Where's the missus?"

Jerod said, "Ella's meeting with her magician friend – I think his name is Jamis. I wouldn't think of letting her come around you, though. You've tried to steal her too many times."

"What kind of name is Random?" asked Caes.

"You aren't shy, are you?" asked Random. "I was a ranger, once upon a time. Random is the name they gave me. I'm not sure why. Maybe because I was a bit unpredictable. What the hell? I survived everything they threw at me. I guess it fits."

The server came with bowls of stew and a platter of buttery bread. "It looks like you found the boss", she said.

"Thanks, Madge", said Random. "Why don't you bring me a bowl also?"

"You bet", she said. "Do you want beer to go with it?"

"Of course! Bring one for Jerod too. Water is for kids" he said. When she walked away, he looked at Jerod. "What are you doing in the thriving metropolis of Roc Harbor?"

"Crislan is about to take the Rider Trials. We're picking up some supplies and giving the mayor and his family a ride to watch the event."

"Another birdhead, huh?" said Random.

Jerod looked at his sons and said, "Random grew up with me. His parents died when he was a baby, and my parents raised him in our house. He's like an ugly weaselly little brother to me. It figures he decided to take the ranger path instead of being a real man and becoming a rider."

Neither Crislan, nor Caes had ever heard this story before. This whole trip to Roc Harbor was full of surprises.

"Yeah, you and the other birdheads always thought you were better than everyone else", said Random.

"It's true. You rangers tried hard to be as good as us, but you know how that goes."

Random just sat and chuckled. "It's good to see you, brother. How long are you in town?"

"We're leaving this afternoon. At least as long as Ella gets her lessons wrapped up in time", said Jerod.

"Well, if you're afraid to bring her by, please give her a big hug for me", said Random.

Jerod said, "You know I'm not really afraid. She's just out doing her own thing right now. If we have time, I'd be happy to bring her by for a visit. If not, then maybe next time we're here."

He looked at his sons. "To clear the air, you both should understand Random dated your mother before we met. She obviously picked the better man."

Random leaned back and laughed. The boys both secretly decided they liked the little man. He seemed fun.

The four ate their stew and bread. It was delicious. They all talked for a while longer, and then it was time to leave.

Random refused to let Jerod pay for their meal. "I don't charge family, you know." He looked at Caes and Crislan. "Your money isn't any good here either. Stop by and see me any time you're in town."

They all stood. Jerod and Random embraced. It was obvious they loved each other. It reminded Caes of his relationship with his own brother.

On the way back to Corwin's, they stopped at the Tinker's shop. The shop had several shelves with small decorative items on them. To Caes and Crislan, it looked like nicknacks a woman might decorate a house with.

A bell rang when they entered the building. Shortly after they entered, a man walked in from a back room. When he walked, a *clump clump* noise was heard. He walked around the corner of the counter and they saw he had a wooden leg. Every time he stepped down, it made a *clump* noise. "Good morning, folks!", he said.

"Good morning, Tinker", said Jerod. "My name is Jerod. We're just looking around. The boys haven't met a tinker before, and I'm showing them what you have."

"Ah, good. Good. My name is Quain, and I make all this stuff", he waved his arm around as he was talking. "Is there anything in particular you're lookin' for?"

"Oh, not really", Jerod said. "I assume you have lightstones?" "Of course", Quain said. "Those are probably my best sellers. I have a whole shelf of them over on the far wall."

Jerod asked, "Can you explain to the boys what a tinker does?"

"Sure", he said. "Do you boys know about magic and colors?" Both Caes and Crislan nodded. "We both have brown gifts", Caes said. "Well, I have brown gifts. Crislan has brown and green."

"Okay, good. So, I am a yellow adept. Have you learned about yellow?", asked Quain.

"I haven't", said Caes. Crislan was shaking his head. "I know brown is animal magic. Green is plant magic. Red is fire. White is healing."

"Yes. And yellow is permanent magic. As a yellow adept, I can take an item – either one I make or one I buy somewhere – and infuse it with magic, making it permanent. Light spells are pretty easy to case for most colors of magic. I have talents for grey, as well as the yellow. Grey is air magic, if you haven't learned that already. I find pretty rocks and have them embedded in glass balls, for instance, like this one over here", he pointed at a glass ball on a shelf. "I work with the objects to make them accepting of magic, and then I cast the spell I want it to have and make the object absorb the spell. That's the short description, folks. In reality, it's more involved – a lot more."

"That's cool", said Caes. "How long does it take you to make something?"

"Ah, that varies quite a bit", said Quain. "A lightstone is pretty simple. I can make a couple of those in a day. Other things take a lot longer." He looked at Jerod. "Sir, can I ask what you do?"

"I'm a rider", said Jerod.

"Oh yes. Good! Here's another example over on this hook here." He pointed at a pouch with a belt.

"That looks like a rider's pouch", said Jerod.

"It is. Yes it is. The net in here automatically tries to snag the closest tree when it's thrown. It's fun to watch – even for me. When you toss it, it springs open and then moves sideways towards the first tree it finds, and entangles itself quickly."

"Interesting!", said Jerod.

"Yes it is", said Quain. "It takes almost a month to make, and costs about what a rider makes in six months. Are you interested in it?"

"Maybe if I had that much money with me, but no. Thanks for the information, though. Maybe I'll stop back with more money one of these times I'm back in Roc Harbor", said Jerod.

"Sure, sure. Do you boys have any other questions?", asked Quain.

"I have a couple", said Caes. "Um… What happens when someone wants an item you don't have the magic for? Like, I don't know… what about if someone wanted an arrow to catch fire when it hits something? That's red magic, right?"

"Well, that would be a pretty dangerous arrow to have around. But, if someone wanted one, I'd make it so you had to say a certain word or phrase while holding the arrow to activate the spell. And then, I'd have to work with a red adept. I would prepare the arrow, and then have a red adept cast the fire spells at the arrow. Then, I'd use my own magic to make it permanent", said Quain. "Does that make sense to you?"

"Yeah it does. Thanks", said Caes.

"What was your other question, lad? You said you had two?", asked Quain.

"Yeah. Um. Uh, this one is maybe too personal. I was wondering what happened to your leg", said Caes.

"Ah, yes. It's pretty personal, but that's okay. You see, I used to live in one of the villages. Do you know where Eastvale is?" said Quain.

"I've never been there, but I've seen it on a map", said Caes.

"Okay. So, I lived there for a lot of years. Anyway, I'd gone looking for things to work with to make magical items. You know, like stones and nice looking sticks, and things like that. Well, I saw a ripplefruit vine, but it was on the ground at the bottom of a tree when they're normally up in the top. I went over to it to find some fruit and didn't notice it grab my leg. It turned out to be a crawling mantrap and not ripplefruit. Well, it got me pretty bad. I wished I had green or red gifts. Maybe I could have gotten free quicker. But by the time I cut myself free, my leg as pretty bad. It was bleeding all over the place and I couldn't feel anything in that leg anymore. The ranger I was with… well, let's just say he was a little preoccupied at the time. He, uh, was a little ways off answering the call of nature, if you get my meaning. When he came back and saw me, I'd fallen down and the vine was coming back at me. He picked me up and carried me away, but by the time we made it to a healer, they said it was too late to save my leg. The had to cut it off."

"Oh man, that's scary!", said Caes.

"Make sure you remember my story, young man. Don't ever go in the forest by yourself. Always take a ranger with you", said Quain.

"I will", said Caes.

"Thank you, tinker – uh, Quain", said Jerod. "You have some amazing things in here. I'll plan on coming back when I can."

"You bet, Rider. It was nice meeting you", said Quain.

8
Flying Home

Caes, Crislan, and Jerod were back at the guesthouse relaxing in the living room when Evvik came in the front door.

"Rider Wind, I have a message from your wife", he said.

"Hello Evvik. Is everything okay?" asked Jerod, standing up. Evvik answered, "Yes, I believe so, sir. She sent a messenger saying her class was taking longer than expected, and was it possible to fly home tomorrow rather than this afternoon."

Jerod scratched his short beard. "Yes, that should be fine. Can you get ahold of the mayor and let him know we'll leave in the morning instead?"

"Certainly, Rider. I'll let him know right away", said Evvik, and then he nodded and went back out the door.

Jerod looked at Crislan and Caes. Leaving tomorrow would probably be better anyway. Depending on how heavy the carriage was, they might have had to spend a night on the ground anyway so the birds could rest. This would give them the ability to rest on the ground tomorrow for an extended break instead.

He looked at Crislan. "Crislan, go get your leathers on. I think we should take the rocs out to the countryside and let them hunt rather than just eat the sheep being brought to them." He paused. "Caes, you can go with us if you want, unless you'd rather stay here."

"I'll go. I can wear my new leathers." He jumped up and headed to his room to change.

Ten minutes later, the three guys were headed to the roc house. When they got there, Caes stood by the door and watched his dad and brother both slip harnesses over the birds' heads and saddle them. Both were talking softly to the rocs while they worked. He realized after a moment they were soothing the birds not only with the soft voices, but there was a bit of calming magic happening as well.

The rocs were saddled. Crislan and his dad walked the birds out the barn door. Jerod motioned for Caes to climb onto the back seat of his saddle. Once positioned, Caes belted the safety strap around his waist. His father climbed into the front seat, tapped his boots against the side of the roc, and it leapt into the air. Behind them, Crislan did the same with his roc.

In just moments, they were high above the city. Taking off had been quite the rush. Without a carriage beneath his father's roc, it took off much quicker. They turned towards the north, and flew past the city and the surrounding farmland. It only took about 15 minutes to be past all buildings and farms, and over the wild forest of the Cragwoods. Jerod found a meadow and brought the roc down low over it. They circled a couple of times while all three studied the meadow for any dangerous animals. Seeing none, they landed in the center of the meadow.

"Don't wander around in the meadow", said their father. "And, keep your knife handy, just in case. He reached into a scabbard on the right side of his saddle to pull a bow and arrow out." He stepped out of the saddle. Once Caes and Crislan were both on the ground, his father took his flute and played a hunt command.

The huge birds leapt into the air and were quickly gone from sight, leaving the three alone in the large meadow. "I've waiting here in this meadow several times in the past", Jerod said. There's a circle of boulders just over that way", he pointed his finger, "where we can sit and wait for the birds to finish eating."

They walked in direction he'd pointed and found the large boulders in a circle around an old fire pit. They took seats and enjoyed the quiet of the meadow. Caes hadn't realized how noisy it had been in Roc Harbor.

Jerod pulled some jerky strips from his pack and handed them to his sons. The three sat quietly, enjoying the serene setting and munching on jerky.

"How are you feeling about the Trials, Crislan?" he asked.

Crislan shrugged, swallowed his jerky, and said, "Pretty good, dad. I'm looking forward to it. It'll be nice to work instead of just training all the time."

"You're going to do great", said Caes.

"Brun says I'll probably haul cargo once I complete the Trials. He said I have a knack for it. I can't wait for my first long trip. Maybe I'll go all the way to Daener City."

"You'll go there eventually, I'm sure", said Jerod. "You won't go alone, though. It's a long flight over the crags. Daener City is a good three-day ride if you're carrying cargo."

Jerod reached into his pack and pulled a water skin out. "Drink anyone?"

He passed the skin around so they all take a drink.

Caes said, "What did Corwin mean when he said he couldn't be called Stormcloud anymore?"

"You haven't learned about that yet, huh?" said Jerod. "New riders, once they pass the Trials, are encouraged to pick a rider name. It becomes their new surname. When he passed the Trials, Corwin chose Stormcloud. He and everyone in his immediate family became Stormcloud. Just like I'm Wind, and so are you boys and your mother.

"My dad was a Wind, and so was his dad. We've had the Wind name for generations. I'm not even sure who was the first. As long as you boys become riders, you'll be able to remain Wind, and so will your mother and I, even when we retire. When Corwin retired, he didn't have any kids to carry on his rider name. I don't like it, but that's the rule. Like I told him, though, when I get home, I'm going to insist he be given his rider name again."

"Will the other riders agree with you?" Crislan asked.

"I don't know for sure", Jerod said. " but I think so. Corwin risked his life to save me and only retired when he was injured too badly to keep flying. I'm pretty sure I can convince everyone."

"If he moved back to Westvale, would he still be considered a rider?" asked Caes. "I mean, like if he wanted to go to the aerie and ride a roc?"

"That's a good question, son. Honesty, if he acted the part, I think he'd be accepted back without issues. If he tried asking for permission, they'd probably say no." He took a drink from his water skin. "I don't see him moving back, though. I don't think he'd want to sell his leather shop, but who knows what he'd decide."

"Do you think the rocs have eaten by now, dad?" asked Crislan.

"Yeah, I think they probably have. Let's call them back", said Jerod.

He stood and pulled out his flute, which hung from a strap around his neck. With the flute in the short position, he put it to his mouth and played a silent tune. Crislan did the same with his own flute. In the distance, they heard a screech. "Here they come", said Crislan.

In minutes two large rocs appeared above the trees and landed in the clearing not far from the circle of stones.

Twenty minutes later, they landed again in Roc Harbor, and walked the big birds back into the roc house.

The following morning, just after breakfast, the Winds and the Halvorsons stood outside the roc house. The birds were saddled. Jerod's roc was connected to the carriage with a long set of straps, and was resting just in front of the carriage.

Ryan and Melony stood visiting with Ella and Jerod. Pi stood with Crislan, giggling about something Crislan must have said. Caes worked with Evvik to load the Halvorsons' bags into the front and rear storage compartments of the carriage. His father had told him it was very important to keep the front and rear compartments equally weighted and, if they couldn't be exact, it was best to load the rear compartment just slightly heavier. Before loading any of the bags, his father had picked up each bag to check their weight. Satisfied it would be light enough for the roc to carry, he'd nodded his approval to Caes to load them. Rocs could carry very heavy loads, but they didn't want to injure a bird with too heavy a weight, or make the trip longer by requiring more rest stops.

As he was finishing loading the bags, a horse-drawn carriage rolled up, and a beautiful blonde girl about his age climbed out, carrying a small duffle bag. She was maybe 3 or 4 inches shorter than Pienna. "Hi Ronni!" yelled Pienna, waving.

"Hi Pi!" said the blonde. She walked over to where Pienna and Crislan stood. Caes walked over there, as well. Introductions were made. Caes had a hard time not staring at the petite girl. He felt tongue-tied and embarrassed at the same time.

His mother called to him, "Caes, did you want to ride in the carriage or with Crislan?" She grinned at him.

"Uh, um… I'll ride with Crislan", he called back. That was a tough question. Part of him really wanted to ride in the carriage and talk to the new girl – Ronni. The other part wanted to impress her and ride on the roc. The deciding factor was the part about how fun it was to ride on the bird.

With everything loaded, Jerod directed the passengers into the carriage, and carefully sat the passengers so the weight was spread equally. Ryan and Melony sat in the rear seat, facing forward. Pienna and Saffron sat in the front seats, facing to the rear. Jerod made sure the four of them fastened their belt straps, and they each had snacks for the ride and a water skin. Satisfied, he wished them a safe flight, and shut the door, latching it locked from the outside.

He called through the door, "It's going to be bumpy when we take off. Don't worry, it's normal."

Jerod motioned towards the two rocs, and the rest of the Wind family climbed onto the saddles and took their places, with Ella and Caes belting themselves on. Jerod and Crislan took the front seats in the saddles. They all waved at Evvik and the other servants and carriage drivers.

Jerod played a silent tune on his flute, and his big bird leapt into the air, giant wings flapping heavily. The slack in the straps disappeared, and the carriage lurched forward, dragging on the ground. With each flap of its wings, the roc pulled the carriage farther across the ground until it finally took to the air after about twenty feet or so.

Crislan gave a thumbs up to Evvik, smiled, and gently put his boots to the side of his roc. It leapt into the air and quickly passed Jerod, whose roc was slowly gaining altitude. The two birds turned to the west and started flying towards Westvale.

It was late afternoon when they spotted the large platform in the top of the trees at Westvale. They'd taken one long break about halfway there. Jerod's roc was pretty tired, so he and Crislan swapped the straps from one roc to the other. Jerod rode the bird Crislan had been riding, and Crislan took the one his father had had.

They landed on the platform, with the carriage landing first, and the roc landing just past it. Crislan landed his roc to the left of the carriage. Caes jumped out of the saddle and onto the platform. Crislan patted his bird and whispered to it a moment, and then looped the lead rope around a peg on the ground. He went over by Caes and helped unload the bags from the front and rear compartments.

Jerod held the lead of his roc and scratched the head of the giant bird, while Ella unlatched the door to the passenger compartment. "We're here, everyone! Go ahead and climb out", she said. "Caes and I will show you to a guesthouse you can use while you're here."

When the carriage was unloaded, Crislan and his father took off again to return the carriage and the rocs to the aerie. Caes and his mother led their guests down the ladder to the maze of branches and bridges beneath the platform, and showed them to an empty guesthouse. Guests almost always stayed in houses closest to the trunks. City folks weren't used to the way trees moved in the wind and sometimes got motion sick, especially if a storm came in.

As they were entering the house, Ronni turned and took his hand in both of hers. "Thank you, Caes. Are you going to be a rider also?"

He stammered, "Uh, yes. Yes, I am. I sent my letter in a couple of weeks ago."

"Oh good! Maybe we'll be in the same classes", she said. She smiled at him, and followed the Halvorsons into the house, shutting the door behind her. Caes stood staring at the door for a moment.

"She seems nice, Caes", said his mom. "She's pretty, too!"

Caes felt his face flushing. He grinned at his mom, and then turned to head to their house.

9
The Rider Trials

The next few days went by quickly. The whole village was occupied with the upcoming Trials. The students who were participating had individual meetings with Brun. The teacher reminding them of their tasks that had to be accomplished in the Trials, and gave them last-minute coaching and other suggestions.

The students who weren't yet ready for the Trials spent their time helping the construction workers finish assembling seats, shade structures, and a better set of stairs than the rope ladder for the final climb to the platform.

Caes' mother kept him busy, as well. He ran food, dishes, and assorted baskets to the guesthouse a couple times each day. She also had him run all sorts of errands to get flowers, wine, vegetables, fruit, and more. He felt like he didn't have any time at all to just sit and think. That girl, Ronni, kept popping into his head, and he wanted more than anything else to have time to visit with her, but his mother seemed to know just what he wanted to do, and always had other tasks to keep him busy. Even when he took things to the guesthouse, she gave him a time-limit, and was watching for him to return so she could give him something else to do.

The next day, riders from Red Cliff Village and Eastvale showed up with a few students. Riders from Sea View arrived the following morning. Lastly, riders from Northridge landed. Altogether, it looked like eight students were flying in the Trials.

All too soon, the preparations were complete, and the day of the
Trials was here.

The eight students gathered on a lower platform, known as The
Study, beneath the one at the top of the trees and near the
ground – only about 40 feet up from the ground. This was a
quiet area away from homes, and was often used by different
classes for lectures, whether by riders, rangers, or any other
crafts. The small platform, which was maybe 20 feet on a side,
had benches built onto it. The students each took seats.

Brun and the teachers from the other villages stood facing the
students. Brun stepped forward a step and said, "Alright you
all. Listen up." The students sat up and watched him. "Okay,
I'm not much for speeches, but I want you to listen anyway. For
those who don't know me, I'm Brun Updraft. I've been the
teacher here in Westvale for the past six years. Those of you
from the other villages have your own teachers here beside me.
We take turns hosting the Trials, and it's our turn this time.
You all know what's expected of you today.

"You're each going to reach into a hat and pull out a stone.
Each stone has a number on it. That's your place in line. If you
draw number one, you're going to be the first to show everyone
how much you've learned.

He paused and looked at each of the students. Five boys and
three girls sat watching him. "I don't want any drama. I don't
want any showoffs. Got it?"

The eight students nodded their heads and mumbled
affirmative answers.

Brun continued, "There will be twelve rocs tied to the platform. All of them are unbroken. Unbroken, do you hear? These aren't the well-trained birds you've been practicing on. These birds to not like you. Remember they want to carry you away to the Crags and eat you. I'm not trying to scare you, but… well, actually, yes, I'm trying to scare you! If you respect these birds, and use the training you've had, you'll all do just fine. If you show off, well, you're going to get hurt. Or worse…

"Do you all have nets in your pouches? Let me see them."

All eight of the students stood up and pulled nets from the pouches on their hips.

"Okay, good", Brun said. "Now take a few moments and fold them properly and put them back." He walked to a table and picked up a glass of water and drank some. He turned back to the students.

"Take your seats again, folks. These birds we have for you – all twelve of them – like I said, they're unbroken. It's your job to break them. When your number is called, you're to stand up and slowly make your way to the center of the platform. You will state your name and the village you're from. Then, you will study the rocs and decide on which one you will break.

"A little advice… No one cares which bird you pick. Just pick one you think will be easy. If I were you, I'd avoid the smaller ones. They've probably got some wood roc in them, and they tend to be harder to break. Your goal is to successfully break a roc and complete your ride. Your goal is absolutely NOT to show off and pick a small bird just because you think it will look good. Do you hear that, Crislan?"

"Yessir!" said Crislan. It irritated him that Brun called him out like that.

Brun continued, "Okay then. When you pick your roc, approach it like you mean it. Not too fast, but not too slow. Too fast, and the bird will get defensive. Too slow, and it'll think you're afraid. You want to approach slower than a normal walk, but not too slow. If you know cantrips or spells that will help, feel free to use them. Get the harness over the roc's head without it biting you, and it'll be a good start. Once the harness is on, saddle it, hop on, and hold on tight. The bird is going to be pissed off, and it's going to try to dump you.

"Take your roc up into the air and teach it who's boss. When you feel like you have control, pull out your flute and tell me you're ready. I'll answer with a set of instructions. Follow my instructions. If all goes well, you'll be landing again in less than ten minutes, and you'll be a rider!"

The students all cheered.

"Alright, one more thing", Brun continued. "If you look to the north, you'll see a nasty looking landmark about 500 yards away we call The Scar. Lightning struck there about ten years ago. It burned a bunch of trees and they haven't grown back yet. There are large rocks in The Scar. If you need to bail off your bird, don't do it there!

"That's the only place close where your net will only find air."

He looked at each student, one at a time, until they each said, "Yes sir!"

"You'll notice some other riders flying around. These are safety riders, and their job is to keep any roving wild rocs away. If you get thrown off, they'll watch where you land so we can retrieve you as quickly as possible.

"Okay. That's it for me. I think Jerod Wind has a few things to say, as well. Jerod is senior rider here."

Jerod stepped forward. "Hi everyone. As Brun said, I'm Jerod Wind, and I'm senior rider at Westvale. I'm also Crislan's father. Please be safe, all of you. Make us proud of you." He paused for a moment. "If you don't know already, you each have two attempts to pass the Trials. With your teacher's recommendation, sometimes we allow three attempts. If you fail today, you'll likely have another try at a later date and location. Have any of you already taken the Trial before?"

One hand went up from a student. "I'm Dean. I tried it last year."

"Were you hurt last year?" asked Jerod.

"Not bad, Rider Wind. I got thrown and landed in a tree", said Dean.

"Welcome back for your second attempt. Let's hope today goes better", said Jerod. "Okay, I think that's it from me. Let's all head up to the Trials. I heard a flute saying everything was ready. Again, be careful, be smart, and good luck!"

The students stood and headed for the stairs. Jerod shook each of their hands as they passed. He grabbed Crislan and gave him a hug before the boy headed up the stairs. He was very proud of his son, but nervous at the same time.

When the students reached the platform, there were people in their seats on the south side of the platform. Several dozen people were sitting and waiting – maybe as many as a hundred. On the north side, and wrapping around to the east, a dozen rocs were tethered to the platform.

It was a perfect summer day, with not a cloud in the sky, and warm, but not hot, temperatures.

Caes was sitting by his mother. In front of them, on a lower level of the bleachers, were the Halvorsons and Ronni. Caes waved at his brother when he stepped onto the platform. Crislan smiled and waved back.

The students took seats in the eight chairs sitting directly in front of the bleachers. Jerod and Brun walked to the center of the platform. Brun nodded to Maeve, who was sitting off on the side. She walked up to them and moved her hands around while uttering something no one in the stands could hear. Finally, she finished and walked back to her seat.

Jerod spoke, and it was loud, "Good afternoon family, friends and fellow riders!" Even though he seemed to be speaking softly, his voice carried to everyone on the platform as if he were standing directly in front of each person. Maeve must have used a spell to make his voice carry.

Jerod continued, "Welcome to Westvale, to our visitors, and to our annual Rider's Trials. We'll get things started in just a few minutes, but a few announcements first. After the Trials, we'll be having a dinner and dance. It'll take place in the public hall. If you don't know how to get there, just follow the crowd. It's down several levels and over that way…" He pointed his hand off to one side.

"Now, a moment with the rules of the Trials. First of all, once a number is called, please keep quiet. Don't cheer or call anyone's names. This is serious business, and we need the students to keep focused on their task. Please don't distract them.

"Second, please don't leave your seats for any reason. If one of the students is thrown, we have safety riders to see to their safety. Hence, the name. Let the safety riders do their job. If someone is thrown, we'll let you know when they're safe.

"As you know, the students have to complete some tasks to show they have control over their rocs. Brun, here, will be using his flute to give them commands. When they've completed the tasks, they'll land here again. As long as they did everything Brun asks, they'll be riders. Cheer for them all you want once they land. Just please be quiet from the time their number is called until they land again.

"Lastly, the students are going to draw numbers from a hat. It's going to be a completely random order. Okay, Brun, the show is yours. Please give us some new riders!"

The audience clapped and cheered. Brun walked to where Jerod had been standing.

"Alright kiddos, let's get this thing going!" Brun said. He walked to a table and picked up a hat. He went to each of the students and each of them reached in and took a stone out. When done, he walked back to the center of the platform. "Are you all ready to become riders? Number one, it's your turn!"

A brunette girl stood up and walked to the center of the platform. When she got there, she turned and faced the audience. "Hi everyone. I'm Jordyn, from Red Cliff Village." She turned and faced the tethered Rocs.

She looked at each of the birds, and finally walked to a large
brownish-red colored roc. When she was five or six feet away,
she stopped and held a coil of rope in her left hand. She might
have been talking to the bird, or might not. It was hard to tell.
She threw the loop around the bird's neck. It didn't seem
happy at all. When she stepped forward, it tried to bite her, but
she seemed to be ready for it, and side-stepped the beak. A
couple minutes later, she had it saddled, and threw her leg over.
She leaned over and pulled the tether loose, and the bird
launched into the air. She had a wild three or four minutes of
riding before things seemed to settle down, and she gained
control of the huge bird.

Brun stood in the center of the platform when the roc took
flight. When she gained control, he played commands on his
flute. Jordyn took the bird through the required paces, and in
about 15 minutes, landed again on the platform. When she
dismounted, Brun called out, "Ladies and Gentlemen, please
give a cheer for Red Cliff's newest rider, Jordyn! Young lady,
have you picked a rider name yet?"

Jordyn stood with a big grin on her face. She turned to Brun
and said, "I would like to be known as Jordyn Redsky, in honor
of my uncle who went by the same name before he passed away
last year."

Brun grinned, "Nick Redsky was a good friend of mine, Jordyn.
That's a great name!"

Jordyn sat down on her seat, and Brun called out, "Number
two!"

Crislan's good friend, Jatt, stood up and walked to the center of
the platform. He turned and faced the audience. "Hello, I'm
Jatt from Westvale."

Jatt turned and looked at the rocs tethered to the platform. He took a harness and made his way to a large ebony colored bird. It was so dark as to be almost black, but with a hint of dark brown mixed in. He threw the loop over the roc's neck, and when it opened its beak, Jatt pulled down hard on the rope. He stepped on the rope and held the bird's neck down until he got a saddle on the big bird. He climbed onto the bird, pulled the tether free, and it started spinning around in circles while still on the platform. Jatt nearly fell off the side from the unexpected twisting. Then the roc jumped into the air and started climbing rapidly.

Caes looked around at the audience. Everyone's eyes were glued to the pair performing the crazy dance in the air. He looked back up and saw the bird suddenly dive straight down, wings folded back against its sides. Jatt didn't have any sort of control yet, and Caes doubted he'd gain control anytime soon. The wings opened again, and the big bird started a climb again, and then started twisting and turning in the air. Jatt looked like he was about to fall off the side. He heard Brun's flute playing *"Take control Jatt"*. He could see Jatt struggling with the reins, and the bird started climbing again. Suddenly, it turned to the left and spun. Jatt went flying off the bird, and screamed!

As Jatt fell, his hand pulled his net out of his pouch and tossed it in the air. The net opened, and Jatt wrapped his arms around his chest and twisted his ankles together right before plunging into the treetops.

One of the safety riders flew over where the boy had fallen. Another safety rider threw a loop over the now-riderless bird's head, and started guiding it away from the platform.

The audience on the platform was completely silent as they waited to find out Jatt's condition. They could see the safety rider's roc circling over the area he'd fallen. Finally, he put a flute to his mouth and played, *"He's okay. Get runners to free him from the tree."*

Brun smiled, and told the audience, many of whom couldn't understand the flute language, "Alright folks, young Jatt seems to be okay! We're sending some helpers to get him out of the tree, but it looks like his net saved him!"

An applause erupted from the crowd, and a lot of talking.

"Okay everyone, please quiet down!", said Brun. "Jatt will be able to take the Trials again on another day if he so chooses. For now, let's everyone grab a drink of water and get ready for the next student. We'll take a five minute break to make sure the safety riders are back in position."

After about five minutes, Brun called number three. Crislan stood up and walked to the center of the platform. He turned and faced the audience, and said, "Hello, my name is Crislan. I live here in Westvale."

As Crislan stood facing the rocs, Caes felt nervous. His brother was the best student rider in his class, and Caes knew, KNEW, he'd do great, but he was scared, all the same. The big ebony roc was gone now, and Caes was happy about that. Caes' mother grabbed his hand and held it. So, she was nervous too.

Crislan reached down and picked up a harness, and started walking towards a large light grey roc, and then changed his mind and headed towards a smaller brown roc. He was saying something softly and then threw the loop over the bird's head. *No, that one's part wood roc!*, thought Caes. But it was too late. Crislan had made his choice.

The roc grabbed the rope with its beak, and Crislan yanked it free. Then, the roc kicked out with a talon, hitting him in his left leg. A gasp came from the crowd. Crislan stepped back, looked at his leg, and then pulled the bird's head toward the ground. He whispered some more, but Caes couldn't understand what he was saying. It was too soft to understand.

The roc seemed to relax just a bit. Crislan stepped on the rope, and grabbed the saddle, and placed it on the bird's back, quickly reaching under to grab the belly strap and fastened it tight. He released the tether and let the bird take a step forward, and then stepped into the stirrup and threw his right leg over. Caes saw blood on his leg. The talon must have cut the leathers Crislan was wearing. Suddenly, the bird vaulted into the air.

Crislan held on tightly to the reins. The roc wasn't happy about him riding on its back. His leg throbbed, but he couldn't worry about it now. He was sure he'd be okay until he landed. In the meantime, he needed to get control of the bird.

He knew the roc would do everything possible to make him fall off, and he wasn't about to let that happen. The bird went straight up, and then dove – just like Jatt's bird had done. Crislan was ready for that.

The bird went straight up again, and then spiraled toward the treetops. That was different! He pulled the reins the other direction, and ended the spiral.

The roc twisted its head back and tried to bite Crislan. He was ready for that too. He pulled both reins straight down, and the bird headed down as well. But, its head was looking where it was going now. Crislan pulled up slightly, and the roc straightened out.

He let the bird fly straight for a couple minutes, and then turned it in a gentle circle. The roc seemed to be resigning itself to being ridden, but Crislan wasn't going to let his guard down. As he completed the circle, the roc twisted and dove again. *I knew that was coming*, thought Crislan.

He regained control of the stubborn bird, and got into level flight again. He heard Brun playing in the distance, *"You just had to pick a woody. We'll talk when you land. When you're done playing with the roc, come back overhead of the platform and circle clockwise."*

They flew over the Scar, and Crislan realized he was farther from the platform than he should be. He turned the bird and headed back to the platform, flying about 500 feet above the trees. As he was turning, he got a sudden feeling of vertigo. He blinked his eyes and tried to focus. The vertigo went away gradually.

He looked down and realized he'd flown past the platform. *"Clockwise circles!"* he heard from below.

Crislan turned the bird back towards the air above the platform and vertigo hit again. The earth tipped and spun, and he shut his eyes. *What's happening?*

The vertigo went away again. He looked around and found the platform, and then put the bird into a gentle clockwise turn. From below, he heard, *"Are you okay up there? Use your flute and answer me, Crislan".*

He fumbled for his flute's string around his neck and had trouble pulling it from his shirt. The vertigo hit again and this time the world spun and went black. He leaned forward and grabbed the bird's neck.

Crislan regained consciousness just as he felt himself slipping from the saddle. The last thing he saw was blood pouring from his left leg. He felt the darkness coming again and did the only thing he could think of. He tossed the net from his pouch. Then everything went black again.

Caes was holding his mother's hand tight. Something was wrong with Crislan, but he wasn't sure what. He heard Ronni whisper, "He's bleeding bad. Oh man…"

That was it! Crislan was hurt from the roc's talon.

About that time, Crislan leaned forward and grabbed the roc's neck. The bird straightened out and flew away from the platform. Five or six seconds later, Crislan went limp and fell from the bird, his net fluttering above him.

Crislan fell like a rag doll. It looked like he was directly over the Scar again. Safety riders were coming towards him fast, but they weren't going to get there in time. He disappeared behind the trees, and Caes heard his mother scream.

He looked at his father, and saw him drop to his knees on the platform, watching where his son had fallen. Other rocs with riders flew overhead, heading towards the Scar.

Caes' mother was crying, and his father was still on his knees. He heard a flute playing, *Bring a litter, quick! He's hurt!*.

From above, he heard multiple flutes playing, one after another. It was coming so quick, he had trouble following the conversation. A roc flew overhead carrying a human-sized basket. The litter.

He heard, *Get a healer to the aerie. We're taking him there.*

Brun called out to the audience, "Folks, we have a situation here. We're going to delay the rest of the Trials for a bit." His voice sounded shaky, and there were tears in his eyes. "Please keep your seats, everyone. We'll give you an update in about an hour."

Caes felt cold anger hit him. How dare that roc attack his brother! He stood up and his legs started shaking violently. He dropped back into his seat and looked at his mother. Ella was crying, and pulled him into a big hug. Tears started flowing from Caes' eyes.

When she finished hugging him, Caes looked up and saw old Catscratch standing in front of him. "Ella, Caes, come with me. Let's grab Jerod and getcha all up to the aerie. The old ranger had tears in his eyes, as well. "Crislan's tough. I hope he pulls through. If he's gonna make it, he needs his family close."

10
Trauma

The riders unhooked the litter from the roc's straps and carried it, with Crislan in it, through the doors of one of the cave entrances and into a dimly lit room. The village's healer stood inside and directed them to set the litter on a table.

The healer, whose name was Camron, looked at the boy in the litter and was worried. Crislan was unrecognizable. Where he'd always looked strong and confident in the past, Crislan now simply looked broken. His right arm was bent at odd angles. His face was swollen. Blood leaked from his ears. His left leg had a blood-soaked bandage wrapped around it. His right ankle was bent sideways. He was missing teeth. He was unconscious, which was probably a good thing. If he woke up, the pain would be unbearable.

Camron was a young healer, and moved here from Roc Harbor after finishing his training just three years ago when the former healer had died of old age. He'd treated many people since moving here, but Crislan might be beyond his abilities.

He looked at one of the riders. "Did any other healers come to the Trials? I'm going to need help."

"I don't know, Camron", the rider said. "I'll check. Do you want one of us to fly to Roc Harbor or one of the other villages to find another healer if one's not here?"

Camron thought for a minute. As bad as Crislan looked, it might be better for him to be allowed to pass on. "Yes, please. Antony, from Sea View, is better than me. Go get him if another isn't here."

"Okay. I'll send someone", the rider said. Camron couldn't remember his name. "Crislan's family will be here soon. What should we tell them?", the rider asked.

"Ah. Um. Let Ella in. She might be able to help for now. Keep the others outside until I call for them", Camron said. "Get Maeve up here also. Okay?"

"On it", said the rider, and he left the room.

Camron reached into his bag and pulled out a knife and some shears. Before he could start the work of healing, he'd need to see the injuries. Judging from the blood leg and saturated bandage, there was significant blood loss. He had head injuries, as well. Several broken bones, too, but those were less important than the head injury and blood loss.

He was cutting the leathers off Crislan when Ella rushed in. "Crislan!" She moved to the boy's side. Camron saw tears on her face. Ella looked up at Camron with a questioning look on her face. "How bad?"

Camron didn't know how to respond. He cut some more leather and answered, "He's bad, Ella. I don't know if he can survive. How far did he fall?"

She wiped her eyes and nose with the back of her hand. "Several hundred feet. His net slowed his fall when it caught some branches but they were too small to hold him. He landed in the Scar on some rocks."

"Okay. I called for Antony – another healer from Sea View. I can't heal him by myself. Help me cut these leathers off. Here's another pair of shears." She took the scissors and started to cut.

"Let me pull his boots off, if I can." Crislan was wearing his new shadow cat boots. She thought she could get them off without hurting him. She'd have to be real careful with his broken ankle, though.

When the boots were off, and tossed into a corner, she resumed cutting the leathers. His broken body broke her heart. If anything, he looked worse when the leathers were off.

"He's low on blood, Ella. I have to try and replenish it, but we need to close the gash on his leg first." He reached into his bag and pulled out fresh bandages, a needle, and suture material. As he was leaning back over Crislan, Maeve came in.

"Oh my… I'm sorry Ella. Camron, can I help?" she asked.

"Hi Maeve. I need to close the gash on his leg. There's a severed artery, though. I clamped it to keep it from bleeding, but I have to try and close the vessel. I think I can stitch it together. Can you start a fire? I need to heat a rod so I can cauterize it once it's stitched."

"Just hand me the rod, Camron", Maeve said. She took it from him and started whispering something. She wrapped a piece of leather around one end of the rod as it started getting hot.

"Ella, wash your hands in the sink, and then come back over here. I need you to pull the artery together while I stitch it."

A few minutes later, the three of them managed to get the artery sewn together and gently, carefully, cauterized it with the hot rod. He pulled the gash closed and put more stitches in the leg, before wrapping a bandage around it. "That'll work for the time-being", he said. "I'll need to reopen it later and clean it if he survives the first hour or two." He paused. "Okay, let me work on replenishing his blood…"

"How can I help?" Maeve asked.

"Are you familiar with healing magic?" he asked.

"Just the basics, Cam", she said. "I know it's draining for you."

"Yes, very", he said. "While all other magic comes from outside the body, healing magic comes from within. You can cast red magic all day long and might just get a little tired. A few minutes of healing magic, and I'll be exhausted. This is going to take more than a few minutes. If I start to fall, please catch me and lay me on the floor.

"I'd like to try something, Maeve. Put your hand on my bare skin. Maybe on the back of my neck. When I start my spell, concentrate on trying to give me some of your life. It might not work, but maybe it'll help a bit." He placed both hands on Crislan, closed his eyes, and started a spell. Maeve put her hands on his neck and closed her eyes, as well.

After a couple minutes, Camron looked up at Maeve and Ella. "It's helping", he said, and closed his eyes and continued his spells. There were shadows under Camron's eyes.

Five minutes later, he felt like he was going to collapse. He opened his eyes. The whites were bloodshot and there were large shadows under them. His hands shook. "That's all I can do. I need to lay down. Get someone to bring me some sugary juice." He turned towards the door, but his knees started to buckle, and he sat on the floor, putting his head between his knees.

"What do you need, Cam?" she asked. "Do you need a bed?" "I'm just going to lay here", he said.

Maeve opened the door and called for a pillow and blanket. A moment later, someone handed them to her. She knelt down and handed Camron the pillow. He set it on the floor and put his head on it. A minute later he was sound asleep.

"Is that normal?" Ella asked.

Maeve replied, "Yes, it is. Camron will sleep for several hours. Oh my, I'm feeling exhausted also. Let's get some chairs in here so we can sit."

Ella went to the door and called for chairs. A few minutes later, they arrived. She put her chair next to Crislan's head and took put her hand gently on his shoulder. He was still unconscious. Maeve sat in the corner, closest to the door, and after a few minutes, Ella saw her head droop and Maeve started dozing.

About 20 minutes later, there was a tap at the door, and Jerod came in. Ella stood to meet him, and the two embraced quietly. Jerod looked at the healer laying on the floor, and Maeve sleeping in the chair. "What happened, El?"

"They were trying to replenish Crislan's blood. It wore them out", she answered.

"Did Camron tell you anything?" Jerod asked.

That got the tears going again. "He doesn't think Crislan will survive", she said, and then started crying. Jerod held her and let her cry.

"Caes is outside with Catscratch and Jatt", Jerod said. "He's having a rough time."

Ella sat back down in the chair. "You should go talk to him, Jerod. I think another healer is on the way. Watch for him, okay. I don't remember the name, but he's from Sea View."

"I will", Jerod responded. "I love you, honey."

"I love you too", she replied.

He left the room and went to find Caes.

Caes was sitting on a bench in the courtyard of the aerie. Catscratch sat to his right. Jatt sat on his left. He felt overcome with worry, but was trying to keep a strong face.

"Ya know, wish I could say things like this never happened, but cha know ridin' is a dangerous job", Catscratch was saying.

"Why'd he have to pick a woody, Catscratch?" asked Caes.

"Dunno", Catscratch answered.

"Crislan said he was going to pick a woody if there was one there", Jatt said. "Brun didn't want him to, but you know your brother. He wanted to prove he could do it." He paused and then continued, "He was doing okay riding him, you know. Way better than me. I don't think he realized he was bleeding, and then he just ran out of blood and passed out."

"I saw it that way too", said Catscratch.

Jerod walked outside, and walked over to the three guys.

"How's he doing, dad?" Caes asked.

"Hi son, the healer did what he could, but had to rest. Crislan's unconscious still. It doesn't look good to me. He's pretty broken. The healer from Sea View Village is on the way and he's more experienced than Camron. Let's hope he can help."

"What about mom? What's she doing?" Caes asked.

"Mom and Maeve were both helping Camron. Maeve is resting now too. I guess it's hard on you to do healing magic. Mom's sitting with Crislan until the Sea View healer gets here", said Jerod, as he sat down on the bench, squeezing between Caes and Jatt.

The four of them chatted for a while. Someone came out of the aerie with some water, sandwiches and fruit. Jerod thanked them, and they started eating. None felt hungry, but it was good to eat.

At one point, Jerod went back inside to check on Ella and Crislan. Nothing seemed to have changed. He left a sandwich with Ella and went back outside. As he was sitting down again, he heard a bird landing, and got back up to see who it was. An older man was climbing off the rear saddle of the roc. He was dressed in a warm leather jacket and held a cloth bag.

The man walked over to where Jerod stood by the others. "I'm Antony, the healer from Sea View. Where is the injured boy?"

"Thank you, Antony. I'm Jerod – Crislan's father. Come with me", said Jerod.

He took Antony inside to Crislan. When they entered the room, Ella stood and took his hand. Jerod said, "This is my wife, Ella. She's his mother."

Antony looked over Crislan, and then over at the sleeping Camron and Maeve. "What did Camron work on?" he asked.

Ella answered, "He stitched his leg and worked on giving Crislan more blood. He lost so much."

"Okay, okay", he said. He leaned over and lifted one of Crislan's eyelids and looked at his eye. Then, he ran his hands over his head, feeling and prodding. He took Crislan's unbroken arm and felt for a pulse, and then put his hand on his chest and felt the breaths. "His pulse is weak, but he's breathing. Has he stirred at all?"

"No, not at all", answered Ella.

"Hm. That's not good. He has a skull fracture. I need to see if his mind is working. Please give me some room." Ella and Jerod moved away from the table Crislan was laying on. Maeve opened her eyes.

"What's happening?" she asked.

"Maeve, move over here, okay?" Ella said. "This is Antony. He's the healer from Sea View."

"Oh sure", she said. She rubbed her eyes and stood up and walked over to Ella and Jerod.

Antony reached into his bag and took out a candle. He put it into a small candlestick from his bag, and snapped his fingers towards it. The candle came to life. A pungent smell came from it. "Sorry about the smell. My magic works better with this burning." He gently placed his hands on Crislan's head, closed his eyes, and started speaking words none of the others understood.

After a minute or two, Antony stopped. He opened his eyes and frowned. "I need to try it some more. I'm not feeling his mind."

Ella held her hand to her mouth and tears started again. Antony closed his eyes again and started another spell. He chanted the strange words for several minutes. When he was finished, he opened his eyes again and looked drained. His legs shook. He sat down in the chair Ella had been in earlier and looked up at her and Jerod. His eyes were bloodshot and his hands shook slightly. "I tried to wake him. I'm sorry. It's not working."

"What do you mean?" Jerod asked.

"I tried to find his mind, but couldn't. So, I tried to forcibly wake him. There's nothing there. I'm very sorry, but he's brain dead. His body is still working, but I feel it shutting down as well. He won't make it through the night."

Ella started sobbing. Jerod felt tears running down his face. This couldn't be true.

"I wish I could do more, but he's beyond healing. I'm sorry." Antony said.

Jerod and Ella went outside to talk to Caes. They found him still sitting with Catscratch. The old ranger had his arm around the boy's shoulder and was talking quietly to him. Jatt wasn't there.

Caes looked up at his parents and knew they had bad news. His dad and mom both had red, bloodshot eyes. His mom's nose was red, which always happened when she cried. He stood up and faced them.

"Caes..." his mother started. "Crislan..." She shook her head and tears poured down her cheeks.

His father cleared his throat. "Caes, your brother is gone. He didn't make it."

"What? No! The healer was here!"

"He couldn't help, Caes. Crislan hit his head on a rock and broke his skull. His brain probably died before we even got him here for the healers", his father said.

Caes felt like his heart was ripped from his chest. He felt cold and sweaty at the same time. He sat down on the bench and looked around desperately, like there was something around he could do something with, or that could help him. Tears came from his eyes, and then anger felt like it would rip him to pieces. His brother, gone? It couldn't be.

Catscratch looked at the family and his heart ached. There was nothing he could do to make anything better.

Caes stood up again and started walking in circles, around the courtyard. He screamed in anger. "I hate those stupid birds!" he yelled.

11

Changes

It had been a week since the funeral service for Crislan. As Antony predicted, he never woke up, and passed away the evening of the accident. Life seemed pointless now.

Everywhere he turned, he kept expecting Crislan to be there with his cocky smile and messy hair. His mother didn't talk much, and spent a lot of time by herself in the gardens. His father occupied his time walking throughout the village. Caes sat in the bedroom he'd shared with Crislan and just felt empty inside.

He was sad. Jory had stopped by a few times, but Caes wasn't in the mood to hang out. His emotions went back and forth between sadness, loneliness, and anger. He was sad about his brother dying. He was lonely because his brother wasn't there. He was angry at the rocs.

Caes got up and went outside. He started up the stairs, and decided to head for a small platform he and his friends often met at. He'd just made it, when Jory showed up.

"Hey buddy", Jory said. "How are you doing?"

"Life sucks, J", said Caes.

Jory sat down on the bench, and Caes sat beside him. "Wanna go grab some ripplefruit?" asked Jory.

"Oh yeah, and get eaten by a passing roc? No thanks", said Caes.

"We could go practice archery. What do you think?" asked Jory.

"No. Not unless I can shoot at giant birds", said Caes. He didn't want to do anything fun. He'd been contemplating something for the past week but hadn't mentioned it to anyone yet.

Jory said, "I heard we should hear back from the riders any day now on who got selected."

There it was. That was exactly what Caes had been thinking about. He couldn't get excited about riding anymore. He didn't even want to look at a roc.

"I'm pulling my name, Jory", Caes said.

"What do you mean, 'pulling your name'?" asked Jory.

"I don't want to be a rider anymore. I don't want to be around rocs anymore. I don't want to do the Trials. I want to do something completely different", said Caes.

"What? That's crazy!" said Jory.

"Oh, I'm crazy now?" asked Caes.

"No, I mean, I understand, but are you sure about that? What's everyone going to think if you quit?" said Jory.

"I'm not quitting. I'm not going to start. It's different", said Caes.

"Oh man, if you do that, your parents are going to freak", said Jory.

"Yeah, I don't care. I don't want to be a rider", Caes responded.

"Well, what else would you do?" asked Jory.

"I don't know. I'm thinking about asking to join the rangers", answered Caes.
"Oh man. I mean, I don't blame you, but... dang. I just figured we'd be riders together", said Jory.

Caes shook his head and looked down. "I just can't, J. I won't ever be able to stop thinking about Crislan and the way the roc tore open his leg and how he bled all over and how he fell..." He trailed off. Tears came to his eyes again, and he quickly wiped them away. "I don't care what mom and dad think. I'm going to write a letter to the rangers and hand it to Catscratch."

"Ben said Catscratch isn't teaching anymore", said Jory.

"I know. But, maybe he can give my letter to someone else", Caes said.

"Yeah, I suppose", said Jory. They sat together in silence for several minutes.

Caes stood up and looked around. "I'm going to go write my letter now, Jory. I can't be a rider." He grabbed Jory's shoulder and patted it and then headed back home.

That evening, at the dinner table, Caes sat with his mother and father, silently eating their food. He was dreading the conversation they were about to have. After writing his letter to the rangers, he'd gone to the aerie and found Brun. The riding teacher had been sitting and visiting with Jordyn when he got there. When Brun saw Caes, he abruptly ended the conversation, and went outside to talk to Caes.

Caes had explained to him his plans to pull his letter and apply to the rangers instead. Brun had been disappointed, but said he understood. He'd suggested waiting a year and submitting a new letter to the riders, but Caes had been firm about wanting to take a different route.

After several minutes of talking, Brun had agreed to find the letter and throw it away.

"Does your father know about this, lad?" asked Brun.

Caes answered, "No, but I'm going to talk to him and mom tonight."

"That won't go well, you know", said Brun. "There's a lot of prestige in a rider's name. If you become a ranger instead, well, you won't be a Wind anymore. Are you okay with that? Rangers are given weird-ass names. They might call you Asscrack or some other stupid name."

Caes laughed. For such a serious man, sometimes Brun came up with unexpected humor. "I'll be okay with that. Thanks for listening to me, Brun."

"I'd still love to have you as a student, but each man has to pick his own path", said Brun.

"Isn't that a ranger saying?" asked Caes.

"Yeah, I think it is. It makes sense though, don't you think?" said Brun.

"It does. Bye Brun." And with that, Caes started back to the village. When he got there, he went to Rangers Cottage – a small house near the base of one of the largest trees. It was where rangers tended to hang out, and sometimes sleep and eat, when they weren't out in the forest. Outside the door was a box with a slot on the top. *Here goes*, thought Caes, as he reached into his pocket and pulled out the letter he'd written to be a ranger. He looked around to see if anyone was watching, and seeing no one, slid the letter through the slot and turned and headed home.

Now it was dinner time with his parents. His father would find out about him pulling the letter to the riders soon - if he didn't already know.

"Ahem", he cleared his throat, and looked at his parents.

They looked up from their plates, and he said, "Mom? Dad? I pulled my letter from the riders today. I hate those birds. I don't want to be a rider anymore."

"Are you sure, honey?" his mother said. "You don't want to just wait for a while?"

"I'm not doing it, mom", he said. "I gave my letter to the rangers this afternoon. If they don't pick me, then I'll do something different. Maeve said I had brown talents. If I can't be a ranger, then I'll write a letter to a brown magician and see if I can do that instead. If that doesn't work, I don't know. Maybe if that doesn't work, I'll just move to Roc Harbor and learn a trade. I don't know any brown magicians, but I'm sure I can find one."

"People will say you're just afraid", said his father. He looked upset.

"If I was afraid, dad, I wouldn't become a ranger", said Caes.

"Our family has always been riders, Caes. You can't do this",
said his father. His dad looked angry now.

"I already did, dad! I already gave them my letter."

"Well, I don't like it. Listen to you mother and take time off and
apply later. Maybe next year", said Jerod.

"I don't want to wait for next year. I hate rocs, and I'm still
going to hate them next year. I hate them for what they did to
Crislan! Why can't you understand?"

They argued like this for most of the evening. Before he'd first
brought it up, he knew it was going to be a fight. He hated the
prestige in being a rider. He hated the expectations that he
follow in his family's footsteps. But most of all, he hated the
stupid rocs.

By the time the argument ended, it was late. His father was still
angry, and his mother was crying. It seemed like she did a lot
of that lately.

Part II

12
Caes the Ranger Student

It had been a little over two months since the terrible day Caes' brother Crislan had died during the Rider Trials. Caes missed his brother so much his heart ached almost constantly, but it was starting to dim just slightly. Summer was nearly over. The evenings had started cooling off, and occasionally he even needed to wear a jacket at night.

His parents stopped trying to talk him into resubmitting a letter to the riders, but he could tell they weren't happy about his hope to train as a ranger.

They were at the table, in their house, eating breakfast, when his father said, "Caes, I heard both of those girls you met in Roc Harbor – Pienna and Saffron - were accepted for rider training."

Caes looked up, suspiciously. He expected his dad to try to change his mind again. "Yeah?"

Jerod continued, "I just thought you'd like to know." He put another bite in his mouth and chewed. "Jatt told me yesterday he wants to do the Trials again. I don't think there'll be enough students yet, so he'll probably wait a year. Maybe even more. We won't do it just for one student."

"I don't really care about the Trials, dad", said Caes.

Jerod started to say, "Well, you know that…" and a knock came at the door. Ella was closest to the door, and went to see who was there.

They heard, "Good morning, ma'am". It sounded like Catscratch, and then the old ranger walked in.

"Ella. Jerod. Good morning." Catscratch looked at Caes and winked. "I'm here on official business, I guess", he said.

"Well, good morning, Catscratch. We haven't seen you since… well, since Crislan died", said Jerod.

"Yup, and my heart aches for ya folks", said Catscratch. "I'm sorry."

"What can we do for you?" asked Jerod. He was eager to change the subject.

"I'm wantin' to talk to Caes", he said. "Ya know I've been saying I'm retirin' once Ben finishes the Ordeal. Well, he's headin' out tomorrow to start it. He's better than I was at his age, and he's probly gonna make it back. Once he does, well, I been thinkin' I might take one last student and put off retirin'." He paused and looked at each of them. "Caes, I'll take ya as my apprentice if Ben makes it back."

"You will? Wow! Thank you, Catscratch!" said Caes.

"Don't thank me yet. Ranger trainin' is tough. Yer gonna hate me sometimes", said Catscratch.

"I'll work really hard. I'll do good!" said Caes.

Catscratch asked, "Ya know how ta play yer flute, son?"

"Not very good yet, but I can play some words. I can understand better than I play."

"Okay", the ranger said. "Ya got a picco?" A picco, like the flute the riders play, is a small instrument used to communicate across distances. The only difference between the two was the picco was a fixed-length, and the rider's flute could change lengths, depending on whether the rider was playing for people or for a roc.

Caes answered, "No, not yet. I don't even have a flute yet. I've been practicing with Crislan's."

The ranger said, "Take this one then." He pulled a picco out of his belt pouch and handed it to Caes. "Practice with it. When - I mean if - Ben gets back in 'bout a week, I'm gonna call ya and ya gotta answer. Got it?"

"Yes, Catscratch, I understand", said Caes.

"Okay. Now, why don'cha scrounge me up a cuppa coffee, and let me talk to yer folks?"

With that, Caes jumped up from the table and got coffee and a cup for Catscratch. When he set it down on the table, the old ranger waved his arm towards the door, and Caes understood he was dismissed. He hugged his mother, and then his father, and ran out the door to find Jory.

Over the next week, Caes spent a lot of time sitting around with Jory. He'd been selected to be a rider, but hadn't started training yet. That would start soon. For now, he was working on the flute with Caes. They were in their hideout west of the roc platform. While Jory wasn't fluent with the flute, yet, he was better than Caes.

"Put that cotton in the end of your flute, Caes", Jory said. "It'll be quieter that way."

"It's called a picco, Jory", Caes said, grinning.

"Whatever. It's a flute. Okay. Now, play your name", said Jory.

Caes put his picco to his mouth and played a series of notes. "How's that?"

"Close", said Jory. "Like this", and he played *"Caes"* with his own flute.
Caes repeated is with his picco. *"Caes likes ripplefruit"* came from his picco.

Jory laughed. "That's good! Maybe we'll have to sneak up and grab some in a bit. Now, play 'Catscratch, are you hungry'".

Caes played another set of notes, and Jory laughed again, and then said, "Oh man, you just said 'Catscratch are you pissy'". He laughed some more and said, "I don't think you're holding it right. Your little finger keeps covering the wrong hole. Here, let me see your hand. Like this…", and he adjusted Caes' fingers. "Try it again, and don't make me pee myself this time."

Once more, Caes played the notes, and this time it came out correctly. "Thanks, Jory."

"I'm ready for ripplefruit! Let's go sneak some", said Jory.

The two of them got up and put their flutes in their pockets and made their way back to the main pathways. As they started up the stairs to their favorite ripplefruit vine, they ran into Jatt.

"Hey guys", Jatt said. "Ben made it back from the Ordeal just a few minutes ago. There's going to be a party tonight. He brought a boar out of the woods."

Wow! If Ben is back, then I'm starting ranger training any day now, thought Caes.

At the party that evening, everyone had pulled pork, potatoes, and plenty of fruit. Wine was uncorked, and it flowed freely among the adults. Catscratch had his fair share of wine, and looked very happy. Even Caes' parents seemed happier than they had since Crislan had died.

Ben wandered around saying hi to people he knew. He was walking with a limp, and had a bandage on his right leg. Apparently, he'd been injured during the Ordeal.

Caes sat with Jatt and Jory. Pi and Ronni showed up after a while, as well, and joined the three boys. The group of them talked with excitement about training starting up soon. Of course, Jatt was an old hat, but for Jory, Pi, and Ronni, starting riding school was exciting. Caes was excited to start training to become a ranger.

When everyone was done eating, and things started to quiet down a bit, Catscratch stood up and whistled. The crowd became quiet and turned to look at the old ranger.

"Hey folks. I'm happy to welcome Westvale's newest ranger, Hops. Ya might know 'im as Ben, but from this point, 'is new name's Hops. You all know we give names to new rangers. Hops, here, had a nasty-lookin' gash on 'is leg from the boar you all've been eatin'. He wrapped it with a bandage, but when 'e got back to the village, 'e was hoppin' on his good leg." He chuckled for a moment. "Hops probly don't 'preciate the name, but then I din't like Catscratch either. Don't worry, Hoppy, it'll grow on ya!"

He stopped and waited for the crowd to laugh and talk a bit, and then shouted out, "I got one more announcement!" The people stopped talking and looked at him again. "Caes, come up here with me."

People looked around and their eyes landed on an embarrassed Caes, who was standing now and making his way to Catscratch. When he got there, Catscratch spun him around to face the crowd.

"I been tellin' anyone who'd listen I'm retirin' when Ben finished the Ordeal, but I decided t'give it one last 'prentice. Tomorrow, Caes starts trainin' with me. Well, that is… I guess Caes will start trainin' with me once I get over the hangover I'm probly gonna have in the morning. So… tomorrow or maybe the next day, I'm gonna take Caes out into the woods and make a man outta him."

There were cheers then, and clapping. Hops limped over and gave Caes a hug, and said in his ear, "Congratulations Caes. Your brother will be watching over you from the spirit world."

Caes didn't hear from Catscratch the next morning. He supposed that meant the ranger drank quite a bit the night before, and his head wasn't ready for him to talk to others. Instead, Caes spent the morning with his friends – Jory, Jatt, Pi, and Ronni. Then, in the afternoon he went looking for Ben, um… Hops. He found the new ranger at Rangers Cottage, which was the first place he looked.

He knocked on the door, and Hops answered after a moment or two. "Hi Caes, come on it", he said, and then limped over to the chair he'd apparently been sitting in.

"Hi Ben – I mean Hops. Oh man, that's going to take some time to get used to!" said Caes.

Hops laughed, and said, "Tell me about it. It's a stupid name, but Catscratch says it'll be normal to me in no time."

"I guess. Brun tried to talk me out of becoming a ranger by telling me they'll name me something like Asscrack", said Caes.

"They might. I figured they'd give me a cool name, but that's what I get for figuring. What's going on?"
"I was just hoping to find out what it's like being an apprentice to Catscratch. Oh, and I wanted to see how you're doing", said Caes.

Hops laughed. "Well, first of all, you'll know he likes you when he tells you to call him Scratch instead of Catscratch. It's easier to say, you know."

"He talks funny", said Caes. "Why is that?"

"He's not from Westvale. He moved here from Northridge a while back. That's where he took his ranger training too. I guess they all talk like that, there. Northridge is so far up in the mountains, they don't talk to people from other places very often", said Hops.

They talked for quite a while, and Caes learned a lot. Catscratch didn't talk very much, apparently. He liked to use sign language or the picco, especially when they were in the woods. Oh, and they were going to spend a crazy amount of time in the woods. If Caes had questions while they were in the woods, he should ask, quietly. Use sign language if he could. He also suggested learning to whistle like a bird. Catscratch apparently did that a lot because it blended into the forest more than the picco did.

Hops suggested finding someone to waterproof his boots. Someone with brown talents would be best, if he could find someone. If not, then coating the boots with grease would help, but wouldn't be as good as the magic. When Caes asked who'd waterproofed Hops' boots, he said it was someone from Sea View Village. He thought it was a magician named Rylee, but wasn't positive about it.

Caes said he'd ask his mother if she could do it, or if she knew someone who could. Otherwise, he'd use grease.

When Caes asked about food and water, Hops told him to always have a waterskin or two ready to go. Always keep them full, even when he thought he'd be here in Westvale.

Apparently, Catscratch liked to grab his apprentice at odd times of day or night and head out to the forest. For food, he suggested keeping some jerky or pemmican in a pouch at all times. They'd hunt for whatever they needed while out in the forest, but sometimes they went hungry.

Hops also asked if Caes had a good knife. If not, he should get one right away.

When Caes asked about the wild animals he'd been hearing about all his life – shadow cats, wolves, mountain lions, bear, and more – Hops just nodded, and told him yes, he'd see all of them. And more.

Caes was nervous, but excited all at the same time.

"What do you do now? You know, now that you're a ranger?" asked Caes.

"Honestly, I'm not sure. I guess I wait for my leg to heal", said Hops.

"What happened, anyway?" asked Caes.

Hops answered, "I heard the boar crashing through the woods, and found a spot to hide where I could see him coming through the trees. I guess I picked the wrong spot. I thought I'd be off to the side, behind a tree, but he came out of the brush right in front of me. I tried to climb up a tree, but he hit me with his tusk. I thought I was dead! And then he just ran further into the trees. I wrapped a bandage around my leg, and followed him. I mean, you know, I couldn't finish the Ordeal without bringing home some meat!

"I lost him for a while. And then, right when I was about to give up, he came out of the brush again. This time, I threw my spear at him and hit him perfect! It went right through his heart." He chuckled a bit. "My leg hurt so bad! For a while I thought I'd failed. I'd die in the woods with the boar right next to me."

"Did you see any shadow cats?" asked Caes.

"Not during the Ordeal", said Hops. "There aren't really that many near Westvale. And honestly, most of the ones I've seen were in the Waha. That place is scary. I'd never, ever, go there without some other rangers. It was crazy going there with Catscratch." He shook his head. "Those cats are freaky!"

"What do you mean?" asked Caes.

"Well, the cat will be standing right in front of you, staring right in your eyes. You have your spear or arrow lined right up on 'em, and all of a sudden that cat's gone! Now it's behind you. Or beside you. Or up in a tree above you. They don't run or anything. You blink and they're in a different place. Your blood will run cold the first time it happens. Crap, your blood will run cold every time you see one of the damn things!"

"Serious?" asked Caes. For a minute, he was rethinking the whole crazy idea of becoming a ranger.

"I'm serious", said Hops. Listen to Catscratch. That old guy knows a ton about the creatures out there and how to survive. That's the best advice I can give you. Listen to him. Don't argue. Don't second guess him. If he says to do something, just do it exactly like he says. He's really good! I think he's the best ranger we have, and you and I are lucky to train under him."

13

Basic Training, Ranger Style

By the time the sun rose the next morning, Caes was as ready as he could be. His pack had two waterskins – both full of fresh water. He had jerky and pemmican, both, in his pouch.

According to his mother, pemmican was a mixture of meat, fat, and fruit, mixed together and dried like jerky. It sounded weird, but when he tried a bite, he decided it was pretty good. He especially liked it when it was mixed with huckleberries or ripplefruit.

He'd bugged his father for a knife, and after his dad grumbled a bit, produced a knife for his belt.

His mother said she knew a good waterproofing spell. It wouldn't be permanent, and it wouldn't work as good as Rylee could do. She knew Rylee, and said she'd do a better job, but at least his boots wouldn't stink from grease. He could ask Rylee to do a new spell if he ever got a chance to meet her.

Caes was just sitting down to eat, happy in the knowledge that he was prepared for whatever happened when Catscratch knocked on the door. His mother opened the door and the ranger stepped in.

"Let's get goin', Caes", he said.

Caes almost asked if he could finish his breakfast, but remembered what Hops had said the day before. He shoved one last bite in his mouth, drank a big gulp of orange juice, and jumped up.

"Let's go, son. Get movin'," said Catscratch.

Caes bent down and grabbed his pack, and headed for the door behind the ranger.

As they walked through the paths in the trees, Catscratch said, "First rule is 'no complainin'. Not now, and not ever. Got it?"

"Got it!" said Caes.

"Good. Ya know sign?"

"No I don't", said Caes.

"Figgers. Well, learn this to start. Watch my hands and fingers. This means 'go'. This means 'stop'. This means 'drop to your stomach'. Now, while we head for the aerie, I wantcha to practice."

Three or four minutes, later, Catscratch held up a hand with 'drop to your stomach' held up. When Caes just stopped and looked at him, Catscratch turned and said, "Ya payin' attention, ya addlebrained wanna-be?"

Caes dropped to his stomach, feeling like he'd already let Catscratch down.

"Better. Now, when I give ya a command, ya do it without waitin'. Got it?"

"Yes, Catscratch. I got it", Caes said.

"Okay good. We're almost to the stairs to the aerie. I'm gonna sit here in the shade by them trees over there. If I see or hear a critter, I'll be up IN the tree instead. I wantcha to climb to the top, as fast as ya can. When ya get there, grab a bucket from the water trough and bring it back down to me. Got it?"

"Got it!" said Caes.

"Okay, then git. Git goin'!"

Caes took off as quick as he could. It was a long climb to the aerie – a small community of caves and buildings at the top of a cliff. The riders lived here with their rocs. Caes wasn't sure what he and Catscratch were doing, but he suspected it had to do with him exercising while Catscratch sat and watched.

He made it to the top of the stairs, and ran over to the trough to grab a bucket, and then paused. Was he supposed to fill it with water or just bring it down empty? For some reason he suspected he'd be wrong regardless of his choice, so he filled it with water and started back down.

When he made it to the bottom, Catscratch looked at him and said, "A little slow, but not bad. Dump the water out. I din't tell ya to grab water."

Once Caes dumped the water, Catscratch said, "Okay, now dunk that bucket in the creek over there and fill 'er up. Now, carry it up and dump it in the trough at the top of the stairs. Hurry now. I don't have all day."

Oh boy, Caes had a bad feeling about this, but filled the bucket and proceeded to climb back up to the aerie. When he got to the top, with his legs shaking, and sweat in his eyes, he dumped the water in the trough and headed back down.

At the bottom, Catscratch glanced up at him and said, "Okay, now drop for 40 pushups. When ya finish 'em, pick that bucket back up, go fill it in the creek, and carry it back up again. Hurry up. Unless ya get faster, ya'll never get ten trips done afore lunch."

Ten trips? How in the world was he going to survive ten times climbing the steps?

The rest of the day was like that. He did ten trips to the top of
the aerie, and lost count of how many pushups he had to do.
After lunch, Catscratch had him pulling himself up ropes,
climbing over logs, climbing up rocks, and running across the
creek over fallen logs.

By dinner time, Caes was ready to fall over and collapse. He
hoped his mother made something big to eat because he was
starved!

Finally, Catscratch said, "Well, I'm 'bout tuckered out. Let's get
dinner and a good night's sleep." When Caes turned to head
towards home, Catscratch called out, "Hey, where ya goin'? Ya
quittin' on me?"

Caes turned and looked at him. "No, you said we were done,
Catscratch."

"I said we was done exercisin'. Ya stayin' with me now. Ya eat
what I eat. Ya sleep where I sleep. Got it?"

"Uh, yes, I guess I understand now. I just thought..." said Caes.

"Ya thought wrong. Now, come on. We're headin' to a camp a
few miles in the woods. We'll eat and sleep there. Grab yer
junk and let's go."

Feeling overwhelmed, Caes grabbed his pack from the ground,
and hitched it up over his shoulders. He ached. His arms hurt.
His legs shook. He was seriously doubting his decision to
become a ranger. He wanted to jump in a tub of cool water, eat
a big dinner, and get some sleep. But apparently that wasn't in
the plan.

The hike through the forest took another couple hours. It was a winding path, and throughout the hike, Catscratch randomly signed stop and go quite a few times. He also made him drop to his stomach three times. Once, Catscratch also dropped to his own stomach. That time, they stayed that way for a few minutes. Afterwards, Catscratch held a finger to his lips, signaling Caes to be quiet. Afterwards, the ranger whispered in Caes, "mountain lion just crossed in front of us".

Caes hadn't seen anything and didn't know how the ranger knew. It was scary knowing the predator was close.

Finally, they arrived at a small cabin 20 feet up in a tree. Caes was anxious to get off the ground and up in the relative safety of a treehouse. A rope hung down from a small deck at the front of the house. It dangled about eye level. "Pull y'self up that rope, Caes", said Catscratch.

Caes reached as high as he could and started pulling himself up. After the exercises that took up most of the day, he could barely pull his weight up. It got easier once he was high enough to use his feet to help. When he made it to the deck, he saw a rolled-up rope ladder. He was just about to ask if he should drop it down when Catscratch said, "An'time now. Hurry up and drop the ladder."

That answered his silent question. He loosened the strap holding the roll together and dropped it over the side. It fell to just above the ground. Catscratch put a foot on the ladder and started climbing up. When he got to the top, he told Caes, "Roll 'er back up and come inside."

Inside, Catscratch had lit some candles. It was getting dark, and it would have been like a cave in there without the candles. The house was a single room. Near the door was a table with three chairs. On the right wall was the kitchen. He saw a stove and several cabinets. On the left wall was a couch and easy chair. At the back were two sets of bunkbeds.

Catscratch opened a cabinet and vapor came out. Catscratch reached in and grabbed a paper-wrapped package and tossed it to Caes. It was cold. Caes started to unwrap it, and Catscratch told him, "Take it to the counter or ya'll spill blood all o'er the place. That's dinner. How ya at cookin', young man?"

"Um… I've never cooked before", answered Caes.

Catscratch grumbled a bit, and then said, "Yeah, that figgers. Parents don't teach kids to cook anymore. I keep hopin' for an 'prentice with chef skills. I guess I gotta just keep waitin'. Okay, so now ya gonna learn to cook." He pointed at a cabinet. "There's pans in there." He pointed at another cabinet. "There's spices there. Ya see the stove. Lucky for ya, we had the stove replaced last year. The one Hops learned on used wood fire. This new one is magic. Ya don't even need a spell to light it. Just touch the stones on the front."

The stove had three stones in front of the burner. Caes touched the top one but nothing happened. He looked back at Catscratch.

"Ya need to touch all three at the same time to make it work. Then, touch the top one - that red stone – if ya want it hot. The middle one – the orange one – for medium. The bottom one – the yellow one – well, ya can probly figger that one out. Ya touch all three again to make it cold again."

With Catscratch giving him instructions, he managed to cook the steaks from the package. He was pretty sure it was barely edible, especially when compared to his mother's cooking, but as hungry as he was, it was amazing.

After eating, Caes cleaned up and put things away. Finally finished, he sat down in a chair. Catscratch spent the next hour on sign language. Caes learned 'climb', 'run', and 'be careful'. After that, it was time to sleep. They each took a bed. Caes was asleep as soon as his head hit the pillow.

Caes awoke to the smell of freshly brewed coffee. He looked around and it was still dark outside, but a little brightness was starting to appear in the sky. He sat on the edge of his bunk, rubbed his eyes, and stood up.

"About time ya woke up", said Catscratch. He was sitting at the table sipping his coffee. "Pour y'self a cup and get breakfast goin'. I think ya'll find smoked ham in the cold box. It's edible cold, but I like it warm. There's prolly some taters too. Dig 'round and see what ya find."

Caes was irritated. "What days do you cook?"

"Ha, yer a funny 'prentice", laughed Catscratch. "'prentices cook and clean. Get used to it. Yer 'sposed to make coffee too, but I 'spose ya don't know how, right?"

"Um, no. I don't. I've never had coffee before", said Caes.

"That figgers", said the ranger, "well, after breakfast I'll walk ya through it. Tomorrow mornin', ya get up 'fore me – that means when it's still dark – and make coffee. The smell'll wake me, so don't start it too early."

"Uh, okay", said Caes. He poured coffee and started to sit at the table.

"Nope", said the ranger. "Ya can drink and cook at the same time, can't ya? I'm hungry."

"Uh, yeah, I can do that", answered Caes.

He took a sip of the coffee and almost spit it back out. *Bitter! How do adults drink this stuff?* He sipped from his waterskin to wash the taste away.

Caes dug in the cold box and found ham and potatoes. There was even an onion. He held it up to Catscratch with a question in his eyes. Catscratch said, "Sure! Mix it with the taters. Chop it all in li'l pieces, but make sure ya peel the skin from the onion! If ya find some oil or fat in the cold box or one of the cupboards, put it in the pan first."

Fifteen minutes later, breakfast was done. Caes sat at the table with Catscratch and they ate in silence. When they were finished, Catscratch said, "There's rules here in the cabin. In all cabins, really. Ya'll find these places scattered 'round the Cragwoods. Any ranger who eats the food hasta replace it. Courtesy says it happens in a few days. Sometimes ya can't do that. Ya gotta come back in a week or two. Anyway, ya gotta 'place what ya eat so the next guy 'as somethin'." He drank some more coffee, and continued, "We'll grab onion and potatoes in Westvale when we get back. Maybe we'll find a boar and smoke our own ham. If we don't, we can smoke deer or elk or jus 'bout anythin' else. We jus need ta 'place it with at least as much meat, right?"

Caes nodded. He was slipping his boots on because he doubted they'd hang out in the cabin very long. His muscles all ached from the day before, and he suspected he'd be sore again tomorrow, as well.

Catscratch pulled his picco from his pocket. "Alright son, yer learnin' sign language, but let's work on yer picco skills too. Hoppy said ya talked to 'im, so I guess ya know how I work. I don't like ta talk when wer on the trail. Animals hear it and know wer coming. If we see each other, we sign. If we don't see each other, we picco." He pulled a piece of cloth from his pouch and stuffed it into his picco. "We do this to keep it quiet. We don't want other rangers to hear us and think wer callin' to 'em, right?"

Caes nodded and looked for a piece of cloth he could use, but didn't find any.

Catscratch said, "Just cutta piece of the curtain. Ya won't be the first to do it."

For the next hour, they carried out a pretty rough conversation with their piccos. He understood most of what the ranger played, but had a hard time playing the right tunes. Catscratch told him he was doing good. Better, even, than most new apprentices. That felt good. He felt like praise didn't come often from the old ranger.

The ranger quizzed him on the sign language he'd been taught so far. He got the answers correct, so he was taught some more words. 'Right', 'left', 'forward' and 'back' were pretty easy. He wanted to learn more, but Catscratch told him the rest could wait for another time.

They gathered their gear and straightened up the cabin. Catscratch looked around carefully before climbing down the ladder. When he hit the ground, he said softly, "Roll up the ladder an' come down."

Caes made it to the ground and Catscratch grinned at him. "Now, climb it again. Git all the way up on the deck and then come down again. Do it ten times. Go!"

Groaning, Caes grabbed the rope again, and climbed up. After ten times, his arms felt like they were about to fall off.

Catscratch said, "After a week, I wantcha to start climbin' with only yer arms. Fer now, yer not strong 'nough. Okay, follow me. We're headin' out." Catscratch started off along a small trail. Caes followed.

It had been a month since Caes and Catscratch headed into the forest. Each day went like the first, for the most part. They slept in ranger cottages in the trees. The cottages were similar but different, and always off the road where they couldn't be seen by passing travelers. They only way to find one was to accidentally stumble on it, or know where it was. Some had magic cold boxes and magic stoves. Others didn't. Some had wood stoves. Some didn't have any sort of cold box, and instead had a cellar dug into the ground beneath the cottage somewhere. The ones without cold boxes only had jerky, smoked meat, canned vegetables and fruit in glass jars, and potatoes and other roots.

Over the month, Caes became somewhat proficient at cooking, and began looking forward to the taste of coffee each morning. He noticed his clothes fitting differently. His pants were getting loose. His shoulders were getting tight. He'd had to cinch his belt farther than normal. Climbing ropes had gotten easier. He no longer needed to use his feet on most of the cottages. Some of them were higher, and on those, he sometimes cheated near the top and used his feet.

His sign language vocabulary had grown significantly. He knew dozens of words and phrases now. He also had gotten much better with the picco. He wasn't fluent in either way of talking, but he was definitely on the way achieving it.

They'd seen a lot of animals. Most were harmless. Lots of small critters, like squirrels and such. There were a lot of deer and elk as well. They hunted several of these during their travels.

Every three or four days, Catscratch told him it was time to hunt again. At first, Catscratch shot the animals with his bow and arrow. He taught Caes how to skin and clean the kills, and how to cut the best parts of meat from the animal. On deer and elk, the best part was always the backstrap. That was the muscle that ran along both sides of the spine from the shoulder blades to the hindquarters, and Catscratch always made him cut it free before anything else. He said it would shrink if he didn't cut it free quickly. Then, they'd spend a day or two in a cabin, smoking the meat and tacking up the hides to dry in the sun. This always happened high in the trees to keep the skins from big predators.

There were days when they didn't wander far. These days were usually spent learning skills, like shooting a bow and arrow or throwing a spear. Then came the day, about a week ago, when Catscratch told Caes, over their morning coffee, "Today is gonna be yer first kill. There's a l'il lake close by. Game likes ta go there and drink. When we get there, ya take the lead and find a place to hide. Use yer bow and shoot a deer if ya see one. I'm gonna climb a tree behind ya somewheres and keep watch. If I see somethin', I'll tell ya like this." He cupped his hands over his mouth and whistled a melody. After a moment, Caes realized he was whistling the same tune he'd play on his picco. He could understand it! *Kill a deer. You're fixing fresh meat for dinner tonight.*

The whistle sounded just like a songbird. "Can you teach me to whistle like that, Catscratch?"

"In time, youngster. When yer master of the picco and sign language, we'll start on bird whistles. For now, it's 'nough ya understand me."

That day, they'd arrived at a small clearing near a lake. There were plenty of bushes to hind behind. As he slowly crept up behind a bush, he heard a bird calling. *"I'm in a tree. There's a deer on its way to the water. Watch for it."*

Caes nocked an arrow, which meant putting an arrow to his bow's string, and watched the clearing. A buck came out of the bush, looking around to see if it was safe. It was too far away for a good shot, so Caes started crawling closer. He made it another 10 feet and the deer still hadn't seen him. He pulled himself up and started to draw the bow. Behind him, he heard Catscratch whistle, *"Danger!"*

He dropped down and looked around. A large, dark, cat-like shape appeared behind the deer. Something was stalking his deer!

The bird whistle came again. *"Shadow cat. Hold still."*

That's a shadow cat? It was the first he'd seen one of these apex predators. It was larger than he expected. The cat's body must have been at least 5 or 6 feet long, and the tail was another 3 feet. Just looking at it, he felt a wave of terror. It was a dark charcoal grey and very scary looking. Caes couldn't imagine facing one on his own.

As he watched the cat creeping up towards the deer, the deer's head pivoted and it saw the cat. He bounded to his right to get away, but suddenly, without even seeming to move, the cat appeared right in front of the deer, and only about 20 feet from Caes. The deer never stood a chance. It basically ran right towards the cat, and it was taken down quickly by the shadow cat's claws and teeth. Caes felt a wave of nausea. He clamped his mouth closed to prevent vomit from coming out. His stomach was heaving. He felt cold sweat all over his body. Caes struggled with the urge to jump up and run as fast as he could. He didn't understand why he was hit by fear and panic and nausea so suddenly.

"Keep still. Don't move. Wait for the cat to leave," came the whistle from the tree.

It was so hard to not jump up and run. Besides the panic he felt about the cat, he also was fighting the urge to throw up. He noticed he was downwind from the cat. The cat wouldn't smell his sweat and fear. He stayed low and waited for the big cat to finish his meal. The feelings of nausea gradually faded. When the cat finally finished eating, and wandered back into the trees, Catscratch whistled to him, *"Come up here in the tree. We'll wait 30 minutes."*

That was a welcome command. He quickly climbed and sat on a branch close to Catscratch. The ranger patted his shoulder when he got close. His fingers moved, *"Fun. Your first shadow cat. Now just wait quietly."* He had to repeat the words again, slowly, but Caes finally understood. He was getting better at sign language, but still had a limited vocabulary.

They didn't get a deer that day. Instead they went back to the cabin they'd stayed at the night before and had jerky and roots for dinner. Over the food, Caes asked questions about the shadow cats.

"Catscratch? How did the shadow cat move so quick? I was watching him, and he was behind the deer, then he was suddenly beside it. He moved 20 or 30 feet when I blinked", said Caes.

The ranger replied, "That's one o' the things makes them cats so dang'rous. Not only hard to see, but hard to escape and even harder to kill. They mess with time."

"Huh? What do you mean?", Caes asked.

"Just what I said. They change time when they need to. Far as I figger, they jump forward or back in time a few seconds. That lets 'em go right where the prey is headin'. Did ya feel sick?" Caes said, "Yeah, I did. It hit me right after he popped over in front of the deer."

Catscratch said, "Yup. That's what happens. Happens to ther prey too. It all works to make it easy for the cats to kill somethin'."

"How do you protect yourself when they can do that? Magic?" Caes asked.

"Nope. Magic don't do much to the cats. They got some kinda 'munity to it, I think. Best ta jus' avoid 'em. If ya hafta fight one, then be unpredictable. It's yer only chance."

"Well, I hope we don't see him again. Once is enough for me!" said Caes.

The next morning, they went back to the same clearing by the lake. Catscratch explained before they left the cabin, "Shadow cats roam a large area. Not likely we'll see 'im 'gain. 'e's probly ten miles from here now. We'll play it the same today. Just find a diff'rent bush to hide b'hind. Hopefully away from the cat's kill. There might be other animals hangin' close or eatin' the guts."

This time, with Caes hiding behind a different bush about 50 feet away from the gut pile, he got his first kill. It was a doe this time, and Caes took it with a nearly perfect arrow to its heart from 30 yards away. He cleaned it, leaving a new gut pile for scavengers, but Catscratch made him take the liver from the pile and take it with him. He wrapped it in a piece of cloth and then picked up the animal. He carried it behind Catscratch as they made their way back to the cabin.

When they got back, the ranger told him, "Good job, Caes. This is yer first kill, and ya hafta eat the liver. It's tradition. All rangers eat the liver of ther first animal. Ya can either eat it raw or ya can cook it. Most rangers like it raw, but I ne'er liked the taste. Ya can do it either way."

Caes unwrapped the liver and looked at it. Then, shrugged and took a bite. Blood ran down his chin as he chewed it. A little sweet but meaty tasting. It wasn't his favorite, but it was edible. He took one more bite and looked at the ranger.

"Good, good!" he said. "Now for cel'bration." Catscratch reached into his pack and pulled a waterskin out. "Wine fer yer first kill." He took a big drink and handed it to Caes. Caes held it to his mouth and took a big drink as well.

"Ha! A few pulls like that and ya'll need ta go ta bed and sleep it off. Take 'nother sip and fix our dinner before ya get too drunk to think."

By the time the month was over, Caes had taken another three animals. All deer. It turned out he was becoming a pretty good shot with his bow.

One morning, Catscratch told him, "We'll be back at the first ranger cabin today. Ya know the one we got to first when we left Westvale?"

Caes told him he remembered. It seemed like a long time ago. Catscratch continued, "T'morrow, if all goes well, we'll get back ta Westvale. Once we get there, ya can take a few days to yerself. Git cleaned up and rested. Hang out with yer friends if they ain't all up at the aerie with ther ridin' classes. Visit with yer folks." He paused for a minute and looked at Caes. "Ya might need to find a razor blade somewhere. Ya got some fuzz on yer chin. It's not 'nough fer a beard, so ya better whack it off."

Caes hadn't noticed the fuzz, and put his hand to his chin and felt it. That day, they hunted again. This time they noticed boar tracks. Catscratch told him boar were dangerous. "We'll hunt this one t'gether, son. We'll use spears. Watch out so's ya don't end up like Hoppy. They lead with ther tusks, and they can kill ya in a second."

When they finally spotted the boar, it charged right at Caes. He threw his spear and hit him in the forehead, which apparently wasn't the best place to hit him. It bounced right off, and Caes was sure he was about to be gored. The boar came right at him, and then Catscratch put his spear right in the boar's side. It spun around trying to get at the spear shaft, and finally dropped dead.

"Next time, don't aim fer 'is head. Ther skulls is like rocks. Nothin' pen'trates. 'member that. Now, clean 'im, and we'll carry 'im back. He's heavy. I'll look fer a pole we can use to carry 'im 'tween us."

They got the heavy animal back to the ranger cabin. The boar was heavy, and both he and Catscratch were worn out by the time they made it. They used a rope to heft the animal up onto the deck, and then proceeded to cut him up into pieces. Some went into the cold box, wrapped in paper. They built a fire on the ground and make a rack to go over it. They wrapped some hides around the rack and placed some of the meat on the rack and proceeded to start smoking it. According to Catscratch, there wasn't enough time to smoke it, so they'd need to stay here another day. In two days, they'd head back to Westvale. They'd take some of the smoked boar and some of the raw meat that was in the cold box right now. The rest would stay for the next rangers who stayed here.

Two days later, the pair arrived back in Westvale. It felt strange being back after so long in the woods. Caes asked Catscratch if the three days off was still okay. The ranger told him yes, it was. In fact, he should take a week, instead. He would call him when it was time to head out again.

Caes made his way back home, carrying a bundle of smoked and raw boar for his parents. The house was empty when he got there, so he put the food away. They had a cold box in their home, as well, so that was where the food went. It was funny, when he was a kid – well, a month ago anyway – he'd never given the cold box a second thought. It was where his mom kept food for meals. He'd never had a reason to get into it before.

He stripped off his filthy clothes and cleaned up in the bath. Then, freshly clean, and in clean clothes, he went off to find his parents.

He found his mother at the garden boxes. She was shocked to see him, and pulled him into a big embrace.

"Caes, you're back!" she said. She smiled big, and hugged him again. "Tell me all about it. Come on, let's go down to the house. Do you want some ripplefruit? I'll grab some and bring it with us."

"Sure. Where's dad?" asked Caes.

"He'll be back in a bit. He went up the aerie to take care of some business. I don't know what. Rider stuff."

"Okay. Do you want me to fix dinner tonight?" asked Caes.

"Oh my, you're growing up!" exclaimed his mother.

"I cook all the time now. That's part of my job. Well, cooking and cleaning too. I didn't realize how much work it is."

He spent the next couple of hours telling his mom all about his training. Then, his dad arrived, and he told it again to him. Both were shocked at his experience with the shadow cat, and also with the boar that nearly got him.

Caes explained he'd be home for about a week, and then they'd be going back out for more training. He said it was hard, but he enjoyed it and was learning a lot. He showed them the sign language the rangers used. Then, he pulled out his picco, stuffed a piece of cloth in the bell of it, and played phrases to them. His dad took his flute out and answered. They had fun talking to each other like that for ten or fifteen minutes.

When that was done, Caes asked about his friends. "Have you seen any of my friends, like Jory or Ronni or Pienna?"

Jerod answered, "They all started rider training about two weeks ago. They'll be busy during the week, but usually have some free time on the weekends."

"What day is it, anyway?" asked Caes. "I've been in the woods so long I lost track of days."

"It's mid-week", said Ella. "You might be able to find them in a couple days, on fifthday."

"Oh, okay", said Caes. "What about Hops? Is he around?"

"Hops? Oh, you mean Ben?" asked Ella.

"It's Hops now. Ben is his childhood name", said Caes.

"Yes, I know", said Ella. "I'm not used to the 'ranger way', I guess. I should try to get used to it."

Jerod said, "I think he's still staying at Rangers Cottage, although he's not limping much anymore. He'll probably be joining the rest of the rangers any time now."

"Thanks, dad. I think I'll head over and see if he's there", said Caes.

"See you at dinner", his mom said.

Caes found Hops at the cottage. When he knocked, Hops answered, smiled, and invited Caes inside. "You're getting skinny now", the young ranger said.

Caes chuckled, and said, "You didn't warn me about all the exercises, climbing, and stuff."

"Yeah, I didn't want to scare you off", Hops laughed. "Are you getting along with Catscratch?"

"I didn't think he liked me at first, but now he's pretty okay", said Caes.

"Are you doing all the cooking?" asked Hops.

Caes nodded, and said, "All the time. Does he ever cook?"

"Only if you get hurt", answered Hops. "Do you want to surprise him? I'll walk you through some of his favorite meals and how to fix them. That'll put him in a good mood!"

They visited for a couple hours, and then Caes went home to have dinner with his parents. It had been great to talk and compare notes with Hops. Caes liked him more and more each time they talked.

When the weekend finally arrived, Caes found his other friends, who were home for the weekend from rider classes. They met at The Study – the smaller platform beneath the one used during the Trials. All of them had stories about their training. Jatt, Jory, Pienna, and Ronni were all there. They told stories about riding the big birds, and cleaning the aerie. Apparently, the first two weeks were all about learning to care for the birds and keep the place clean. Jatt was the veteran, and didn't have to do all the cleaning the newer students did. He sat quietly and listened to the others tell their stories.

When they finished, Caes told them about his adventures. He embellished the story of the shadow cat just a bit. He made it sound like the cat smelled him and looked for him before giving up. When he told about the boar, Ronni exclaimed, "Oh, you almost ended up like Hops!" and grabbed his hand. That shocked him, in a good way. He squeezed her hand before she took it back and put it in her lap.

They all seemed to be liking their rider training, and acted interested in his training, but he felt like they'd drifted apart just a bit. He guessed that was probably natural. He was bummed, just a bit, but what could he do?

The following secondday, he saw Catscratch on one of the paths. "Ah, son", the old ranger said, "I was just comin' to yer house. Wer leavin' again first thing in the mornin'. Meet me at Rangers Cottage for breakfast, okay?"

"Got it, Catscratch", Caes replied. He was ready to get back out there and learn more.

He went home and talked to his parents, explaining he was leaving in the morning with Catscratch. Both were disappointed he was leaving so soon.

His dad asked, "How are your boots fitting, Caes?"

"They're a little snug, but they still work. Maybe I need to get a new pair before long", Caes answered.

"Why don't you try these and see if they fit?" and his dad reached down and picked up Crislan's new boots.

"Uh, those are Crislan's..." he said.

"Yes, they were, but he doesn't need them anymore. I think they're about your size. Why don't you take them - if they fit, anyway?"

Caes wasn't sure what to say, so he simply took them and held them in his lap. It felt wrong to wear his brother's boots. After a few minutes, he mentally shrugged, and pulled his own boots off. He held the soles of his boots up to his brother's and saw the new ones would probably fit, so he put them on and tried them. The fit was perfect.

"I already waterproofed them, Caes", said his mother.

"Actually, Rylee came through the village while you were gone. I had her waterproof them."

"Thank you, mom, dad. I don't know how I feel about having them, but thank you for giving them to me."

15
Personal Responsibility

The next morning, Caes was up before the sun. He made coffee for his parents, and had a cup to himself. His mom and dad were still asleep. Apparently the smell of fresh coffee didn't have the same effect on them as it did Catscratch, so he knocked on the door to their bedroom and announced he was leaving.

There was a rustling sound from the other side of the door, and his mom said, in a sleepy voice, "We'll be right out, Caes."

A few minutes later, his sleepy-eyed parents came into the kitchen. "Oh, coffee!" his mother said.

She poured cups for her and Jerod and sat at the table. "This is early", she said.

"Nah, this is normal time for me to get up and head to the woods", he said. "Catscratch is going to get up soon. I need to hurry and get to Rangers Cottage."

They talked for a few minutes. Things like, "be careful", and "take care of yourself". That kind of thing.

Then, Caes gave them both hugs, and grabbed his pack and other gear and headed for the door.

He arrived at Rangers Cottage in about 5 minutes. It wasn't much of a walk from his parents' house. He walked inside, quietly, and saw that Catscratch was still asleep. He smiled to himself, and made coffee.

Sure enough, as soon as he could smell the coffee, Catscratch woke up. By then, Caes was about ready to pour a couple of cups. The stove was hot, and he tossed some hunks of bacon on it, and grated up potatoes into hashbrowns, smothered with butter, salt, and pepper. He had a jug of ripplefruit juice he'd gotten from his mom. He poured a glass for Catscratch.

"What the…" Catscratch exclaimed. "Where'd ya learn to make hashbrowns?"

Caes laughed, and said, "That's my secret, boss."

"Uh huh… Been talkin' to Hops have ya?" He winked at Caes. "Maybe it's time… Ya can call me 'Scratch' instead of 'Catscratch' if ya want now. My friends call me that. Yer a 'prentice, but I'm startin' to like ya. 'specially if ya keep fixin' hashbrowns!" He smiled, and then said, "Just don't call me that in front of others. It's only fer friends."

Caes smiled big, and decided today was a great day.

An hour later, with the cottage cleaned up, and their gear loaded, Caes and Catscratch went out the door and down to the forest. The sun was just coming up, but most people in Westvale were still sleeping. As they walked, Catscratch gave him a few more phrases to remember in sign language. It was getting easier, and Caes could almost anticipate what a word or phrase would look like. There was a pattern to it he hadn't seen when he first started learning it.

When they made it to the edge of the village, Catscratch told Caes, "Wer gonna escort a couple wagons fer the next week er so." He pointed to some wagons just up ahead. The traders were hooking up some mules to the wagons. Two rangers were sitting on a rock watching.

"Who're those rangers, Scratch?" asked Caes. It felt a little funny calling him that, but it made him feel good at the same time.

"They just led the wagons through the west pass to here. Wer gonna take 'em from here and let them guys head back", Catscratch replied. "Ther headin' to Forks Village. That's 'bout as close to The Waha as I wancha. Don't be goin' by yerself, ever, to that place. No ranger goes there 'lone."

Caes wasn't sure where to start with his questions. He'd heard of the Waha, but didn't know anything about it except it was dangerous. He'd never been to Forks Village, and wasn't sure what to expect there, either. "How long will it take to get to Forks Village? Is it far?"

"Well, on a roc it wouldn't be. But on foot, ya, it's a trek. Figger 'bout a hunnerd miles. It'll take 'bout a week if wer lucky. Longer if it gets hard."

"Okay", said Caes. What about the Waha? What's that all about?"

"Yup, that's a bad spot. 'void it if ya can. Don't ever go there 'lone. There's more shadow cats and wolves there than ya ever wanna see. Lots a rocs too. It's near the base o' the Crags. Wild place. Ya know, 'lotta rocs hunt all over Cragwoods but nest in the Crags. Sometimes in the Waha too."

"Have you been there before?" Caes asked.

"Yup, sure have. A few times. Not fun. Took Hops there time er two."

They walked for another minute or so, and then Catscratch said,
"'bout escortin'… We do it ta keep the traders safe, ya know.
They pay us fer it. Fixed rate a day. They pay half up front, ya
know, what they 'spect the number a days to be. When we
'rrive, they pay the rest."

"Is that ever a problem? I mean, do they ever try to not pay?"

"Nope. If a trader e'er cheated us, no ranger'd escort 'em 'gain.
Without an escort, they never last a couple days. Okay. Wer
close 'nough fer 'em to hear." He winked at Caes. "Gotta keep
up the myst'ry. Use sign language now when we talk."

Caes answered, *"okay"* in sign language.

They walked up to the wagons. "Folks", Catscratch said. "Wer
gonna be yer new escorts. Name's Catscratch and Caes."

"Hello rangers", the first trader said. "My name's Jack. This
here's my daughter, Ash. Over there at the other wagon is
Pepper – he's the grey-haired ugly one. His partner is in the
back. You can't see him right now. But his name is Doug." He
reached out and shook Catscratch's hand. "Are the other fellas
leaving now?"

"Yup. It's our turn now. We'll go's far as Forks. I dunno where
yer goin' after. If yer headin' south from there, we might go
further. If not, well… We ain't goin' to Northridge. Maybe
Eastvale, but not further north."

"That sounds good, ranger, Catscratch? Is that what you said?"

"Yup. That's me", said Catscratch.

"Okay. Figure it'll take 5 days to reach Forks Village?" asked
Jack.

"Nope. That's a 7 day trip, at least. Ya good on that?" asked Catscratch.

"That sounds fair", Jack said. He dug out some coins from his pouch. "Here's half. Pepper's is in there too."

"Good", said Catscratch. "Well, we'll rest a bit and wait fer ya guys." He turned and walked to the other rangers, signing *"come along"* to Caes as he walked.

When they were close to the other rangers, Catscratch nodded, and sat silently, but his fingers were saying, *"Any troubles on the road?"*

"Not too much", the first ranger signed. *"They didn't like leaving their wagons on the ground to sleep in the ranger cottages. Valuable stuff they're carrying. We ran into …"* Caes didn't understand the signs for a bit. They were words he hadn't learned yet. *"but all good now. They learned a lesson."*

"Thanks for the info", Catscratch replied. *"This is Caes"* he spelled it out rather than signing the word. *"He's my new apprentice."*

"Putting off retirement, eh, Scratch?" said the first ranger.

"Ya know it, Fang. Caes, Fang's my first 'prentice. What was it? 15, 20 years now?"

Fang replied, "I've lost count, Scratch. That sounds about right. Nice meeting you, Caes. Keep your head on a swivel when you get close to the Waha."

Caes nodded and said, "Nice to meet you, Fang."

"This is Chucker. I've been working with him for about 5 years. Good ranger."

Catscratch and Caes both nodded at Chucker. "Hi", signed
Caes.

Chucker nodded back at them both.

"Well", said Fang, "since you're both here, we'll head on out to
find some food and a bed. We'll head back across the pass in a
couple days. Safe travels!"

Fang and Chucker both stood, waved, and walked off the way
Catscratch and Caes had come from.

They sat and watched the traders for a little over half an hour
before they signaled they were ready to hit the road. When the
wagons started moving, Catscratch stood and walked behind
them.

"What do we do?", Caes signed.

"Walk and watch, kid", Catscratch replied.

"Do we just walk behind?", Caes asked.

"Sometimes. If I want you in front, I'll tell you", was Catscratch's
answer.

They walked for a few hours. It was uneventful on the road.
They all stopped at a stream and let the mules drink. Catscratch
pulled some jerky from a pocket and munched on it, so Caes
followed suit.

Scratch put his hands to his mouth and bird whistled. *"Stay here
and keep your eyes open. I'm going to scout a bit."*

Caes replied, in sign, *"Okay"*.

The old ranger wandered over to the creek, and then walked in a circle around the wagons, about 20 or 30 feet away. He called, *"Wolves around. Quite a few. Fresh tracks. Keep your bow in your hand, with an arrow nocked."*

"Wolves?" Caes replied with his picco.

"Red wolves, if I'm reading the sign correctly", Scratch whistled. *"Come over here slow, like you're just wandering. Don't spook the traders."*

Caes slowly, casually, walked over to Catscratch. Scratch waved towards some tracks, and signed, *"See that?"* He knelt down and touched the different parts of the track. "Extra pad here", whispered Scratch.

Caes followed Scratch as he slowly completed the circumference of the wagons, pointing casually at other tracks. Scratch signed, *"Keep knife loose and bow in hand."*

After a few minutes, the traders brought the mules back to the wagons and hitched them up again. Pepper waved at Catscratch to signal they were moving out. Scratch nodded in return.

"I'll take point", he said, motioning to the front of the wagons. "You stay here. Be alert." Scratch walked alongside the wagons, and then took the lead. He picked up his pace until he was 40 or 50 feet in front of the wagons.

Caes followed the wagons, and kept an eye on Scratch. Every time the wind blew, he imagined wolves pacing them and suddenly attacking.

After about two miles, the lead mule neighed and pulled back, his eyes looking wild. Scratch didn't seem to notice, but was kneeling down and looking to the side. Caes got a good grip on his bow, and felt his heart racing.

Jack stopped the wagon and tried calming the mule. "What's happening?" he shouted.

Right then, Caes saw a huge red wolf in the trees to their left. He looked around and saw another behind and a little to the left of the first wolf. He looked to the right and saw another wolf there. They'd formed a circle around the wagons.

Scratch turned around and saw what was happening. His arrow was already knocked, and he drew the string back, taking aim at another wolf close to him. He released, and the wolf yelped and spun, trying to get the arrow. On its second spin, it dropped to the ground, dead.

Caes heard a whistle, *"Take the old one, with grey snout. That's the leader."*

He looked at the three wolves close to him. One was larger and had grey fur on its nose. He pivoted towards it, and released his arrow. It took the big wolf through an eye and it dropped like a stone. The other wolves took note and ran back into the forest.

"Nice shooting, guys!" Jack called from the lead wagon.

"Yup", Catscratch replied. "You all good?"

"We're good, rangers. Glad you were here!" Jack replied.

Once the mules were settled down, the traders started moving again. Scratch knelt down by one of the dead wolves. "Let's skin these fellers, Caes. The pelt's worth somethin'. Nothin' else, yer mom'd like it."

Caes wasn't sure about that, but went to work skinning the one with the grey snout. When done, they rolled the pelts together and quickly walked to try and catch up to the traders.

"Should we leave them alone like this?" he asked.

"Nope. Not norm'ly. Wolves ain't comin' back soon, though. Be okay, right?"

"I guess", Caes replied.

They caught back up to the traders, tossed the bundle of pelts onto the back of the rear wagon, and took their positions again. The rest of the day was uneventful, and they pulled off the road where Scratch told them to, near a large boulder that looked like a bear.

"Thers a cave back that way", said Scratch. "We'll scout it and make sure no critter in there. Stay here folks."

Scratch waved Caes over, and they walked back through the woods about 50 feet to a cave opening. Boards were fastened to the opening to make a sort of door, but time hadn't been good to them. Some of the boards were hanging loose.

Scratch signed, *"Might be dangerous here. Bear, maybe lion, or maybe shadow cat inside. Wolves too maybe. Be quiet. Hopefully it's empty."*

The ranger reached into his pack and pulled a white stone out. *"Spear is probably best now"*, he signed.

Caes put his bow on his back and unhooked the strap holding the spear. He held it in his hand and nodded.

Scratch whispered a word and the stone started glowing. Scratch rolled it through the opening in the doorway and stepped back. They waited a few moments, and the ranger pulled the boards free and looked inside. With the glow from the light stone, he could see the small cave seemed empty of animals. He stepped inside and looked around. The cave was about 20 feet deep and only about 8 feet wide, at its widest point. If they were sleeping in here, it would be crowded. *"Looks good"*, Scratch signed. *"Let's head back."*

They got back to the traders, and Scratch told them, "Well folks, the cave looks good. Pull yer wagons to the front and lead yer mules inside. They be safe there fer t'night. We got a cabin not far from here. We can all sleep there."

Pepper complained, "Wait a minute, you mean we just leave the wagons and mules in the cave? What if someone comes by and takes them?"

"Fine with me. Sleep with 'em. Yer wagons won't fit in the cave." Scratch shrugged and started towards where the cabin was.

"Wait!", Pepper called. "Give us a few minutes to get things situated here."

"Yup", Scratch replied and took a seat on a log. Caes sat beside him.

They watched the traders wrangle the mules into the cave, and they obviously weren't happy to go in there. The traders put the door back in place and pushed the wagons up against the wood, set the brakes on the wagons, and grabbed their packs. When they got to Scratch, the ranger simply stood and started walking past the cliff face, following a small trail. Sure enough, only a few dozen feet away, Caes saw a cabin in a tree, roughly 20 feet above the ground.

Without a word, Caes walked beneath the cabin, and jumped up to grab the short rope hanging down. He pulled himself up, using only his arms, until he reached the deck, and climbed onto the deck. Reaching down, he unfastened the rope ladder he knew would be there and rolled it down to the ground. By the time the four traders and Scratch were up on the deck, he'd gone inside the cabin and lit a few candles.

The cabin was similar to all the cabins he and Scratch had been to, so far. Only four beds in this one. He wasn't sure who'd be on the floor, but figured he'd be one of them. Scratch solved that one for him. "Well folks, us rangers are takin' the bunks to the left. You do whatcha want with the others."

The traders talked amongst themselves for a few minutes and apparently came up with a plan. Ash went to the kitchen wall and started fixing dinner. Scratch signed Caes to just sit and watch.

When Ash was finished cooking, she scooped beans and meat into six bowls, and they all sat around the room, eating. Afterwards, they climbed into the beds and fell asleep. Ash and Doug put blankets on the floor and slept there.

The rest of the trip to Forks Village was similar. They didn't run into other wolves, but did see a mountain lion. On the fourth day, they surprised a huge bear crossing the road. The mules panicked and bolted, overturning one of the wagons in the process. Goods spilled all over the place, and it took quite a while for the traders to get the wagon on its wheels again and reloaded. One of the lead ropes had busted when the mule panicked, and they had to assemble another. The whole experience was interesting to Caes. He started to help right the wagon, but one sign from Scratch stopped him. Apparently rangers were there to protect, not to be laborers. Scratch told him later they'd help if asked, but the traders would need to pay them more, first. Since the traders didn't ask, the rangers just sat and watched.

For its part in the matter, the big bear didn't seem overly concerned with the humans. It slowly walked into the woods and they never saw it again.

They made it to Forks Village, collected their pay from the traders, and headed back to Westvale.

On the way, they had plenty of time to work on sign language, bird calls, and picco. They also spent time on archery and spear throwing. And, of course, hunting. Without the traders to fix dinner for them each night, they were back to Caes' cooking and the food they found on the way, as well as what was in the rangers cottages along the road.

After the first couple days, Scratch told Caes he wanted to get off the road and follow trails instead. Apparently, open roads made the old ranger nervous. They wandered quite a bit. It felt random to Caes, but he was sure the ranger had his own plans. This gave Scratch a chance to teach Caes all about edible plants, as well. It was surprising how many of the plants, native to the Cragwoods, that were safe to eat. He discovered the joys of things like wild ginger, nuts, berries, greens for salads, and more. He'd never realized flour could be made from cattails. And, some of the maple trees produced a sweet syrup. His mind roiled with ideas for making better dinners. Of course, he also discovered a scary number of poisonous plants. Some of them looked nearly identical to the edible ones. For example, there were edible mushrooms, and poisonous ones that looked almost the same. There were ripplefruits, which were delicious, and then there was crawling mantrap, which looked like the same plant, but would crawl to you when you weren't looking and eat you.

Caes listened carefully to everything Scratch said and asked plenty of questions, as well.

It ended up taking them about 6 weeks before they arrived back at Westvale.

Back in Westvale, Scratch released Caes for a week of time on his own. He went looking for his friends, but found they were all occupied with rider training. He looked for Hops, but he was out in the woods, somewhere.

That left him with his mother and father. He stayed there for three days before deciding he'd had enough. He went to Rangers Cottage and made himself at home there. A day later, Scratch walked in.

"Whatcha doin' here, kid?" the old ranger asked.

"All my friends are out doing whatever they're doing, Scratch. Even Hops is gone. It doesn't feel right being at home anymore. I figured I'd just stay here until you're ready to head out again."

"Yup, yer turnin' ranger, all right. Figgered it'd happen. We can go in the mornin', okay?"

"That sounds great, Scratch. Thanks." Caes was surprised at how anxious he was to get back out in the woods.

After a minute, Caes continued, "I've been wondering something, Scratch. About the Ordeal, whenever I'm ready for it, anyway… You've been saying, since the day I started training, that rangers never go into the woods alone, and always buddy up with another ranger. Well, if that's the case, then how come, in the Ordeal, you send ranger apprentices by themselves? I mean, don't they sometimes die during the test?"

Catscratch nodded and sat down in a chair, facing Caes. "Ya think it'd be best to send two folks t'gether? Whatcha think that be like?"

"Well, yeah, I think it'd be safer that way. There'd be a better chance of surviving and passing the test, you know.", said Caes.

"Uh huh. An' you think that be better than how we doin' it t'day?"

"I don't know. That's why I'm asking. I guess it would be better. Safer anyway.", said Caes.

"Yup, it'd be safer, fer sure. But, d'ya think you'd have better rangers? Think on it a minute." Catscratch got up and walked to the coffee pot and poured a cup. He came back to the table and sat down. "When a 'prentice 'pletes the Ordeal by himself, ever'one knows he's capable. If he 'pleted it with another guy – or girl, don't matter – no one knows if he's good, or if the other 'prentice helped 'im survive."

"Oh yeah, I can see that", said Caes. "Maybe one guy is really good and the other isn't good enough, you're saying… Yeah, that makes sense. The good guy might be the reason the other is able to complete the Ordeal. He might be the crutch to help the other along."

"Now ya seein' the reason", said Catscratch. "A lesson I hope ya learn is Personal Responsibility." He said it slowly and without his normal accent.

Catscratch continued, "Ever' ranger's ultimate 'sponsibility is to himself. Ya can't 'spect others ta take care a'ya. Fact, ever' human should be 'sponsible for himself – or herself. It's jus' like the forest. D'ya see animals takin' care of other animals, 'cept fer ther litters, I mean? There's strength in numbers, but each person needs ta be able ta take care o' himself."

"That makes a lot of sense, Scratch. Thank you for explaining it like that."

16
Guard Duty

Caes climbed the stairs to his parents' house. He and Scratch got back to Westvale again this morning after another few months in the forest. The sun hadn't set yet, and if he was lucky, his mother would be making dinner. He looked forward to homemade comfort food. Scratch told him to take a week, and really take it this time. Recently, over the past year or so, Caes had shortened his time off and was always ready to head back into the forest. Scratch told him he needed to spend quality time with his parents. Actually, it went something like this, "Son, ya need ta make 'em feel special. Spend time with 'em. Tell 'em all 'bout yer 'ventures, ya know."

He grinned. He and Scratch had gotten real close since he'd become his apprentice. He told the old ranger his whole life's story, several times. Scratch had told him all about himself as well.

He'd learned that Scratch grew up in Northridge – a remote village in the far north of the Cragwoods. His parents had passed away years ago in the Battle of the Crags. He'd apprenticed as a ranger and learned from Eagle Eye, who you might guess was missing an eye from an unlucky encounter with an eagle. Caes' first guess had been that he had amazing eyesight, but that wasn't the case.

Eagle Eye had apparently been a very good teacher, but didn't survive an encounter with a shadow cat that approached from his blind side. Scratch was still in his first year of training when that happened, and apprenticed to another ranger, named Slim, afterwards. Slim was named because of how skinny he was when he finished the Ordeal. He'd struggled to find food, and drank some bad water. After getting very sick, and holing up in a cave for nine days, he'd nearly not survived the test. When he walked back into Northridge, the other rangers assumed he'd died during the Ordeal. He ended up being a good ranger, but Caes had the feeling Scratch didn't have a lot of respect for him.

He opened the door to his parents' house without knocking, and scared his mother badly. She didn't know he was home, and must have been deep in thought. He opened the door. She screamed. He felt bad, but privately thought it was very funny!

"Hi mom!" he said, after she finished screaming.

"Caes!" she screamed (again) and threw her arms around him in a huge hug. "Where've you been? It's been, what? Three months this time?"

"It's been a long time, mom. We've been all over. We spent some time at Eastvale. Then, I think we went to Forks Village, and then Sea View. We even took some traders over the North Pass to some little village on the other side. I tried talking Scratch – I mean Catscratch – into taking them all the way to Daener City, but he didn't want to go that far."

"Well, you've been gone a long time. I've missed you – we've both missed you", she said.

"Where's dad?" he asked.

"Believe it or not, he's in Daener City for a political meeting. I guess Eastlund is causing some trouble again, and the other countries – and Cragwoods – are talking about how to deal with it. I wish they'd held it in Roc Harbor, but I guess some of the leaders from other countries called the meeting."

She smiled again, and gave Caes another big hug. "Please don't be gone this long next time!"

"I'll try not, mom", he said.

"I was just fixing a stew. How does that sound?"

Caes felt his mouth watering. "It sounds amazing. Can I help?"
"No, I've almost got it done. You can talk to me, though."
He pulled a chair into the kitchen and visited with his mother while she fixed the stew, and then made homemade biscuits. He told her all about his adventures. He tried not to scare her with stories about the dangerous animals, and instead tried to talk about edible plants and the people he met.

In all, they had a great visit.

When dinner was finished, and Caes was cleaning the dishes, Ella said, "Did you hear they're having a Rider Trial next week? Jatt is trying it again. It'll be his second attempt, you know."

"Oh yeah?", he said. "Riding has kind of lost its glamour to me."

"I know, Caes, but some of your friends will be doing it. I think Pienna is going to, and that other girl – Saffron? – is doing it also. Jory might, or he'll wait until next time. I understand he hasn't decided yet."

"Ronni and Pi are both taking the Trials?", Caes asked. "I'm surprised they're ready already."

"Yes, are you going to watch?", she asked.

"I don't know, mom. I… I just don't know. I don't know if I could see one of them… you know."

"Yes, I know. No one wants a repeat of what happened to Crislan. But, and you know this already, riding is dangerous. Just like being a ranger. Sometimes people get hurt.

"You should go up to the aerie and visit your friends. They're not here in the village much anymore, you know. Not with all their training. But, I'm sure they'd like to see you."

Caes thought about it, and then said, "Okay, I'll go up there in the morning. I'll see how they're doing."

Ella smiled, and hugged Caes. "That's good. I'm sure they'll be happy to see you."

"We'll see", Caes said.

His mother said, "How about your magic? Have you seen Maeve at all?"

Caes answered, "Well, no. I just haven't had time, mom. You know, with all the time in the woods."

"You think I don't know you've been here a few times so far, and stayed in the Rangers Cottage?"

"Uh, um… I didn't think you knew", Caes said.

"I know most of what happens around here, Caes. Magic is important. Go see Maeve after you see your friends, okay? She'll be happy to see you, and might have some good cantrips you can use as a ranger."

Caes said, "Okay, I'm convinced. I'll go see her tomorrow also."

Afterwards, the two visited, told stories, and generally gossiped about people they knew, which was basically everyone in Westvale. It wasn't a very big village.

In the morning, Caes awoke early and made coffee. He was just finished making breakfast of ham and hashbrowns when his mother came into the kitchen. "I could get used to this, you know", she said. "Coffee and breakfast as soon as I wake up? That's nice!"

He grinned and said, "This is just gratitude for the dinner last night!"

"Ah, that's nice", she said.

They ate, and visited, and then Caes stood up and said, "I'm gonna head to the aerie and see if my friends are there."

"Have fun, Caes!"

He grabbed his waterskin and headed out the door. It took about 15 minutes to reach the stairs to the aerie. It was a few hundred feet up the cliff face, and Caes remembered the times Scratch made him climb it during his first weeks as a ranger apprentice. He climbed to the top. It was a much easier climb now than it had been back then. The past couple of years really improved his strength and endurance.

At the top, he asked the first rider he saw where he might find them. The rider told him, "They all went on a flight at first light this morning, but they should be back in an hour or so."

"Thanks, Rider", Caes said. "Do you mind if I wait up here until they return?"

"Shouldn't be a problem", the rider said.

Caes wandered around and found a comfortable-looking bench in the shade. He sat down and daydreamed for a while. He must've dozed off for a bit, because all of a sudden her heard a commotion. Rocs had just landed, and the riders were all climbing out of their saddles.

"Caes?" he heard. Jory saw him and waved. He yelled, "Caes! I'll be back in a few minutes. I have to put my roc away first." Caes waved back at him and smiled. He was happy to see his friend, and looking forward to sharing stories. He looked up and saw Ronni looking at him.

"Hi stranger!" she said. He jumped up from the bench. Ronni looked amazing. Her blonde hair was pulled back in a casual ponytail, and she was wearing leather riding gear, but somehow she made it look great.

"Uh, hi Ronni! I didn't see you walk up", he said.

"Well, yeah, I noticed", she said. "Do I get a hug?"

"Yeah! Yeah, of course", he said. They hugged, and he realized it was the first time they'd ever hugged. "Your boyfriend probably won't like that."

"Which boyfriend is that?", she said.

"I dunno", he said. "I just figgered you had a rider boyfriend."

"'Figgered'? What kind of word is that?", she laughed.

He felt really embarrassed. "Oh man, I've been around Scratch, I mean Catscratch, too long. I'm starting to sound like him. I'll try harder. I meant to say, 'I just figured you had a boyfriend already'".

"Well, I don't, you know. Pi does. She and Jory are dating", she said.

"Really? That's great. I mean, that's great they're dating, and… and it's great you're not." He laughed. Caes felt like he couldn't say anything right.

"Well, there is a guy I kind of like, but I'm not sure he's interested", she said.

"Oh", he said. "Well, he'd be dumb not to like you. Is he a student too?"

"Yes, he's a student", she said. Caes felt his heart drop, and he didn't know what to say. He thought anything he'd say would just come out wrong.

"Oh, well, um… who is it?"

"You're really dense for your age, you know?" she laughed. Her laugh was as pretty as her face, and he was starting to feel like a fool. "I kind of like YOU, big dummy. I just wish you weren't gone all the time."

"What?" Caes got a big grin on his face. Suddenly things started to make sense. "Really? I mean, yes! I'm interested!"

"Can we hug again?" she asked.

"Oh yeah, of course, yes!"

He'd woken up feeling like it was going to be a great day, and it was turning out even better than that!

About that time, Jory, Jatt, and Pi came out of the room they'd been in, and went to where Caes and Ronni were standing. "Did she tell you about me and Pi?", Jory asked.

Caes laughed hard. "Yes, she did. Oh man, I'm happy for you guys!"

They all went into a dining hall for the riders and sat and visited for the next two hours. It was great being around his friends after such a long time. It had been almost two years, and he couldn't believe he'd let such a long time pass without visiting them.

They shared stories of riding. He shared stories of hunting. They talked about feeding the rocs. He talked about cooking and cleaning for Catscratch. It was a great couple of hours. Ronni sat next to him the entire time. Never before had he felt so aware of someone sitting right next to him. His whole being felt happy for the first time since his brother had died.

Eventually, it was time to leave the aerie and head back to the village. They said their goodbyes and promised to find each other whenever they could. Caes whispered a promise to Ronni that she'd be the first he came to find. They all gave hugs, and he went back down the steps to the village, and made his way to Maeve's house.

When he got to her house and knocked on the door, she opened it, and smiled. "Caes, it's good to see you! How is your ranger training going?"

"Hi Maeve. It's going well. I've spent a lot of time in the forest with Catscratch. I got back last night, and mom said I should come see you." He was feeling a little awkward about how much time had passed.

"Well, come on in, young man." She opened the door wider and waved him through the door. "I'm guessing you haven't kept up on magic studies?"

"No, I haven't. I'm sorry."

"You know you need to practice regularly and improve your skills. Do you remember what I already taught you?"

"I think so", he said. "I use the calming cantrip all the time when I'm hunting. I don't know if it helps, or if I'm too far away, but I always try it. Well, not when a lion or wolf is running toward me, but you know, when I'm hunting deer or elk mostly."

"Uh huh. Okay. Well, let's see what other things you might be able to learn." She waved him to her table, and the two of them sat and practiced what he'd already learned. Satisfied he still remembered most of it, she proceeded to teach a couple other cantrips to him. Stun was pretty cool. It allowed him to temporarily (very temporarily) make an animal forget what it was doing. The other was Animal Smell. It let him smell the air the same as a small animal. He was shocked at how things smelled different to squirrels and other small animals. He supposed it might help him hunt, too.

She told him the lesson was enough for today. Maybe he could come back in a few days and learn a little more. He agreed to come back, unless of course, Catscratch had something he had to do.

The next morning, Caes awoke early, and fixed coffee and breakfast for his mother. She came into the room, hugged him good morning, and sat to eat. They were just finishing when he heard a bird whistle. *"Caes, come to Rangers Cottage."*

He looked at his mom with a question in his eyes. "Yes, Caes, I heard it. Catscratch wants you to go see him. Go ahead and see what he needs. And, thank you for breakfast."

He grabbed his pack, strapped his knife on his waist, and ran out the door. A few minutes later he was at the cottage. He tapped on the door and then went inside.

Catscratch was sitting at the table with a cup of coffee. Brun was sitting across from him. "Hi Scrat… I mean Catscratch. Good morning, Brun. How are you guys doing?"

"We was just talkin' 'bout the Trials this week, Caes. They gonna put the steps in place t'day", Scratch said. He chuckled, and said, "And, so ya know, Brun 'ere's a friend. 'e calls me Scratch too."

"Oh yeah?", Caes responded.

"Yeah, that's right", Brun said. "And, we need to keep kids off the platform while the workers finish getting the bleachers installed. You know kids. They think about the ripplefruit growing near there, and they sneak up and get in all kinds of trouble. I don't suppose you've ever done that?"

Caes laughed. "Well, maybe once or twice, I guess."

"Once or twice, my butt", Brun said. He chuckled. "You kids always thought you got away with it. I didn't jump on you but I knew you were swiping fruit." He sipped his coffee. "So, here's the deal. I normally have ranger students – I mean 'apprentices' – guard the platform. Scratch is going to round up a few others and you can all take turns. Mostly, I need someone there when the builders and riders aren't. That means night and early morning, mostly. Are you going to have a problem with that after what happened with Crislan?"

"I can handle it, Brun", Caes said. "When do we need to start?" He wasn't looking forward to this, but Scratch wanted him to do it, so he was going to.

"This evening. Scratch will put together a schedule for you and the others. All you need to do is sit up there under some tree branches and keep watch. Chase off any kids that climb up. Thanks.", and Brun got up, shook both their hands, and headed out the door.

When Brun was gone, Catscratch looked at Caes, and said, "This is prolly as good a time as ever. Yer doin' real good as a 'prentice. If ya hadn't re'lized, it's a'most time fer ya ta do the Ordeal. I'm proud of ya, Caes."

Caes wasn't sure how to respond. After the talk about his brother's accident, the idea he was nearly finished with ranger training made him a bit emotional. "Thanks, Scratch. I hadn't thought about it. I guess it has been about two years, huh?" "Yep, it has. Keep yer head in the right spot and we'll prolly take ya out in a week or two.", said Catscratch.

"I won't let you down, Scratch. I'm ready. Hopefully you won't decide to drop me in the Waha…", Caes said.

Catscratch laughed. "I promise ta drop ya somewhere 'sides the Waha. I kinda wantcha ta s'vive it, ya know!"

"Thanks, Scratch!"

"Well, I 'spose I better scrounge up more 'prentices", Scratch said. "Stay close, son."

17
Danger, Danger

The sun was starting to rise, with orange colors starting to color the eastern sky. Caes figured it was still an hour or so before most of Westvale started waking up. It had been a long few hours so far. His shift started two hours after midnight. He occupied himself with daydreams about Ronni and disbelief that she liked him. When he got tired of that, he dug jerky from his pouch and chewed on the tough meat, washing it down with water from his skin.

He had another hour or so before the workers showed up, and he'd be able to go grab a little sleep. Guard duty was boring, and it was uncomfortable wearing his pouch. He took it off, as well as his pack, and set them in a pile under the tree branch that was overhanging the platform at one end.

On top of the boredom, now that he could start seeing the platform in the early morning dimness, he kept feeling anger, guilt, and sorrow over what happened with Crislan. The emotions cycled through his mind. Thinking about Ronni helped for a while, but his thoughts always came back to Crislan. He remembered where he'd been sitting. He remembered his brother's ride on the stupid ugly roc. He remembered the blood pouring from his leg. And, of course, he remembered his brother losing consciousness and slipping off the side of the big bird. Then, anger started all over again. Tears started flowing from his eyes, and he slapped himself in the face to get his mind off it. *Would the magic net from Quain's shop in Roc Harbor have saved him?*

Caes looked over the platform again. Big and empty with some partially-assembled bleachers, the platform was a place of excitement for much of the village. To him, it was a place of sorrow. His mom wanted him to watch the Trials and see his friends become riders – or die trying. He just couldn't get his heart into it. If Jory, or… oh man, if Ronni got hurt or died during the Trials, he could never handle it.

No, I'm not going to watch. I can't.

But, his mom and dad would pressure him until he agreed. Oh man…

He looked across the platform again, and saw something sitting on the far side. *What's that over there?*

Something small was on the opposite side of the platform, but he couldn't tell what it was. It was little. Maybe a tool of some sort?

Scratch had told him, in no uncertain terms, "Stay off the damn platform. Stay under the tree branches and watch." Curiosity and boredom were getting him, though.

He looked around. No one was there. No kids. No workers.

He looked in the sky and tried to see birds – mostly rocs – flying around. Nothing. The sky looked empty, but it was still pretty dark.

The sun was getting higher, and brighter, all the time. He should just wait until the workers got here and let them check out whatever was on the platform over there.

But, it was really bugging him.

I can just run over and grab it, and run right back. No one will know.

He checked his pack to make sure it was secure and wouldn't
fall from where he was sitting. He shoved it just a bit further
from the edge, and then looked around the sky again.

Nothing. *The sky is clear – I think.*

Okay, he'd do it. He took one last look and then ran across the
platform. It only took a few seconds, but it seemed a lot longer.
He made it to the object and looked at it. It was a Rider's Flute.

How in the world did this get here?

He squatted down and picked it up. It looked just like the one
his brother had had. For that matter, it looked just like his
dad's, as well. *That's weird. I wonder who dropped it.*

It must've been one of the riders working on the platform. He,
or she, was probably worried about where they lost the flute.
Caes shoved it in his pocket and made sure it was secure. Most
riders kept them on a string around their neck, but some just
kept them in a pocket. He stood up and started back to the
other side of the platform.

He forgot to look at the sky first, but maybe it wouldn't have
mattered. He'd taken three steps when WHAM! Something hit
him hard.

Pain shot through his entire body. Then, a feeling of rapid
movement. Then the world went black.

Construction workers arrived at the roc platform shortly after sunrise. They went right to work. First, working on a handrail for the long flight of stairs they'd already installed to get from the walking paths to the platform – replacing the rope ladder that was used the rest of the time. Then, they started working on the bleachers for visitors to watch the Trials from.

No one noticed the pack and pouch piled under the branches, and no one noticed the missing ranger apprentice.

The workers continued working on their tasks, unaware of the drama that happened in the early hours of the morning.

After about an hour, one of the workers hollered out, "Hey Masen, whose stuff is this over here?"

"Dunno", yelled Masen. "What's it look like?"

"Um. I'm not sure. Maybe ranger stuff. It's none of ours."

"Well", said Masen, "just leave it alone. Someone will come for it soon enough."

And so the pack stayed in its pile under the branches.

Ella woke up, and rubbed her eyes. She looked to her right, but that side of the bed was still made up. Jerod hadn't made it home yet, apparently. She sniffed the air, but didn't smell coffee. *I guess Caes is still up on the platform.*

She got out of bed, got dressed, and went into the kitchen. It didn't look like Caes had been here, so she made coffee and sat down to enjoy it at the table. It'd been nice having him around this week. She hoped Scratch was staying here a little longer before taking Caes out into the woods again.

When she finished her coffee, she decided to run some errands, and then get some work done in the gardens and paths. There'd been some requests to add handrails to a section of path, and she'd been studying some spells that might encourage the trees to grow limbs formed into handrails. It was a tough spell, but she thought she might be able to do it, especially after the extra training she'd had in Roc Harbor.

Before leaving, she peeked into Caes' bedroom to make sure he wasn't just in there sleeping. It was empty, so she shrugged and headed out the door.

Ella returned home at about noon. The spell seemed to have worked. New branches were growing where she trained them. She'd return tomorrow and 'encourage' the tree to do some more. These types of spells didn't work immediately, but instead worked over the course of a few days.

She called Caes' name when she came in the house, but there was no answer. She peeked into his room again, but it was still empty. Scratch probably had him doing something, but she was surprised he hadn't come back to get some sleep after this shift on guard duty.

A few minutes later, she heard a picco call, *"Caes meet me at Rangers Cottage"*. That was odd. She wondered where Caes was. *Maybe he's with his girl, Saffron.*

Catscratch sat in Rangers Cottage, chewing on a piece of jerky. *Well, time to get the kid up,* he thought. He reached into his pocket and pulled out his picco. He went to the door and stood outside, and played, *"Caes meet me at Rangers Cottage"*.

Then he went back inside and sat down to sharpen his belt knife. It didn't make much sense to have a knife on a belt if it wasn't sharp. A dull knife was more likely to cut you than a sharp knife.

After about 15 minutes or so, he looked up and wondered why Caes wasn't there yet. It was about lunchtime, and the boy'd had plenty of time to catch some sleep. He hoped it hadn't been too traumatic, watching the platform. He had to admit he'd grown fond of the boy. He was glad he'd taken him on as an apprentice. He was a quick learner, and always seemed eager to do the next thing.

He waited another 15 minutes, sharpening one of the kitchen knives as he waited. After that time passed, he decided to go find the delinquent apprentice.

It was a short walk to the Wind house, and that was a logical first place to look. When he got there, he knocked on the door and Ella opened it.

"Mornin' Ella", he said. "Is Caes inside?"

"Hi Scratch", she said. "No, I haven't seen him today. I heard you call him. Didn't he go to the cottage?"

"Nah, ain't seen 'em yet today. Kinda odd, ya know. He's norm'ly early. Whatcha say we go fer a walk and find 'im?"

"I'm happy to, Scratch. Where should we look?", she asked.

"Ah, I think we might check the platform first. If not there, maybe head up ta the aerie? Whatcha think?"

She nodded, and they started for the platform. It took several minutes to get there, mainly due to all the stairs they had to climb. When they arrived, the climbed up the newly-constructed steps, and peeked their heads over the edge. Caes wasn't there.

"He's not here", Ella said.

"Yup, let's go to the aerie next", he said.

They walked towards the aerie, keeping a watch for Caes along the way. Catscratch figured they'd find him there, visiting his friends. He was getting a little irritated at the boy for playing hooky today and ignoring his call.

It was about a 15 or 20 minute walk to the aerie from the village. They were nearly there when they saw Saffron walking towards them. When they got close, Saffron said, "Hi Ella. Hi Catscratch. Is Caes at home?"

Ella looked at Scratch, and then answered, "We were coming to the aerie to see if he was there. No one's seen him all morning."

"Well he's not up there. Did you look on the platform?", she asked.

"We looked there already. Is he with Jory, maybe?", Ella said.

Saffron said, "No, I just talked to him. He's hanging out with Pi right now."

"Okay, Saffron. I guess we'll look around some more", Ella said.

"Alright. If I see him, I'll tell him you guys are looking for him. Oh, and just call me 'Ronni', okay?"

"Thanks, Ronni", Ella said, and then turned to Scratch. "Come on old friend. Let's look around some more."

"Yup. Maybe we should talk ta the workers. Let's go back t'the platform."

On the way back to the platform, they stopped at the Wind house, and then Rangers Cottage, to make sure he hadn't returned while they were gone. Not finding him, they continued to the platform.

They climbed the steps again, and both stood on the platform, looking around. They saw several workers, and walked over to the closest. The man saw them coming and turned to face them.

"Hey friend", Scratch said.

"Hello ranger", said the worker.

"Wer lookin' fer the 'prentice who watched the platform 'til this mornin'", Scratch said.

"We haven't seen anyone. The platform was empty when we arrived this morning", the worker said.

"Hm", said Scratch. "Ella, I dunno where ta look next. Whatcha think?"

They started back to the stairs, and the worker called after them, "Hey ranger! Masen, over there, found some ranger gear. Is it yours?"

"What?", said Scratch. "Where?"

"Masen!", yelled the worker. "Show this guy what you found!"

Catscratch and Ella walked over to Masen, who motioned for them to follow him over to the tree branches overhanging part of the platform. When they all got there, Masen said, "This gear was here when I got to work this morning. I don't know whose it is."

Scratch knelt down and looked it over. "This is Caes' stuff. His pack an' pouch both."

"Why would he leave it here?" Ella asked. She was starting to feel panicky, but didn't want to show it.

"He wouldn't." He stood and looked around the platform.

"We gotta 'sume maybe a roc got 'im. Need ta round up some Riders. Have 'em look 'round fer 'im."

Oh no! Not Caes too!, Ella was thinking. Her panic was rising, and she really wanted Jerod to be home.

As quickly as they could get there, Ella and Scratch made it to the aerie. Huffing and climbing all the stairs in such a hurry, they walked across the courtyard looking for a rider. Jatt came out of a doorway and saw them. They explained the situation to him, and asked him if a rider was around. Jatt said he'd run and find Brun, and he took off.

A few minutes later, Brun and Jatt came up to them. Ella and Scratch took turns explaining how Caes was missing, and that they were worried a roc might have snatched him from the platform.

"Oh, that's not good", Brun said. "I'll organize a search party. If a roc got him, we'll likely not find him, though, I have to warn you. They like to take their morning meals back to a nest in the Crags, or sometimes the Waha. I'll have a bunch of riders and all the students fly up that way to look." He paused and looked at Ella, "I'm real sorry, Ella. Um. I'll have someone fly to Daener City too. It's a long flight, but let's get Jerod back here. Again, I'm real sorry."

"Yup. I'll get some rangers ta walk the area too. Ya know, in case he fell or somethin'", said Scratch.

18

The Crags

Caes came awake to the sensation of flying. Wind was beating him in the face. His body ached. He felt disoriented. He opened his eyes and panic hit him. He was hanging below a huge roc – it's talons held him tight. It was difficult to breath, with as tight as the talons held him.

He twisted his head and looked down. The trees were a long ways down!

He looked around but didn't recognize anything. Then, he saw the cliffs of the Crags. It looked like the roc was headed there. If they were this far, then he must've been out for over an hour or maybe two. He'd heard Scratch telling him once, during one of the times in the woods, that rocs often hunted far away from their nests, and carried the meat back to their roclings. Was he going to be food for little birds?

If he was carried to a nest, he'd be ripped apart, alive, by the nasty birds. He needed to come up with a way to escape, but how to do that when he was hundreds or maybe even thousands of feet in the air?

He saw a large lake coming up. Would he be lucky enough for the roc to land, or at least fly lower? It didn't seem like the bird was interested in that. Several minutes later, they were over the lake, but the roc wasn't flying any lower. Even if he managed to squirm free, it would be death to hit the water from this height.

Caes struggled to come up with a solution. He couldn't think of anything. Both his arms were pinned in the talons. He tried squirming and trying to pull an arm free. The bird just clamped down harder. He felt like he was going to pass out again with as tight as the talons got. He had to try again.

He pulled hard, and the bird squeezed again. The blackness came again...

Caes wasn't sure how much time passed this time, but when he woke up again, the Crags were really close. If he hadn't been dangling beneath the huge bird, the view would have been amazing. Huge cliffs and pinnacles were everywhere. Some were thousands of feet high. Others were lower, but they were everywhere.

He looked down and saw a river below. It looked like it started at the base of a cliff. They were coming in pretty low above the top of the cliff, and it looked like a small lake was at the top. *Was that Hidden Falls Lake?*

He'd never seen it before, but had heard stories from his dad about a lake in the Crags that drained through the rock and fed a river below it. It must be it. If so, that meant he had been over the Waha, and entering the Crags now.

He had to find a way to get free. It looked like they'd be low enough he might survive a fall into Hidden Falls Lake. That would be better than certain painful death in a roc's nest. His arms were still pinned, though. If he could somehow get one free, maybe he could reach his knife. It was worth a try.

He thought about the spell he'd learned from Maeve recently. Could Stun affect the big roc? He closed his eyes and remembered the lesson. Time to try it.

Caes whispered the cantrip, releasing it towards the roc.

The big bird stopped flappy its wings, and loosened its talons! Quickly, before it could recover, Caes pulled first his right, and then his left arm free. *Yes!*

A second or two later, after dropping altitude while stunned, the roc recovered, and started flapping again. It squeezed his chest again with its talons. *Ugh. That hurts!*

Caes moved his arm around, and tried to find his knife. There it was! It took a couple minutes, but he managed to get a good grip on it – reaching around a talon to get to it. He looked down, and saw they were nearly over the lake. It looked like they were only 20 feet or so – maybe 30 feet – above it. It was now or never.

He pulled the knife free and tried to stab the roc's talons.

Nothing! The knife just bounced off the hard surface.

He chanced another look down and saw they were almost past the lake. He had to try again.

Caes twisted as far as he could and stabbed the knife into the roc's leg, above its claws. The knife sank deep and the bird gave a piercing screech. And, the bird let go!

Suddenly, he was falling towards the water, and hit it hard, feet first luckily. His breath was knocked out of him, and he felt like he was going to pass out again. He fought hard to stay awake. He was under water and couldn't tell which way was up. His feet hit the bottom of the lake and Caes pushed hard to try and reach the surface before he ran out of breath.

He broke surface and gasped some big breaths and scanned the sky with his eyes. There was the bird! It was circling back to get him again!

He took a deep breath, and right as the talons extended to grab him, he dove as deep as he could and kicked hard, trying to get lower in the water. He felt the water surge above him, and felt the talons scrape his lower legs before the bird flew high again.

Whew! It almost got him.

He swam underwater as far as he could, and then surfaced for
another gulp of air. He twisted around, looking for the bird. It
was circling, but looking away at the moment. Caes took
another breath, and dove again, heading for the edge of the
lake. It was still 50 or 60 feet away. When he surfaced again,
the roc still didn't seem to see him, and he was near a marshy
area with a lot of cattails growing. Perfect. He swam into the
cattails and waited.

The roc circled the lake several times over the next 20 minutes,
and finally grew tired of looking for him, and flew off to the
cliffs.

Caes pulled himself up onto the bank and lay there for a few
minutes before realizing he was just waiting to be eaten. Who
knew what predators were nearby. He looked around and saw
a tree not far away. It was tall, and there were limbs near the
ground. He should be able to climb up in it to think.

A minute or so later, a wet Caes sat in the tree. He couldn't
believe it had all happened to him. Now, he was in the middle
of nowhere, lost. He didn't even have his pouch or pack. At
least he still had his knife. He reached down to touch it, and it
wasn't there. *Oh no! It's still in the roc's leg!*

He had no pack, no pouch, no weapon of any sort. How would
he survive?

He thought back to his lessons with Scratch. He supposed he
could find a good stick that could be used as a spear. That
would be pretty easy. With all the rocks around, he should be
able to sharpen it enough to kill a deer if he could get close
enough. If he could kill a deer, he could make a bowstring from
the entrails. Of course, he didn't have anything to cut with.
That would make it tough.

He thought some more. If there were obsidian, he could make a stone knife, but was there obsidian around here? He wasn't sure. He'd have to keep his eyes open. In the meantime, maybe he could find a sharp rock and grind it against other rocks to shape it. Or maybe he could break it with other rocks?

He'd need water. With the lake here, that would probably work for a while, if he didn't get sick. Scratch had drilled into him the need for fresh water. Lake water was not good enough. If he could make it down the cliff to the river, that would be better. Rain water would be best, but it hadn't been raining lately.

He'd need food, also. That was going to be a bit tougher. *Why didn't I keep my pouch on? I have plenty of jerky in it.* He recognized some of the plants as edible, but others he wasn't sure about. He'd get pretty hungry just eating leaves and such. Maybe he could catch fish? Scratch had showed him, once, how to make a fish trip using reeds, sticks, or cattails. Assuming the lake had fish, maybe he could trap some.

He'd need shelter. That would be tough. He didn't know about any ranger cabins in the Crags or the Waha. Maybe he could find vines and make a sort of rope. Then, he could fashion a bed of sorts in trees. It wouldn't be comfortable, but it would be better than becoming dinner or breakfast for a shadow cat or wolf or something.

Okay, he had a plan. Now to execute it.

His clothes had mostly dried. He looked around, from up in the tree, looking for any of the items he'd need. It would probably be best to start with food. He cautiously climbed back down from the tree and made his way to the lake. He scanned the sky, but didn't see any rocs. He pulled some cattails up and made a pile on the shore. He also saw some small sticks on the ground. He tossed those into the same pile.

Once the pile was big enough, he started poking sticks and
cattails into the mush in the bottom of the lake, making a sort of
fence in a rough circular shape just next to the cattails. On one
side, he left an opening and created a funnel shape leading into
the circular shape. It looked something like this:

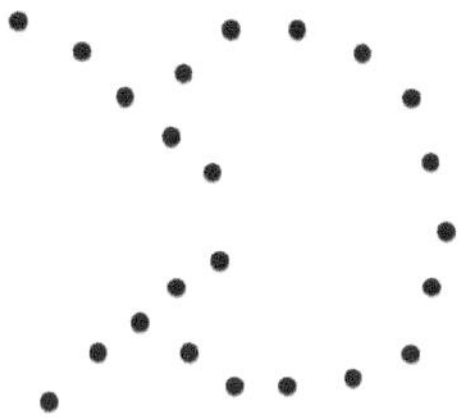

The idea was to get fish to swim in from the left, which was
where the cattails marsh was, and they'd follow the sticks,
reeds, and cattail stalks into the circular area and be trapped. In
theory, and according to Scratch, it would work. It was time to
try it out.

He was wet again, but that didn't matter. He'd wanted to get
back in the water again anyway.

He sat on the shore for a bit, and then quietly walked to the far
side of the marshy area. On the way, he picked up a bigger-
sized stick. He walked into the far side of the marshy area and
started walking through the cattails, smacking the water with
his stick.

When he got to his homemade trap, he looked inside and saw a
few fish. Awesome!

He stepped into the trap and tried to catch a fish with his hands.
Two of the three fish were pretty small, and swam right
between his the reeds in his fence. Crap. The last one, a trout,
was too big to fit, but it'd be hard to catch with his hands also.

Caes went back to the shore, and started working on weaving together a net out of the cattail reeds. After half an hour, he had a workable large portable fence. His plan was to take it into the trap and move it in front of him to trap the fish in a smaller area so he could grab it with his hands.

After several frustrating minutes trying to corner and grab the fish, he realized this wasn't going to work. He left the trap again and found a long stick and a rock. He spent several minutes grinding one end of the stick into a point. Now he had a spear he could try to stab the fish with.

Back into the trap, and this time he was able to corner the fish and after several attempts, stuck the thing with his spear. He took the fish, his spear, and the portable fence back to the shore. He quickly gathered some small sticks and some dried moss from the bark of a tree, and piled them together into a fire pit of sorts. Then, remembering how to use the flame cantrip, he managed to get a spark burning in the dried moss. It finally spread to the sticks. Caes added some larger sticks, and finally had a fire burning. He stuck his spear down the fish's mouth and held the whole fish over the fire.

It had taken quite a while to finally get the food, but at least he had a trout cooking.

When he was satisfied it was cooked enough to eat, he used some sharp rocks to scrape the skin from it, and took a shallow bite. He wasn't too thrilled with the idea of biting too deep and getting bones or guts. When he was finished eating, he went to the lake and dipped his hands to take a few drinks of water, then went back to his tree and climbed it for safety.

It was getting close to evening by now. The sun was getting lower in the sky, and he'd need to figure out a way to sleep in the tree without falling out.

After spending about an hour gathering sticks and trying to keep them from falling out the tree, and then gathering reeds and trying to weave a rope, he realized he didn't have time. It might work if he had more time, but it would be dark before he had something strong enough to hold him. In the end, he took off his pants and stuck the legs on some of the branches to make something strong enough. He tentatively laid back on the pants and bounced. It seemed like it was going to work. Hopefully if wouldn't get too cold tonight because his legs were bare.

The fire had long burned out by now, and it was dark. He got as comfortable as he could and fell asleep.

19

The Search

Ella was sitting in one of the rooms in the aerie, talking to
Maeve. The magician had heard about Caes, and went there to
offer her support to Ella. The riders all seemed to be out
searching. Catscratch had grabbed all the rangers he could find,
and they were searching, as well.

The sun was setting, and she hadn't heard anything from the
searchers yet.

She heard a commotion from outside, and stood up to see what
was happening. She walked into the courtyard, and saw Brun
climbing off a roc. He saw her and walked over.

"I wish I had better news, Ella. We haven't seen any sign of
Caes yet. Today we mostly circled around Westvale and over
around Red Cliff. We're going to stop searching for the night
and start back up again tomorrow. We'll head up towards the
Crags."

"Thank you, Brun. I appreciate you looking. I guess I'll head
home for the night. Would you send a runner if you hear
anything", Ella said.

"I will. Try to sleep, Ella", Brun said.

They said goodbye, and then Ella and Maeve walked back to
Westvale. Ella was sick with worry, and really wanted her
husband to come home. She hoped a rider had gotten to him in
Daener City.

"I can stay with you tonight, dear", Maeve told her. "You don't
want to be alone at a time like this."

"Thank you, Maeve. I'd love your company."

They went inside Ella's house and worked, together, on a small dinner. Neither had much appetite for a big meal. Ella wasn't hungry at all, but Maeve convinced her to at least eat a little. They sat and ate, and each had a glass of wine. Eventually, they both got tired. Ella went to her bed, and Maeve slept on Crislan's old bed.

The next morning, after coffee, Ella went back to the aerie. Most riders were already out searching for Caes. Ronni was there, sitting in the room Ella had been in the day before. Her eyes and nose were red. She'd been crying.

"Did they find Caes?", Ella asked.

"No, they didn't. I'm just upset. I can't believe he's lost out there and maybe dead."

"We need to be strong, Ronni. At least until they say he's gone for good", Ella said. "Until then, we need to assume he's alive. I've been struggling with the same worry all night."

"I know. It's just… I don't know. I'm just afraid." She sat quietly for a minute, and then said, "I should get my roc and join the search."

Ronni gave Ella a hug and left. Ella sat in the chair and put her head in her hands. The worry was almost overwhelming. She had to stay strong.

Caes woke early, much earlier than normal. His back ached, and his legs were freezing. His entire body felt like it was a big bruise. The sun wasn't up yet, but it was starting to glow in the eastern sky. He rubbed his legs to get blood flowing again and provide a little warmth. Then, he pulled his pants off the branches and he slipped his legs into them.

As the sky brightened over the next hour or so, Caes scanned the sky, watching for rocs. He also scanned the ground, looking for predators. He thought he might have spied a big cat near the bank, but it was too dark to tell, exactly. It was something big, anyway.

As he was looking up, he noticed what looked like ripplefruit vines in one of the trees not far from him. That would make a great breakfast. He climbed down his tree and went to the other one. It didn't have any low branches, but eventually he was able to wrap his arms around the trunk and fight his way up to the first branches. From there, it was easy to climb up.

At the top of the tree, where the branches started to get small, there was, indeed, ripplefruit. Some of them were ripe. He twisted a couple of the fruit free and stuffed them down his shirt. Then, he climbed down to a lower branch where he could sit and eat them. He took his time and enjoyed the fruit, and sat to watch the sun rise completely. Every few minutes he saw another roc fly overhead. Whenever he saw one, his stomach climbed into his throat. He was very glad to be in a tree, with leaves as concealment.

Eventually, when there weren't any rocs in his view, he climbed down and looked into his fish trap. Another trout was in there. At this rate, he'd have plenty of protein, but might get tired of fish. He went back to 'his' tree and gathered the spear and portable fence and went back to the trap. After several minutes of frustration, he finally cornered the trout long enough to spear it and bring it to shore. When it stopped flopping around, he took it off the spear and shoved the spear down its throat. Then, he started working on starting another fire.

He got the small fire going, and then went to the tree line to look for larger sticks. As he was carrying them back towards his fire, a roc appeared in the sky above him. He wasn't sure if it was the same one that had grabbed him, but he dropped the sticks and dove into the lake. The roc dove at him, but missed when it tried to grab him with its talons.

Caes treaded water in the lake as he watched it flying overhead. The lakeshore was nice, but he wanted to start making his way towards home. The lake was too open to the big birds. If he counted the roc that had taken him from Westvale, this was the second to try and pick him from the water.

The roc came back towards him, and Caes saw it swooping down. He took a big breath and dove. As he swam downwards, he saw something shiny on the bottom. It was a long way down, so he surfaced again and got a deep breath, and then dove again. His ears started hurting after about 10 feet. He pushed further and reached the bottom. He stuck his hand into the murky bottom and found the object. Pulling it up, he realized it was his knife! It must have come dislodged from the roc's leg when it tried to pluck him from the water. He pushed off the bottom and went back to the surface. He was almost out of air. He took a few breaths, and then shoved his knife back into the scabbard at his waist.

This would make thing easier!

As he was swimming back to shore, he spied a group of rocs flying overhead. His first thought was to dive deep again, but then noticed they had riders on them. It looked like a search party!

He tried waving his arms around, but they didn't see him. The small fire he'd started had burned out, so they wouldn't see any smoke. *The flute! Play the flute!* Oh yeah, that would work. He reached his left hand down and felt for the flute.

It was missing.

Oh no. That was disappointing. He waved his arms some more, and shouted as loud as he could, but they didn't seem to notice. After a couple minutes, they were gone from his sight. He made it back to the shore. It was warm out, but he was soaked. He decided to dry his clothes in the sun while he cooked the trout that was still lying on the ground, stuck on his spear.

He took his pants and shirt off and wrung them out as much as he could, and laid them on a big rock to dry in the sun. He set his boots next to the fire pit to dry in the heat it would make. Then, he got to work again on the fire. He got it going, and added the other sticks he'd scattered across the shore, and eventually got it hot enough to cook the fish.

With his knife, he gutted it, and removed the skin. Then, got it balanced on his spear and held it over the fire to cook. Once he was done cooking it, he moved back into the bushes and sat quietly, waiting for his clothes to dry. While he was there, he whittled on the spear to make the tip sharper.

After about an hour, his clothes looked dry, and he snuck back to them to give them a shake and put them back on.

He spent the rest of the afternoon cutting vines and cattails, and weaving a sort of net to hold him in the tree.

He never saw the searchers again, and by nighttime, he was back in the tree, leaning against his new sleeping matt. He slept much better that night.

20

Roc for Dinner?

The following morning, Caes awoke with the early sunlight.
After watching the sun rise for a while, Caes climbed down his
tree and drank some water from the lake, and then climbed the
other tree – the one with ripplefruit in the top – and found
another three ripe fruits for breakfast. He sat in that tree, eating
his breakfast, until the sun was all the way above the horizon.
Today, he decided, was going to be a travel day. He hoped to
find a way off the cliff he was at the top of and find a way down
to the bottom, by the river he'd seen. He contemplated lashing
his knife to his spear, but in the end, decided to stick with two
separate weapons. He couldn't afford to lose his knife again.

Looking around, he found another stick that would make a
decent spear, and spent the next half hour or so whittling on it.
Eventually, he had a second spear.

He walked back to his tree and climbed up to retrieve his 'bed'.
He'd carry it with him if he could. It took too long making it to
want to make a second one. When he tried to climb down the
tree, it snagged in a branch, and then he lost his grip on it, and it
fell to the ground.

Great… I hope I didn't break it.

He got to the bottom of the tree and walked over to pick up the
mess of reeds and vines. It was still mostly intact, but what was
even better was what he found underneath it. The flute was
there in the bushes. It must have fallen from his pocket on the
first night, when he'd used his pants as a bed. Well, now he had
a way to call the riders when – or if - they came back.

He went over to his fish trap and looked for a fish in it, but it was empty this time. That was too bad. Fish for the trail would have been good, but he'd have to look for something else.

Caes looked at the sky, and then at his shadow, and determined the directions. Straight ahead was south. To his right was west, and to his left was east. The river would be south, so he started off in that direction, keeping to the brush and trees as much as possible.

The lake wasn't very big. At most it was half a mile long, or maybe a little longer. At the slow speed Caes was walking, it was 15 minutes later when he reached the end of the lake, and then another 5 minutes or so to reach the edge of the cliff. What he saw when he got there was depressing. He was at the top of a nearly sheer cliff. The ground, below, was at least 1,000 feet below him, and he didn't see any path leading down, and no place to climb. Without a very long rope, it simply wasn't passable.

For the next hour, he walked first to the west, and then to the east, looking for possible routes down. Every 5 or 6 minutes, he had to duck under a bush, or hide against a rock, because a roc flew by. Sometimes he saw 4 or 5 flying at the same time.

Finally, after walking quite a ways to the east, he found a sloping hillside, and decided to walk down it, hopefully, all the way to the base of the cliff. It was a tough slope, with loose rocks scattered here and there. At one point, he started sliding, and right as panic hit, he was able to grab a bush and stop his slide. He rested for a few minutes, and then started down again.

The route he'd selected seemed to be going near the base of the cliffs. He'd dropped at least 500 feet in elevation so far. It would be a tough climb back up if he ended up needing to. Hopefully, that wouldn't be necessary.

The slope gradually leveled out, and he was on a small plateau on the cliff. There were several trees on the plateau, and he was grateful for them. Rocs were in the air, and frequently passed overhead. He stuck to the trees for concealment. None of the rocs had riders on them, so they must all be wild.

Caes spent several minutes under some brush, waiting for the air to clear. Finally, it looked clear and he went to the edge of the plateau and looked down. He was still a few hundred feet above the base of the cliffs, at least. It looked like he might have to climb back up the slope he'd come down because he didn't see a way down from the plateau. That wasn't going to be an easy climb.

Rather than starting right up, he went to the the east and west sides of the plateau to see if he could find a way down. It'd worked up above, and maybe it would work here, as well.

On the east, he didn't find anything, and on the west side, he didn't either, but he did see a roc nest right below the edge he was looking over. It was maybe 10 feet or so below him, and there was a young roc sitting in the nest. The roc was much smaller than the others he'd seen, and not even close to the huge one that had grabbed him from the roc platform in Westvale. He ducked back away from the edge and a thought occurred to him.

I think that's my dinner down there!

If he could drive a spear through the bird, he could kill it. Then, since he'd found his knife, he could cut it up and cook it over a fire. There was enough brush, moss, and small trees on the plateau to make a fire. After two days of trout, roc sounded delicious.

He crept back to edge and looked again. This time, he was
looking to make sure there was a way back up once he killed the
roc. It wasn't going to be easy, but it looked like he could
probably make his way up. So, he went back to his gear, pulled
out his knife, and gave his two spears sharper points. He
planned to hold the spear, point down, and jump off the edge,
driving the spear through the bird with his body weight. He'd
never done something like this before, but was confident it
would work.

He waited a few minutes, back away from the edge, and took
deep breaths, visualizing what he was about to do and
preparing for anything that went wrong. Ready, he crept
forward again and looked down at the bird. He held the spear
with the point facing downward, and leapt off the edge. The
roc moved, just slightly, as he was in the air, and it was just
enough for the spear to miss and plunge through a mass of
feathers – missing the body of the roc. Caes landed right on its
back.

Uh oh! He tried to lift the spear back up and stab it, but the
stupid bird jumped off the cliff – with Caes on its back!
Suddenly, Caes found himself about 300 feet above the forest,
hanging on for his life to the neck of the roc. The spear fell to
the ground.

The wild roc was not happy about having an unexpected rider.
It spun its head trying to reach Caes. All Caes could do was
twist away from the beak and smack it with the palm of his
hand.

Then, the roc twisted to the left and start spinning in the air. Caes would have flown off the bird if he hadn't already had a death grip around the bird's neck. When spinning didn't dislodge him, the bird tried diving to the ground instead. It tucked its wings and dove, head first, directly towards the ground. At the last second, it put its wings out and pulled up, flapping its wings hard. They gained altitude at an amazing rate. In seconds they were several thousand feet above the ground, and the bird twisted its neck to try to reach Caes again. Once more, Caes twisted away and smacked the bird's head with his hand. He wanted to grab his knife and stab it, but was afraid he'd be thrown off, so he just held on as hard as he could. The only time his hand came loose was when he needed to smack the bird when it tried to bite him.

The roc didn't seem to have a limit on the energy it could expend. It tried all sorts of moves to throw him off. It twisted to the right. It twisted to the left. It tried to bite him. It climbed straight up. It dove straight to the ground. It spun in the air. At one point, Caes was certain it flew upside down and started tumbling. Each time, when Caes held on tight enough, the bird eventually changed directions.

At one point, the roc flew several thousand feet high again, and Caes took the risk to cast his stun cantrip. Briefly, very briefly, the bird stopped fighting and just fell. After a couple of seconds, though, it regained control and tried throwing him off again.

Caes tried whispering the calm cantrip. He did it once and the bird seemed to relax. When it tensed up again, Caes whispered it again. Again, the bird seemed to relax. While relaxed, Caes chanced loosening one hand and stroking the neck, whispering, "It's okay. Just land and let me off. It's okay."

Eventually, the bird seemed to realize Caes wasn't going to fall or jump off and stopped fighting as much. Either that, or it was getting tired and conserving its strength. Caes started to relax and loosened his hands just a bit. He realized the bird wasn't a baby roc like he'd thought. He realized it was an adult wood roc. *Of course,* he thought, *wood rocs were much smaller than great rocs.*

Now, how to get off the stupid bird?

He thought about the reins riders used on their rocs. He didn't have any reins, but maybe he could emulate them by pulling or pushing on the roc's head and neck. Turning seemed the easiest thing to try. He tried pulling the neck to the right, but the roc took that as a signal to try and bite him again. He smacked its head again, and whispered the calm cantrip again. As soon as he finished it, he tried pulling the neck to the right again, and this time the bird gently turned to the right! *Yes!*

He tried the same thing on the left, but again, it tried to bite him. He tried the cantrip again and pulled to the left. This time, the bird gently turned to the left.

He was getting tired, and he wasn't sure how many more cantrips he could cast before he became too tired to use any more. So, he resorted to calmly talking to the bird and stroking its neck. The roc seemed to like that and wasn't trying to throw him off.

Caes tried pushing its neck forward, and the roc started descending towards the forest floor. *Okay, maybe I can do this without killing myself...*

He looked for a meadow or river bank or something like that
and spied a rather large bank on the east side of the river. He
aimed the roc at it and continued to push his neck forward. The
roc continued descending. "Good roc!", Caes whispered to the
bird. "That's it, keep heading to the clearing. There we go."

Caes didn't have any idea if the talking was helping, but it
didn't seem to hurt. He started considering his strategy to get
off the bird. It was possible – even likely – that it would simply
grab him for dinner as soon as he jumped off its back. He
decided he'd need to try one more cantrip and decided on stun.
When he was getting very close to the ground, he started
whispering the cantrip, holding back the final word until the
roc put its claws down and landed. Then, Caes release the last
word of the cantrip and jumped off the bird, running quickly to
a cluster of trees.

The roc turned and looked at him, and then shook its head.
Then, without hesitation, it leapt into the air and flew away.
Caes collapsed to his knees behind the trees. His entire body
was shaking. *How did I survive that? That was crazy!*

When he finally stopped shaking, he started thinking about the
other things in this forest who'd happily make a meal of him,
and grabbed a tree and climbed as high as he could.

He sat in the tree for over an hour before deciding to climb
down and find food and water.

During this time, Caes contemplated his situation. He needed a
better way to hunt than throwing a simple wooden spear. He
might be able to catch more fish in the river with another fish
trap, like he'd made at Hidden Falls Lake, but he couldn't
follow the river all the way. He wasn't sure where it went, and
what dangers he might find following it.

As far as he could tell, he was probably in the area of the Cragwoods known as the Waha, and likely in the most northern part of it. He needed to make his way south and west to find his way back home. That meant he needed to find a way across this river, since he was on the eastern side of it. He could maybe find a shallow stretch. If not, he'd need to swim it, or maybe make a raft of sorts. On the other side, he should look for materials to make a bow and arrows. That meant looking for straight wood and something for a string. He and Scratch had discussed this in the past, and even made their own strings. Scratch preferred fibrous plants, but Caes knew it was also possible to use animal hide or tendons. He'd have to keep his eyes open for things that would work. Feathers would also be needed. He'd seen several, and would likely see more. Next time he saw some, he'd gather them in his pockets.

What else do I need?

Hm. He supposed he could sharpen the tips of the arrows, once he made them, but some type of arrow head would be best. He hadn't seen obsidian yet, but maybe he could find some rocks that he could form into points. It would also be good to find some big enough to use as an axe.

Now, to find some food.

Caes climbed down from the tree and started looking for sticks to use as spears again, since he'd lost the two he already had. With all the trees around, it didn't take long to find a few good-sized straight sticks. He leaned them against the tree he'd been sitting in, and went to the river for a drink of water. There weren't any cattails here, unfortunately. Fishing would be tough until he found a good spot and some good reeds. He supposed he could just use sticks to build his fish trap. Maybe later. For now, he went back to the tree and climbed back up, carrying one of his sticks with him.

For the next hour, he whittled away on the sticks, making them the right length and with a sharp point. At the end, he had three spears. The sun was getting low in the sky, and he needed to find food soon. A squirrel ran across a log by the river and Caes had a thought.

He climbed down and slowly walked closer to the log and sat down about 10 feet away from it. Then he just waited. The squirrel had disappeared when he approached the log, but after sitting there for ten minutes, it came back out, chittering away.

Caes waited until it got closer, and then tried throwing the spear at it. The squirrel ran away, and stopped on the side of a tree, and chittered again. It was like it was making fun of his attempt to spear it. Caes threw a spear again at it, and again, it didn't even come close to hitting the squirrel.

The squirrel just ran to the other side of the tree and chittered some more.

Apparently, the spear wasn't going to work against the squirrel. He'd need to try something else.

While he sat, thinking, the squirrel came closer and ran onto the log again. Caes held his remaining spear and watched. If he didn't move, the squirrel didn't feel threatened and ran around, chittering.

If only Caes could get the squirrel to hold still.
Wait! What about a cantrip? Would that work? Maybe Calm? Possibly. Hey, what about Stun? Yeah, that might work!

He started mouthing the words to the cantrip, very softly, and almost silently. He kept watch on the squirrel and made his spear ready to throw. When it came a little closer, he whispered the last word and released the spell at the squirrel. It immediately fell off the log and laid still. Caes ran up with the spear and stuck the squirrel right as it started to move again. It wiggled for a moment and died.

Meat! Caes took his knife from his scabbard and proceeded to gut and clean the squirrel. There wasn't a whole lot of meat in it, but it would be good.

Caes made a fire. While it got going good, he skinned the squirrel and found some sticks to use for cooking it. While it was cooking, Caes picked up the guts and was about to throw them into the bushes and stopped. He wasn't sure if it would work, but maybe it would make a good fish bait?

He set the guts back down, rinsed his hands in the river, and went back to his fire to eat his squirrel meat. It was delicious! When he finished dinner, he tossed some of the squirrel guts into the mud in the shallow water at the edge of the river and stepped back to watch. After several minutes, he saw some movement around the guts and crept forward to see what it was. There weren't any fish, but it looked like crawdads were eating it. That would work! Tomorrow, he'd make a basket of sticks or reeds or whatever he could find and kill another squirrel. After that, maybe he'd eat crawdads.

It was getting late now, so he retreated to his tree and worked on a bed of sorts to prop on the branches of the tree. He finished right as the sun dropped behind the trees. He leaned back on it while testing the strength as he held onto the tree trunk. Satisfied it wouldn't break, Caes laid back on it and drifted to sleep.

Caes awoke at first light. He looked around from his bed in the tree. There was a doe drinking at the river. He glanced at his spears, sitting on a cluster of limbs above his head, but the deer was too far away for him to have a chance at it. Plus, if he threw it hard enough to try and hit the deer he'd likely fall out of the tree. If only he had a bow and arrow. Then it would be an easy shot.

Okay, so today I need to make a bow and arrow. That's my top priority.

The deer drank for a few minutes and then her head looked around and she darted into the trees. Something had scared her. Caes pulled a spear down into his hands and waited. Several minutes later, a wolf came out of the trees and approached the water. A second wolf came out a minute or two later. Caes waited, silently, as he watched the predators. They didn't stay long. After drinking some water they both silently went back into the trees. This was a good reminder to watch for dangerous animals.

After the wolves left, Caes waited another 20 minutes and then climbed down the tree. With his spear in one hand, and his knife in the other, he wandered downstream several hundred feet, looking at the river and the vegetation on both banks. He couldn't tell how deep the river was, but it looked shallow enough to wade across. It was moving pretty fast, though. He returned to his camp and picked up his other spears, and then started walking downstream again.

About a mile downstream, the banks started getting steep, with big boulders on the sides. The river got narrower and deeper. He started back upstream again and looked for the best place to cross the river. A few hundred yards seemed about the best place. The river was wider here, and looked shallow enough. Caes started walking across. About a third of the way across, he got to his waist in the water. The current was stronger than it looked, and he was careful not to fall over.

He kept pushing across, and when he was nearly halfway, he was up to his ribcage. He paused for a moment to get his footing, and then took another step. His foot found a deep spot and he lost his balance and fell. He went completely under water and fought to get his head back above the surface. The current caught him and carried him down the river. He tried swimming, but his spears were interfering, so he let them go. He'd just have to make new ones later.

The river was getting deeper and narrower. In a few minutes, he'd be in the boulder area he'd seen on his walk. Finally, he got his feet on the bottom of the river and stopped his floating downstream. He started walking to the shore. When he was about 10 feet from the bank, and the river seemed to be getting shallower, Caes saw a huge bear coming out of the trees. With no weapons to speak of – and not even his homemade spears – Caes decided to back into the current again and float downstream away from the bear. The bear saw him and rose on its hind legs and let out a big roar. It charged into the water, coming at Caes, like it was going to attack him. The current started pulling Caes downstream, and the bear apparently lost interest. It turned upstream and splashed into the water. Right before Caes went around a small bend in the river, he saw the bear pull a large trout out of the river with its teeth.

Caes wanted to get some distance between him and the bear, and let the current take care of it. Before he knew it, they were in the boulder area. The current picked up and he started moving faster. It was time to head for the bank, so Caes started swimming to the western side of the river. He heard the river getting louder. It sounded like whitewater ahead.

He swam hard, trying to reach the bank. The boulders were in reach, but Caes couldn't grab hold of them. They were big, smooth, and wet. His fingers just slipped away.

The sound of whitewater got stronger and suddenly he was in rapids. There were boulders in the water now, and he was concerned he'd get trapped by one, so he rolled over and put his feet in front of him, trying to keep his toes above the water, and rode the rapids, pushing off boulders with his feet when he came close to them. If it weren't for the panicky feeling he had about being out of control, this might have been fun.

The rapids got faster and then he flew over a waterfall. Luckily, it was only a dozen feet high, but he was sucked under the water and held there for a minute in the turbulence. He struggled to get free of the turbulence, and felt his air running out. Then, when he stopped struggling, the water seemed to release him and his head broke the surface.

Caes looked around. The water was calm and deep here, and it was moving slow. Happy for the relative safety, Caes swam to the bank and climbed out of the river. He was on the western side, at least. He looked around, checking to make sure he wasn't about to get eaten by some animal. Satisfied that he was momentarily safe, he found a good tree, and climbed up about 20 feet to sit on a branch.

He was feeling hungry. He hadn't eaten anything yet, this morning. Caes pulled his knife out to check it, and then put it back in its scabbard. He had several things he needed to work on. First, there was his empty stomach. His hunger would get distracting before too long. He'd need to find something to eat. Second, he needed to find the materials to make a bow and arrows. Third, he needed to make another spear. Sometime today he'd need to find shelter, as well.

He climbed out of the tree and started walking downstream. The river curved to the west not too far from where he'd climbed out of the water. Around the bend, he found a treasure trove. Cattails were along the bank, and just past them, he saw a large cluster of bamboo. This would be fantastic for what he needed to make.

He looked around at the bamboo and found a few stalks that were about an inch in diameter. Using his knife, Caes went to work cutting them down. It took a while. A saw would have been easier, but he finally got the bamboo cut. He carried them over to a good location for a fire. Tall trees were nearby if he needed to climb one.

Caes went back and pulled several cattails out of the water. These, he also took to the fire location. He wandered around a bit and found a nice flat rock, about ten inches in diameter. He picked this up and carried it back, as well. Lastly, he looked for big leaves. This took a little longer, but he finally found some large round leaves from a water plant, and brought them as well.

He gathered a nice bundle of small sticks for a fire, as well as a few larger ones, and then started a fire with a cantrip. After feeding it with small sticks, and moving to larger ones, he got a nice fire burning. He picked up one of the large leaves and then saw a huckleberry bush. He'd been about to go get water from the river, but changed his mind and picked huckleberries instead, cupping the leaf in his hand and filling it with berries. Caes brought the berries to the fire and carefully set the 'bowl' of berries on the ground, away from the fire. Then, he took some of the cattails – the ones with smaller heads on them – and rubbed his hands over them to form a big pile of pollen in another 'bowl' leaf. The fire was getting warm, so he set the flat rock in the coals near the edge of the fire. Eventually, the rock would get hot.

He carried another 'bowl' to the river and put water in it, which he took back to the fire and carefully mixed it with the pollen, using a finger to stir it together. It was too runny, so he gathered some more of the cattails and added more pollen to the mixture. It took a while, but he eventually had a pasty mixture. To this, he added some huckleberries and stirred it some more with his fingers. Satisfied with the consistency, he poured it on the flat rock and waited.

While he waited, Caes went to work on the bamboo with his knife. First, he cut it to the right length, and then worked on crushing some of the bamboo. It would be easier if he had a way to boil the bamboo, but this should work if he was careful. Caes checked his cattail huckleberry mixture periodically. It was going to take a while because the rock wasn't very hot yet, so he went back to his project.

From the crushed bamboo, he gathered long lengths of fiber and started weaving them together, occasionally dipping them in the river to keep them moist. He'd been working on this for some time when he noticed the mixture of cattail and huckleberries was resembling a flat bread. He used his knife and pulled it free from the rock, and flipped it over to cook a little more. When it looked like it was cooked through, he took a bite. It wasn't the tastiest bread he'd ever had, but it was warm and filling. The huckleberries really helped the taste. He finished eating it, and then climbed a tree to be safe while he went back to work on the braid. A little over an hour later, he had what he thought would work for a bow string. If he could find a bee hive, he might be able to get some wax and make it better, but that would have to wait.

He strung the bow string over his piece of bamboo and tested it. It wasn't pretty, but he was confident it would work to shoot an arrow. He went back to the bamboo patch and looked for thin pieces to be cut into arrows. It didn't take long. When he had a dozen shafts cut, the sat down and started sharpening one end, and notching the other end, of each. He didn't have arrow heads, but he could try using just the bamboo. He just needed to find some feathers first. Any feathers would work, but longer ones, like from a goose's wings, would be best.

Caes thought about searching for feathers, but decided to make a spear first. He spent the next half hour whittling a stick until it was sufficient to give him some protection, and then carried it along the river so he could look for feathers.

It didn't take long, and he found some on the bank of the river. Caes wasn't sure if they were goose or duck or some other bird, but they were straight wing feathers. He climbed back up his tree with his arrows and the feathers. He worked for a while on the shafts, cutting slots into them and carefully fitting the feathers in them. Two hours later, he had 8 arrows finished. He climbed down and shot one arrow at a tree. Surprising him, it flew pretty straight and smashed against the tree. Now he had seven arrows, but at least they seemed to work, at least at relatively short distances.

Caes looked at the sun and saw it was getting low in the sky. It didn't seem like it, but he'd spent several hours working on the bow and arrows. And, of course, the spear and flatbread. He was getting hungry again, but didn't see any squirrels. He went to the pile of cattails and started poking them into the river bottom to make a new fish trap. If he'd been thinking earlier, he would have made the trap before starting on the bow and arrows, but that was too late now.

He made the trap with funnels on both the upstream and downstream sides, but offset from each other. Hopefully a fish would swim through and get stuck in the middle. He walked away from the river to the huckleberry bush. He ate several handfuls, and then gathered a handful of leaves from the bush, and carried them and more huckleberries back to his fire. He sat quietly and ate the leaves, mixed with berries. It wouldn't make him full, but it would put nutrients in his stomach.

When the sun started to set, Caes gathered more bamboo and made a tree 'bed', and then laid down to sleep.

22

Still Searching

Jerod landed his big roc at the aerie. He'd flown as quickly as possible getting back from Daener City. The messenger rider had told him Caes was missing and presumed taken by a wild roc. Jerod was afraid of what he was going to discover at Westvale. He was also very concerned about how Ella was doing.

He unsaddled his roc and removed the harness, and then patted the big bird on its neck. Then, he took his flute out and played, *"Go feed"*. The bird leapt into the air and quickly disappeared from view.

Jerod, then, peeked into the room often used for meetings, and seeing them empty, headed for home. When he got there, he found Ella inside talking to Maeve. Ella stood up and came to him as soon as he got inside. He took her in his arms and held her.

When she pulled back, Jerod said, "What happened? The messenger, Tuck, told me they think a wild roc took Caes."

She answered, "Yes, that's it. He was up on the platform, keeping kids from climbing up there. He..." She started to lose composure and stopped to get control. "He never came back down. The workers found his pack and pouch under the tree limbs. I'm... I mean everyone... Oh man, no one thinks he'll make it back, honey. I just can't believe it happened."

"How many people are looking for him?" asked Jerod.

"All of them, I think", she said. "Brun said he has all riders out
searching, plus all the students who're good to ride on their
own. And, Catscratch has all the rangers looking. He asked us
to send riders to some of the other villages to ask their riders
and rangers to look also. I think they did, but I don't know for
sure."

"Okay. I'll find out if it was done. Has anyone seen any sign of
him?"

"No. Nothing at all, so far", she said.

He turned and looked at Maeve. "Hi Maeve. Thank you for
staying here with Ella. I have a question for you. Can magic
find Caes?"

She shook her head. "No, none that I know of. I've never heard
of magic powerful enough to do that. Maybe, possibly, in the
Northern Isles. Other than that, no, there's no one that can do it.
I don't even think there's anyone in the Isles who could, but
maybe."

"Alright. I know it was a stretch, but I had to ask", he said. He
looked down, and then looked back up. "What about magic to
find out if he's alive, even if it can't find him?"

Maeve tipped her head slightly and looked at the ceiling.
"Interesting thought, Jerod. I'm not sure. Let me look through
my books and see if there's anything like that."

"Thanks, Maeve", Jerod said. He turned to look at Ella. "Can I
do anything for you, honey?"

She shook her head slowly. "No, Jer. Just find our son."

Jerod walked into the aerie from the courtyard looking for riders. The place seemed empty. When he didn't find anyone, he pulled out his flute and called, using the longer length to reach humans, *"Jerod here. I'm back. Can someone give me an update? I'm in the aerie."*

"Tuck here. I'll be back in ten minutes", came the reply. Jerod walked into the courtyard and sat down. He didn't want to sit. It made him feel helpless and lazy, but there wasn't anything else to do until he talked to other riders and rangers. It occurred to him, as he was sitting there, that there was a Rider Trials coming in just about a week. He wasn't looking forward to it. He hadn't been looking forward to it before Caes went missing. The pain from losing Crislan was still fresh after almost two years. Somehow, even if they never found Caes, he needed to be at the Trials. As senior rider, it was expected of him. If he couldn't handle it, then he needed to step down and let another rider – maybe Brun – take over. Tuck was another good rider, but probably still too young for that responsibility. *Why am I thinking like this? I need to keep – at least try to keep – a positive attitude until there's no chance at all of Caes returning. I can't be thinking about quitting.*

He shook his head and put his head in his hands. *A shot of whisky would be nice, but I need to keep my head clear.*

He heard a roc approaching and looked up to see Tuck landing his big bird. He was riding Tosh today, a reddish-tinged, black-colored roc. Tuck rode that bird frequently. She was huge, but still pretty young. Jerod had ridden her a few times and was impressed with her speed and stamina. Shortly after Tuck landed, another roc landed. Jerod thought it was Finley, but wasn't sure. It was ridden by a student. Jerod wasn't positive of her name, but he thought it was Leanne.

Tuck took the saddle and harness off Tosh and played, *"Feed, Tosh"* on his flute. The big bird launched into the air. He walked over to Jerod. "Hi Jerod. I'm glad you're back."

Tuck was a tall, slender, young man of about 25 years old. He held his hand out to Jerod. Jerod returned it and they shook hands.

"So, what's the deal, Tuck? What have you and the riders found?", Jerod asked.

"Ah, shit, Jerod. I wish you were talking to Brun and not me. I wish we'd found something – anything. But, you know, no one has seen anything. We've gone to Red Cliff, and all the way to Lake of the Woods. We flew through the Crags. We even went all the way to Northridge – and that's a long flight. The last two days, we've been going back and forth along the western mountains. Brun said he figured that's where a wild roc might have gone. We're going back to the Crags tomorrow, but… oh man, this sucks to say… Most of the riders are saying he's been… nevermind."

"Just say it, Tuck!", Jerod demanded.

 "Uh, shit. I can't say it, Jerod. We'll just keep looking until you tell us to stop. I'll ride for a month if you tell me to", Tuck said.

"You think he was eaten by a roc?", asked Jerod.

"Uh, yeah, I think it's likely. I don't want to say it, but man, yes, I, uh, think it's probably the case", said Tuck.

"Thank you for your honesty, Tuck. I didn't want to hear it, but I appreciate you saying what you think. So, do you think there's anything we could do that we're not already trying?"

"Um. Let me think…" He looked down for a minute, and then continued, "Uh, shit. Um, no, I don't think so. Man, I feel terrible, Jerod. I really wanna think of something, but I just can't!", Tuck said.

Jerod felt tears coming, and turned to look the other way. Nonchalantly, he hoped, he wiped his eyes, and then looked to the ground. He turned and looked at Tuck again. "This is a tough time, Tuck. Please ask the other riders to keep it up until the day before the Trials. If we don't find him by then, I think we have to accept the reality of what's happened."

"Are you sure, Jerod?", Tuck asked.

"No, but it's the right answer. He'll be gone a week by then. If we haven't found him, then he's in some roc's belly. I asked Maeve, you know the magician? Anyway, I asked her if there was any kind of magic that can see whether he's still alive. Maybe… I don't know… Maybe she'll find something." He felt his emotions hitting again, and tears started coming out of his eyes. "I'm sorry, I can't help it."

"Jerod, if you didn't show emotions, I'd think there was something wrong with you. If I ever have a son, oh man, I can't imagine how I'd ever deal with it."

"Thanks, Tuck", Jerod said.

"You're a good dad, Jerod. I wish my own dad had been as good as you. Shit, Ella is an amazing mom. I can't believe two people like you guys are dealing with such a bad situation. I'll do anything I can to make things easier for you. Just tell me what you need and I'll do it", Tuck said.

Jerod grabbed Tuck and embraced him, slapping him in the back. His tears were flowing freely.

Maeve knocked on the Wind's door, and waited. No one answered. She looked at the ground and thought for a minute. She decided to check the garden boxes, and headed up the stairs. At the top of the stairs, she saw Ella with her hands in the garden, tending to her plants. She was talking softly, but Maeve wasn't sure if she was using magic or not. She cleared her throat.

Ella turned around and saw her. "Oh Maeve, I'm sorry. I was lost in thought."

"Hi Ella", Maeve said. "I'm just checking to see how you're doing."

"Oh, I'm struggling, Maeve", she said. "I can't just sit in my kitchen wondering about Caes, but I can't go looking for him, either. I'm just stuck."

"I know, dear. I'm sorry you're dealing with this", Maeve said.

"I found a spell that might work to see if Caes is still alive. I can't cast it, but an adept in brown magic might be able to. I'm just not good enough with brown. Someone with gifts or talents won't be able to, either. There's an adept north of Daener City – her name's Zoe. I think she might be able to. Are any of the riders heading there? From what I can tell, Zoe would need something he's worn recently. Something still dirty, you know. Something you haven't washed."

"Oh that would be amazing. If she can find out if he's still alive, or… well… you know what I mean. If we can find out about him, I'd be so grateful", Ella said.

"Like I said, her name is Zoe. I don't know where, exactly, she lives, but it's a bit north of Daener City. I'm sure people in the area know where to find her", said Maeve. "She's the best brown magician anywhere close."

"Thank you, Maeve", Ella said. "I'll look through Caes' room and find a dirty shirt or socks or something. I can get Jerod to send a rider there."

"Good luck, dear", Maeve said. "Let me know if there's anything else I can do. I really hope Caes makes it back to us all."

23

Venison

The sky was just lightening when Caes awoke the next morning. He rubbed the sleep from his eyes and looked around. It was too dark to see much, so he just laid there for a while. He tried to remember how long he'd been in the forest. He was pretty sure this was his third morning, but he was starting to lose track of time.

It got chilly last night, and he woke up shivering a few times. Caes was wondering if he should chance looking for a cave. It would most likely be warmer in the nights, but he also might run into creatures he didn't want to find. Maybe a blanket would be good. He wondered how he might make something like that. Nothing came to his mind, but he was determined to think on it. Maybe something would occur to him.

He looked over at the river and scanned the bank. *Is that something moving around?*

It looked like an animal was close to the water, but in the darkness of early morning, it was hard to tell for sure. He rolled over, carefully, and picked up his bow and an arrow, just in case.

Caes lay there for a few minutes, trying to get his eyes to focus in the dimness. There was definitely something moving around. He just couldn't tell what it was, for sure. It almost looked like a deer.

He lay there for another few minutes, and the sky gradually got brighter. *Yes, it IS a deer!* He was excited, but he needed to make sure not to spook the animal. In the past few days, he'd had a couple little fish, a tiny squirrel, and some huckleberries and leaves. His stomach was begging for more food.

He very slowly raised himself into a kneeling position and nocked an arrow. The sky got a little brighter. He could finally completely see the buck. It was only about 30 feet away. This should be a pretty easy shot. He put the bow to his cheek and drew the string back to his ear, sighting carefully along the arrow. He aimed for the spot just behind the front leg of the deer, hoping to hit the heart. The deer wasn't moving. Caes took a deep breath and then let half of it out. His aim steadied, and he released the arrow.

It flew towards the deer, but not at the spot Caes had aimed at. It hit him, instead, high and a little forward of where he'd aimed. The deer jumped and darted into the trees. *Shoot!* Caes grabbed his other arrows – there were six left – and his spear, and climbed down the tree. He needed to track the deer, if he could, and see if it fell somewhere. When he got to the ground, he nocked another arrow, but didn't draw the string. He quickly ran to where the deer had been and looked around on the ground. *Yes, there's some blood!*

There was bright, bubbly, blood on the ground and on some of the leaves where the deer had run. It looked like he'd hit it in a lung. With luck, the buck would run for a bit and then die.

Caes saw blood on leaves ahead, and followed further. After about 300 yards, he saw the deer on the ground, and a wolf was creeping up to it. There was no way Caes was willing to give up his deer! He dropped to a knee and took aim with his second arrow. He planned to kill the wolf also.

He wasn't far away, but he was concerned about the aim, especially after the last shot, so he dropped back down and crept closer. Without the weight of an arrowhead, the arrows didn't seem to stabilize. He crept closer and finally was less than 20 feet away. The wolf was entirely focused on the deer.

Caes took aim, again, with his bow, and released the arrow.
This time, it hit true. The arrow took the wolf right through the
heart, and it dropped to the ground, dead. Five arrows left.
Hopefully he'd be able to recover one or two he'd already shot.
Otherwise, he needed to think about making some more.

He slipped his bow around on his back and held his spear as he
slowly walked up to the two dead animals. He poked the wolf
with his spear and it didn't respond. He poked the deer. It
didn't respond, either.

He smiled as he realized he had plenty of meat for the first time
in a few days. Caes knelt down and started gutting the animals.
He was far enough from his camp, so he just left the entrails on
the ground in a pile. It took some time, and his knife was
starting to get dull, but he finally got the animals cleaned. He
tried to pick them up, but realized he'd only be able to carry one
at a time. He picked up the buck and put it over his shoulders
and carried it back to his camp.

When he got there, he balanced it on his shoulders while he
struggled to climb his tree. It took some time, and a lot of
energy, but he finally made it up to his 'bed' and laid the deer
on it. Then, he climbed back down and returned for the wolf.
When he got there, several birds flew away and he picked up
the wolf. It was heavy. He hadn't realized it was heavier than
the deer. It was hard to get over his shoulders so he dragged it,
slowly, back to camp. There was no way he was getting the big
wolf into his tree, especially without rope, so he took it over by
the river instead and left it there, and then returned to his tree.

He'd just climbed up into the tree to start cutting up the deer
when he heard the sound of wind gusts. He looked up and
over at the wolf just in time to see a roc swoop down and snatch
the wolf up in its talons! *Was that the wood roc I tried to kill?* He
wasn't sure, but it probably wasn't. It seemed too big. It was
too late to do anything about it. The roc was already gone.

Caes shook his head and went back to skinning the deer. At least the stupid bird took the wolf and not his deer.

As he was cutting some pieces from the deer meat, Caes realized he wouldn't be able to eat all the meat before it rotted. *I should turn some into jerky to take with me.*

With that in mind, he started cutting some thin strips of meat and hung them over a stick. When he had about 20 strips, he stopped and built a fire. When it was burning good, he fed it more wood and then went looking for cooking sticks. He found some sticks he could use and brought them back and formed them into a cooking rack. It was basically a couple sticks with forks in them that he could poke in the ground on each side of the fire, plus a piece of bamboo he used as a skewer for the hunk of meat. The skewer sat on top of each fork in the support sticks. He watched the meat cook, and periodically rotated the skewer so another side of the meat cooked.

While the venison was cooking, Caes found more sticks and some vines, and assembled a teepee-style cooking rack. It was three long sticks, tied together with vine, with smaller sticks halfway down, criss-crossing the tripod.

When this was done, he wrapped the deer skin around the tripod as best he could. He used his knife to make holes in the skin and tied it in place with vines. He stepped back and looked at his homemade smoker. *I think it'll work!*

When his venison was finished cooking, he took the skewer off
and set the smoker in place over the fire, carefully adding some
more wood to it at the same time. He wanted the fire to keep
burning, but wanted it to be small and smoky. With it in place,
he set the strips of meat he'd cut onto the wooden rack, and
held his hand there for a minute to test the heat. He needed it
warm enough to dry the meat, but not hot enough to burn his
wooden rack. Satisfied, he climbed back up his tree and ate the
venison he'd cooked.

Caes wanted to go look for obsidian or other sharp rocks, but
didn't want to leave his meat smoker. Scratch had always told
him wild animals were afraid of fire, but he wasn't ready to
trust that with his venison strips smoking.

He looked up at the sky to check for rocs. It was late morning
now, and there were rocs flying around, but they weren't close.
He noticed small birds were singing this morning and saw a
yellow bird land in a tree not far away. Maybe he should
practice some of the spells Maeve had taught him. He hadn't
used Call Birds since that first day she'd taught him. It was a
pretty easy cantrip to remember. He thought about it for a
couple minutes and then whispered the words, and released the
cantrip towards the yellow bird.

The little yellow bird flew from its branch and landed on his
arm! He smiled. Caes wasn't sure how useful this would be,
but supposed he might use it to lure some dinner, if needed.
The bird flew away. He looked around again, and saw another
bird in a different tree. He whispered the cantrip again, and
that bird flew over, landing right where the yellow one had
been.

Caes was pretty sure he'd be able to eat bird for dinner if he needed. He'd just need to keep his knife close. He could call a bird with Call Birds, and use Stun to make them temporarily helpless, and then cut off their head with his knife. He wasn't looking forward to eating small birds, but at least had a plan in case he needed it.

He wiggled his arm and the bird flew away.

Caes looked around for another bird. Nothing was close. A roc flew overhead. Caes was curious if the big bird would react in any way to the cantrip. It was very unlikely due to the roc's large size, but he tried it anyway. As he released the cantrip towards the roc, it suddenly changed directions and saw Caes. It swooped down close, but then flew directly over his head, just over the tree top. Caes was very glad to be protected by the tree. *Did the roc feel the magic? Or was it a coincidence when it saw me?*

He needed to try it again to know for sure, but not now. Caes ate the last bite of his venison lunch and contemplated the rest of the meat. He could cut and cook another piece, but without a way to keep the rest of the meat cold, or salt to preserve it, he'd need to dispose of the rest. He took his knife out and cut another piece off to have for dinner.

He carried the rest of the deer back down the tree. He thought about just tossing it in the river to get it away from him. He didn't want predators coming in to his camp if he could help it.

Up in the sky, he saw another roc. This one was smaller than the others he seen this morning. Was it the one he accidentally rode? He thought it might be. The coloring and size looked right. He quickly cast the Call Birds cantrip and released it towards the roc. Just like the first experiment calling a roc, this one turned immediately and came towards him. He turned to run back into the trees, but then spun back around to face the bird, and tossed the rest of the deer onto the bank of the river, and then backed away to the closest tree.

The roc circled once, directly overhead, and then landed at the deer carcass. It looked at Caes and then grabbed the deer and leapt into the air. A feather fell from one of the roc's wings as it flew away. Caes went over to pick it up. It was a beautiful pure white. It must have come from the bottom of its wing.

On a whim, Caes reached into his pocket and pulled out the rider's flute he'd found on the platform. He was amazed it was still in his pocket after the adventures he'd gone through. He played, *"Thank you White Feather"*. He supposed that was better than just calling the roc "stupid bird".

He put the flute away and looked at the feather again. It would make a perfect fletching for arrows, but he didn't want to try it until he found something to use for arrow heads.

Caes went over to his smoker and checked the progress. Things looked good, but it was going to take all day. He added a little more wood and adjusted the deer skin.

Throughout the afternoon, Caes foraged in the nearby bushes and trees. He didn't want to go far, so each time he only walked a few minutes in a direction. He was looking for obsidian, as well as fruit or greens he could eat. There were still some huckleberries on the bushes he'd found yesterday, but they wouldn't last long. It would be good to find some more fruit than that.

Each time he went out, he went in a different direction, and then was back at the fire in less than 10 minutes.

On his third time out, he spied a ripplefruit vine in a tree. He squinted and looked up at it. The sun was in the same direction, so he had to hold his hand to shield the brightness. There were a few fruits on the vine!

He climbed up the tree. The vines were near the top, where the limbs get small. As he climbed, the tree moved with the wind. He had to be careful not to snap a branch. He finally made it to the fruit and twisted it off the vine. He tucked them into his shirt and started back down.

He'd made it most of the way down, and was only ten feet or so from the ground when the branch he was standing on broke and he fell to the ground. He landed hard on his butt in a bush. He wiggled a bit and found that nothing seemed broken. His hind end might be sore for a day or so but he was okay. He leaned back and laughed. Wouldn't it be something to survive being carried away by a roc, dropped in a lake, practically drowned in a wild river, almost eaten by a bear, only to die falling from a tree with ripplefruit in his shirt? For some reason that thought just seemed funny.

Thinking of the ripplefruit made him reach into his shirt to check it. Did it get smashed in the fall?

It felt fine. He took one out and took a bite. Ah, delicious! He sat eating the fruit and felt something on his leg. He looked down, but didn't see anything. Just branches of the bush he'd landed in – and was still sitting in – as well as a small vine on top of his leg. He took another bite and chewed it. The fruit was so delicious. It reminded him of all the times he and Jory had snuck ripplefruit. There simply wasn't a better tasting fruit.

It was probably time to get back and check on his smoking meat. He started to stand up, but his left leg seemed stuck. He looked down at it and saw the vine was now wrapped completely around his lower leg. How did that happen? He reached down to pull the vine off, and it wrapped around his hand. *Oh no! Crawling mantrap!* How hadn't he noticed that before? His left leg and left arm, both, were trapped. He pulled as hard as he could, but couldn't get either his arm or leg free!

Caes looked around and this time saw more vines coming towards him. The roots were actually walking across the ground! He had to get free quick. If the other vines reached him, he'd die right here.

He grabbed his knife from the scabbard and started hacking at the vines. They were tough to cut. Mostly, the knife just bounced off the vines. He started hacking and then sawing, in an alternating motion. It worked a little.

He looked up and the other vines were getting closer. They had been ten feet away, and now were only about 4 feet. *Faster!* He hacked and sawed, over and over. Finally his leg was free. He pulled it back away from the vine and started working on his hand.

Caes finally cut through the vine that was holding him, right as the other one was less than a foot away. If he hadn't had the knife, he'd never have gotten free. He jumped to his feet and stepped away from the vines. He remembered what Quain told them about his leg. This was the first time he'd ever been this close to the mantrap vines. Scratch told him all about them, and warned him to stay away from them if he ever saw them.

They'd even stopped to look at one from several feet away one time. How did he not recognize it when it first came near him today? He knew the answer. He'd been too busy laughing at not getting injured in the fall and then enjoying the fresh fruit to be paying attention. He resolved to always pay attention after this. He couldn't afford another lapse in judgement.

He found the bow and arrows, as well as the spear, that he'd laid on a rock, and made his way back to camp. He'd been gone longer than he'd planned and was worried about animals and his smoker, but everything seemed to be okay. He added another piece of wood and then went to look in his fish trap.

Nothing. He shrugged and went back to his tree and climbed up. He was shaken up by the incident with the mantrap vines, and scanned the ground around his camp looking for any vines on the ground. He didn't see any, but resolved to be much more careful, especially now that he'd seen some in the area.

By evening, the venison he'd been smoking was done. It shouldn't rot anytime soon. Caes filled a pocket with the meat and then put together his skewer rack and cooked the other piece of deer meat he'd cut earlier. While it cooked, he gathered some more huckleberries and leaves to eat with it.

When he was done eating, he sat back and practiced his cantrips again, calling small birds, and then stunning them. None appeared hurt afterwards, but were anxious to fly away after the stun wore off.

When darkness came, Caes laid down on his stick and vine bed in the tree and fell asleep.

24

Alive?

Ella sat in the rear seat of the saddle, riding behind Grayce, one of the young riders on the blonde-colored roc, named Shon. She passed the Trials three years ago - the year before Crislan died. She was cute, with brown eyes and long, dark brown hair. She was quieter and less boisterous than most of the riders. She and Ella always got along well.

They'd flown over the Waha not long ago. Ella had her eyes roaming all over the ground, looking for any sign of her son. She saw a lot of wild rocs, but no people. She ticked off the days in her head, coming to four nights Caes had been gone. It tore her up inside, thinking that he might be injured and hoping for rescue down there. She'd heard, multiple times, from Jerod and the other riders how dangerous it was in the Waha and in the Crags. She hoped he was alive and trying to find his way back to Westvale, but knew it was unlikely. If a roc really had taken him, he almost certainly didn't live through it. She knew it was a fact, but she refused to accept it until she had no other choice.

She looked down again, and saw they were over a small lake at the top of a cliff. Ella tapped Grayce on the shoulder. "Grayce, there's a lake down there. Is that Hidden Falls Lake?"

Grayce nodded. "Yes, it is. There's an underground waterfall or spring or something that feeds the river below the cliff. That's a wild area. Did you want to fly closer to it? I can do that if you want."

Ella thought about it, and said, "No, we don't need to. I was just curious."

"Okay. Let me know if you change your mind or want to see anything", Grayce said.

"I just want to hurry and find Zoe. I need to know whether or not Caes is still alive. I want her to use the spell Maeve found, but I'm scared to death of what she finds out."

"I can't imagine what you two are going through. It's got to be horrible, wondering", Grayce said.

"I… sometimes, I just want to die, Grayce. The fear of what happened is so hard. I just want to know what happened and if he's alive."

Grayce didn't answer, probably because she didn't know what to say.

Grayce and Ella stayed at a small town in the Dark Forest, three or four hours flight north of the Crags. Ella had never been this far from the Cragwoods before. In the morning, they'd fly the last three hours to get to Daener City and find the adept, Zoe. She brought Caes' pouch and a pair of dirty socks she found in his bedroom. Hopefully that would be all Zoe needed to cast the spell to determine if he was still alive. The inn they stayed at was crowded, and the two women caused attention when they walked in. Women traveling alone was unusual, but the riders' leather pants and jackets really got people's attention.

The Dark Forest was a different country than the Cragwoods. Riders were seen on rare occasions, as it was a more civilized part of the world. Dangerous animals were rare here. Sure, they had some wolves and bear, but the temperature on this side of the Crags and other mountains north of them was significantly cooler than in the Cragwoods. As far as Ella was aware, shadow cats did not roam this far north. When the roc had landed, Ella went inside the inn to find out if there was a roc house nearby. If there wasn't one, they could release the giant bird to hunt on its own and find its own place to sleep. However, there was the risk, if they did that, the bird might feed on some farmer's cattle or horses, and then they'd have to compensate the farmer for the animals. It was better to find a place to keep the bird indoors.

There was a small roc house on the outskirts of the town, just three blocks from the inn. They remounted and flew Shon there and bought a sheep from the farmer who owned it. After pushing the panicky sheep into the pen with the roc, they walked, together, back to the inn. The ate dinner in the dining area, drank an ale, and retreated to the room they'd rented for the night.

The next morning, they woke early and left the town before the sun was all the way in the sky. By mid-morning, they'd landed in Daener City. The roc house there was very large, and had a stocked cattle yard full of animals for visiting riders. These were funded by the riders of Cragwoods, themselves, and even staffed by some retired riders.

Grayce led Shon into the roc house and arranged for someone to feed him. Then, they walked down the street, together, to find out where Zoe lived. She'd asked the attendant about Zoe, but just got a blank stare and finally a "sorry, I don't know her" answer.

They found an apothecary a couple blocks down the street and stepped inside. The keeper looked up at the two women, frowned, and said, "Good morning ladies. What can I do for you?"

"Good morning, sir. We're hoping for some information. We've been sent to talk to Zoe, who we understand is a mage near here. Can you help us out?", asked Grayce.

"I know her, yes, I do. She comes in sometimes", said the keeper. He looked them over and asked, "Are you riders? Your clothes are different than most here in the city."

"We are, yes. Can you help us with directions to Zoe?", asked Grayce again.

"Ladies shouldn't be riders, that's my opinion. Anyway, I could, but she doesn't like to be bothered. Not even by riders", he said. "Why don't you just tell me what you need? Mage Zoe comes into town every week or two, and usually stops here while she's in town. You little ladies can just stay in an inn until then."

"Are you serious, keep?" asked Grayce. "We've ridden a long way to come here and it's important we talk to her."

"Well, I don't really care how important it is for you ladies – although I have to say you don't look much like ladies in that leather. Maybe you can go get dresses and ask again. Maybe I'll have more information or maybe I won't. Good-bye", and he turned his back on them.

Ella looked like she was about to explode. She reached for a bottle on a shelf and looked like she was going to throw it. Grayce grabbed her before she got it, and pushed her out the door.

"How dare that son of a bitch talk to us that way!" Ella was practically shouting, when they got back into the street.

"Welcome to my world, Ella. Here in the Daener City, there are more assholes like him than you'd imagine. Women are expected to behave like women. You know, wear dresses, curtsy to men, all that kind of crap. Women don't take jobs meant for men. It's disgusting!"

"Errr! I hate men like that!", Ella said. Her anger was just barely held in check.

"Let's look for someone else. Come on", Grayce said.

They walked further down the street. The delay in getting directions was very frustrating. They asked three different people they met in the street for directions, and all three were rude and refused to answer them.

"We really aren't that far from the Cragwoods, Grayce. Why are people so different here?", asked Ella.

"You remember the Battle of the Crags, Ella?", asked Grayce. "We were attacked by these people and beat them. They've hated us ever since, well, especially our women because we don't act according to their standards."

A wagon was being loaded at a storefront. They stopped by the wagon and waited for the wagoneer – who was in the wagon, arranging some cargo - to notice them. When he did, he jumped and said, "Oh, shit, I dint re'lize you were there!", he said.

Ella said, "Hello sir. Are you from around here?"

He chuckled and said, "I'm from ever'where now'days. Lee, at yer service, riders." He held out his hand and they both shook it. "I'm 'riginally from the Cragwoods, but live in the Dark Forest now. What can I do fer ya?"

Ella smiled back at him. "By any chance are you from the area around Northridge?"

"Yup, sure am. How'd ya know?", asked Lee.

"We have a very good friend who sounds a lot like you, Lee. Just call it a lucky guess", said Ella. "By any chance do you know a mage named Zoe? She's supposed to live a little north of the city."

"I've heard a her. Ya want me to find out?", asked Lee.

"Oh, would you please? It would be very helpful", replied Ella, smiling happily.

"Just a minute. I'll ask." And he climbed down and walked inside.

"That was lucky", whispered Grayce.

"I know. He sounds just like Catscratch", whispered Ella back to her.

A couple minutes later, Lee came back outside. "Yup, I found out where she lives. Lemme see if I can 'scribe it to ya." He paused. "Wait a minute. Who'd ya say ya know that sounds like me?"

"Do you know a ranger named Catscratch?", Grayce asked.

"Nope, I don't. Sorry", said Lee.

"What about Jon Walker. Do you know him?" asked Ella.

"Jonny? Yup, I knew 'im. Ain't seen 'im in ages. He was a ranger after that but I dint see 'im after. How's he doin'?"

"He's a ranger in Westvale now. He's a good friend of me and my husband", said Ella.

"Well, whatcha know… Ya know, maybe instead a ya findin' the mage's house yerselfs, I can juss take ya. I can load later." And he went inside again to talk to whoever was inside. He came back out and tossed a couple bags onto the boardwalk next to the door of the shop. The wagon was empty after that. "Well, hop on up. I'll give ya a ride, yeah?"

On the ride, which took about 40 minutes, he talked their ear off. He talked about the weather, road conditions, shops he liked and didn't like, his last trip to Cragwoods, and more. He was very talkative. This was so much better than the jerk in the apothecary.

They pulled to a stop outside a nice house in a copse of trees.

"Ella, Grayce, nice to meetcha. I hope Zoe can help. Do ya need me to wait?", asked Lee.

"I can't ask you to do that, Lee. Thank you very much for the ride", said Ella.

"Well, how 'bout I stay fer a minute. If the mage'll talk to ya, just give me a wave an' I'll leave. If not, then I'll take ya back to an inn, yeah?", said Lee.

"Thank you, Lee. We appreciate it!", Grayce said.

They walked to the door and knocked. A minute later, a pretty young lady in her young adult years opened the door. She was wearing a long dress. "Good day. What do you need?", she said.

"Are you the mage, Zoe?", asked Ella.

"Maybe. Who are you?", replied the lady.

"Oh, I'm sorry. My name is Ella Wind. My husband is Jerod, the senior rider of Westvale, in the Cragwoods." She pointed at Grayce. "This is Grayce. She's another rider. She gave me a ride here. Are you Zoe?"

"No I'm not. What do you need?", the woman said.

"We've come a very long way, ma'am", said Grayce. "Is Zoe here? If not, can you tell us where to find her?"

"Yes", said Ella. "Our magician – her name is Maeve – said we should find her. Can you help?"

"Just a minute", she said and shut the door. They could hear it latch when she'd closed it.

●

Shortly after, the door opened again, and a different lady was there. "I'm Zoe. What do you need?"

"We're sorry to bother you. I… we have a… I'm sorry. I'm a mess. I have a big favor. Our magician – her name is Maeve – she said we should find you. Can… can we come inside and talk?", asked Ella.

Zoe looked at the two for a minute, and then said, "Sure. Come on in".

Ella turned and waved at Lee. He waved back and shook the reins. His wagon started down the road.

Zoe held the door open, and the two women walked through the doorway. Inside, the house was neat and clean, for the most part, but there were shelves on most of the walls, and they held an assortment of bottles, wooden boxes, and books. Light in the house came from the windows, augmented by candles. It struck Ella as odd that there weren't any lightstones anywhere.

"Would you take some tea?" asked Zoe.

"Yes, please", said Grayce.

"I'd love some, thank you", said Ella.

Zoe called, "Chrystin, bring tea in here", and then looked back at Ella and Grayce. "Chrystin is my apprentice. She's new here, but has promise."

Chrystin came back in a minute with a teapot and three cups. She left and returned again with tea holders, which she dropped into each of the cups, and then poured hot water over them.

Zoe picked up a cup of tea and stirred it with the tea holder. Then, took a sip, and then set the cup back down on a table.

"Now, ladies, what do you need from me? Oh, Chrystin, you might as well sit and listen."

"Thank you for the tea, Zoe. It's been a long morning, and tasts great. Our magician – Maeve, I think I told you that already – well, she said you might be able to help. Um, my son, Caes… Well, have you been to the Cragwoods?", said Ella.

"No, I haven't been there", she said.

"Well, we, uh, live in trees. Uh, in houses in the trees. I guess you'd just call them treehouses. Uh. Well, I don't suppose you know much about riders do you?" said Ella.

"I know enough about them, Ella. Why don't you just tell me what you need. I'm starting to get frustrated with you."

"I'm sorry. Really I am. Well, anyway, my son – Caes is his name – he, uh, was guarding a roc platform. That's a, uh, a place for rocs to land and take off and things. It's where we, uh, test new roc riders." She stopped and took a drink of her tea, and then continued, "My son, Caes, was guarding the platform – they're really big – and, well, keeping young kids from climbing up there and getting hurt or taken by wild rocs. Uh, my son, he, we think, he was taken by a roc and carried away. Um… Oh man, this is so hard." Tears came down her face. "He disappeared about 4 days ago." She stopped and drank some more tea, pausing to wipe her tears with the back of her hand.

"Go ahead, Ella. I'm sorry about your son. What does this have to do with me?" asked Zoe.

"We, uh, were talking to Maeve about magic. We wanted to know if magic could find him, but Maeve said no. Then, she said she knew of a spell from one of her books that might be able to tell if he's alive. If he's alive, you know, we'll keep looking until there's no chance of finding him." She reached into her bag and pulled out a book. She handed it to Zoe. "Maeve gave me this book and said a brown mage might be able to cast the spell in it. She said you'd need some items he'd been wearing. Dirty things. I have his socks and the pouch he always wears. Would you be willing to help us?"

"Let me see the spell, Ella. I'll take a look." She thumbed through the book, slowly, and stopped after about a dozen pages. "This looks like the one. I don't know this spell. Give me a few minutes to read through it."

Zoe leaned back in her chair and read. Occasionally, she took sips of her tea.

After five minutes – which felt like half an hour to Ella – she closed the book and held it in her lap. "Can I keep this book? There are several interesting spells in it."

Ella told her, "Yes, you can keep it. Maeve said you'd probably ask. Can you do it?"

"I'm pretty sure I can", Zoe said. "It'll take an hour or so to gather the necessary components, but it looks possible to me. Refill your cups and relax. I need to go in my back room for a bit."

She stood up and walked out of the room. Ella and Grayce looked at each other. Both were hopeful, but didn't want to say anything. Grayce poured hot water from the teapot into their cups. "This is going good, Ella", and she held Ella's hand.

They sat for quite a while. It felt like hours, but Ella was sure it was less than an hour. The water in the teapot was gone by the time Zoe came back into the room.

"Okay, I think I'm ready. Please hand me the items from your son, Ella."

Ella took the pouch and dirty socks over to Zoe, who placed them in a bowl on the floor in front of her. She then reached into a cloth bag and took out a pinch of some type of dried herb, and sprinkled it over the pouch and socks. Then, she took a bottle of purple liquid and poured a splash of it into the bowl.

Lastly, she lit a candle and waited until wax was melting, and dropped a single drop of hot wax into the bowl. When this was done, she picked up the bowl and set it in her lap. She started chanting something Ella couldn't understand. The chanting went on for over a minute, and then Zoe looked at Ella and told her, "Now I need something from you. Perhaps several hairs?" Ella reached up to her head and pulled 3 or 4 hairs out. "Is this enough?"

"That should be fine", she said. She chanted for another several seconds, and then said, "Say something to him. See if he answers."

"What?", Ella said. "Say something? Uh… Caes, are you there, honey?"

From the bowl, she heard, "Mom? Is that you? Mom? Mom!" He was yelling at the end.

Ella tried to answer, but Zoe held up her hand, palm facing Ella.

"The spell is ended, Ella. It won't do any good to answer", Zoe said. "Your son is alive. I don't know where he is, but he still lives and breathes."

Ella started crying. Tears were pouring down her cheeks. She alternated between crying and laughing. Then, she jumped up and grabbed Zoe and hugged her. Then, she hugged Grayce.

"Can you cast it again, Zoe? We need to ask where he is!" Ella was excited, but wanted more information.

Zoe answered, "Look in the bowl, Ella. The items are gone. They disintegrated with the spell."

"Oh…", Ella looked at the bowl and the powder in the bottom. She sat back down in the chair, and said, "That's too bad. Um… I guess that's all we can do then, huh?"

"Yes, that's all. I can't do anything else to help you find him", Zoe said.

"Well, we have to hurry and get back and tell the others he's still alive. Zoe, I don't know how to thank you! I'll do anything, anything at all, for you. Thank you!"

Zoe wiped a tear from her eye. "I hope you find your son, Ella. Please tell me if you find him. And, thank you for the book. It's more valuable than you probably realize."

"Let's get back to Shon, Ella", said Grayce. "It's going to be a long walk back to the roc house. We need to get going."

They thanked Zoe again, and the two women went out the door. It took more than an hour to make it back to the roc house. They went inside and got Shon saddled. Then, collected some food and water from the attendant, and led the big bird out of the building and mounted up. A minute later, the bird launched into the air, and they started their return flight back to Westvale.

25

White Feather

Caes dreamt of home.

In his dream, he twisted to grab a ripplefruit that was just out of reach. It was the biggest, juiciest ripplefruit he'd ever seen, and just had to have it. Jory was cheering him on, and Ronni was there, too. She was urging Caes to get one for her too, and if she wanted one, he absolutely HAD to get it for her. He was hanging onto a branch and twisting to his right while reaching with his right hand. The fruit was just out of reach. He twisted just a little harder, and his hand slipped off the branch. He was falling!

He woke up to realize he was half out of his bed of sticks and reeds, and about to tumble about 25 feet to the ground. Caes quickly grabbed branches and pulled himself back onto his bed. Oh man, if he'd fallen he might had died!

The sun was coming up. He'd slept a bit longer than most days. He could see the sunrise over the mountains to the east. Caes reached into his pocket and pulled out a piece of venison jerky and chewed on it. Today, he needed to get away from the river and start heading southwest, towards Westvale. As far as he could guess, he was only a few miles south of Hidden Falls, but the river would turn and head to the southeast. That would put him weeks of travel out of the way. He wasn't sure where the Waha started, but suspected he was already in it.

He climbed out of his tree and over to the river to check the fish trap. To his surprise, there was a large trout in it. He hadn't really expected to see one. Caes wondered if the Stun cantrip would work on a fish. He slowly moved as close to the trap as possible and then knelt down and held still. The fish was swimming all over the place. After a minute or so, it seemed to relax and held mostly still. Caes whispered the cantrip and released it towards the fish. Just as he'd hoped, the trout rolled on its side and drifted into the trap wall. He quickly reached into the water with his knife and stabbed it through the gills, and then grabbed it with his hand and carried it to the shore.

The cantrips had helped him immensely so far. *Okay, that does it. I'm studying with Maeve anytime I can - if I ever make it back home.*

Caes looked through the sky to make sure he was still safe, and then gutted and cleaned the fish. He gathered sticks and made a fire. Before too long, the fire was perfect, and the fish was cooking on a stick. When he was done with breakfast, he put the fire out and contemplated whether or not he should take anything with him. He'd definitely want his weapons. He stuffed the white roc feather inside his shirt. He hoped that would prevent it from being damaged or lost. It would be nice to take the deer hide and tan it, but that would take a lot of work and time he didn't want to spend. He went to the fish trap and pulled several reeds out so no fish would be trapped anymore, and then started walking to the west.

After his experience with the crawling mantrap vine yesterday, he was very careful to watch where his feet landed. That was an experience he didn't want to repeat. He decided to walk until midday, or maybe a little later, and was hoping to see obsidian somewhere.

He'd been walking for over an hour. Shortly after leaving the river, he'd come across a game trail. Since it went mostly west, he'd decided to follow it. Besides squirrels, birds, and other small creatures, he hadn't seen any other animals. For the most part, he considered that a good thing. Ahead of him, he heard several birds take flight, and then the forest got very quiet. It was almost like every animal suddenly took a nap. Caes quietly stepped off the trail and ducked behind a rock. A breeze was blowing in his face and he decided to give another cantrip a try. He closed his eyes for a moment to recall the words for Animal Smell. Once he was sure he remembered it, he thought about squirrels and cast the cantrip. It was incredible how his sense of smell changed. Suddenly, he could smell so much more than before. The first thing he noticed was acorns up ahead of him. The smell of nuts was incredibly strong.

Caes shook his head and tried to smell something besides nuts. He could smell something else, but had a hard time… gone. The cantrip stopped working. That was frustrating. He wondered if additional training with Maeve would make them last longer.

Okay, let's try it again, Caes. He repeated the cantrip and again thought about squirrels. The smells came back, and again the smell of acorns was front and center. He tuned it out and tried to find the other smell. *There it is! It smells like… what is it? It smells dangerous!* He looked around and saw a good tree for climbing, and quickly moved to it and climbed up as high as he could. Once in the tree, he cast the cantrip again and tried to focus on the danger smell. It was very musky. Cat-like.

Caes held very still, but looked around as much as possible. There was a lot of undergrowth here, and a lot of trees. He couldn't see very far. He caught a glimpse of something moving just ahead of where he'd been walking. He was almost holding his breath, he was trying so hard to stay quiet.

Right about then, a dark-colored feline moved between some bushes. It was a shadow cat!

Caes' heart was pounding so hard, he was sure the cat would hear it also. When the cat went past him, it turned and looked around. It acted like it could smell Caes and was trying to determine where he was. Finally, the cat moved off behind the next bush, and Caes couldn't see it anymore.

As much as he wanted to keep walking, Caes decided to wait for a while. This ended up being over half an hour before he felt somewhat safe climbing down from the tree. Even then, he fought the urge to just climb back up and stay there for the rest of the afternoon. The cat had disappeared behind the bush, and Caes had no idea where it had gone from there. He nocked an arrow and continued west.

A few hours later, he spied a shiny rock up ahead. When he got closer, it looked like it might be obsidian. He picked up the shiny black rock and saw that, yes, it was sharp on one side and looked like black glass. It was the volcanic glass people knew as obsidian. The rock was about four inches in diameter, and should make nice arrow heads, at least if he could chip it properly. He didn't have a pouch to put it in, so he held it in his left hand and his spear in his right hand. If he needed to use the spear he'd need to drop the obsidian.

Caes continued walking westward. His game trail had ended, but the undergrowth had eased. It wasn't difficult walking between the trails. He kept his eyes on the position of the sun to make sure he didn't accidentally walk in circles. Catscratch had drilled that into him during his first year of apprenticeship. It was crazy how easy it was to get disoriented and lose sense of direction. He kept his ears focused on the sounds of the forest, especially on the small animals and birds. He knew, from his training with Catscratch, that forest sounds could save his life, if he only paid attention to them, and he'd seen it personally just a matter of hours ago with the shadow cat.

He'd come to the bottom of a small valley and was climbing the other side of it when he suddenly heard a change in the forest sounds. He looked around for a tree to climb, and not seeing one close, just dropped to his knees behind a boulder, looking around.

"Say something? Uh… Caes, are you there, honey?", came a voice from somewhere. Was that his mom?

Caes spun around, looking all over. Where was his mother? He didn't see her anywhere!

"Mom? Is that you? Mom? Mom!", he yelled. He looked around more. By now he was standing up and spinning around, looking. "Mom! Mom! Where are you?" he yelled some more.

He didn't hear her anymore. Her voice didn't seem to come from any particular direction. He didn't think it came from in front of him.

Caes took out the flute from his pocket, making sure it was in the longer position – so humans could hear it – and played, *"Mom! Are you there Mom?"*

Then he stopped and listened. He didn't hear a reply.

"Mom! Can you hear me? I'm over here!"

Still nothing.

"Mom! Play something. Yell or something."

Still nothing.

He didn't want to go anywhere and miss her. He looked around again, and saw a good tree for climbing. He ran over to it, dropped the obsidian rock down his shirt, and climbed.

When he got as high as he could – maybe 40 feet in the air – he stopped and looked all over. He took the flute back out and called, *"Mom! Can you hear me?"*

Still nothing.

"Mom! Mom! Do you hear me?", he yelled as loud as he could. Still nothing.

The only thing he could figure was she was looking for him and maybe used a spell to project her voice, kind of like Maeve had done so Brun could be heard during the Rider Trials. If she was close, he was sure she'd call again later. He sat in the tree for about an hour listening and watching. Finally, he decided she wasn't there, and climbed down to continue his journey.

Around mid-afternoon, Caes decided to stop for the day. He'd come to a small meadow with a creek running through it, and he figured it would be a good place. He'd be able to make a bed in a tree and watch over the meadow to make take a deer. In the meantime, he planned to work on arrow heads.

He wandered over to the creek and drank until his thirst was quenched. He'd give almost anything for a good waterskin to have with him. On the bank of the creek he found some rocks that looked like they might work for chipping obsidian. He grabbed a couple and dropped them down his shirt with the volcanic glass. Then, he went back to the tree, picking up sticks on the way. He made a pile at the base of the tree and then went looking for vines. Birds flew up into the air near the edge of the meadow, maybe 100 feet from where he was. He looked to his tree, but it was a couple hundred feet away now. He nocked an arrow and waited. A twig snapped behind him, and he spun to look. Not 20 feet away was a large red wolf! *Crap! How did he get there?*

The wolf was looking right at him, and Caes realized he was supposed to be the wolf's dinner tonight. He looked over his shoulder and saw another wolf creeping up behind him. *Oh no. This is bad…*

With nothing else coming to his mind, he let an arrow fly at the wolf directly in front of him. He hit it in the shoulder, but it didn't go deep. The wolf yelped and jumped into the bushes. Caes nocked another arrow and looked behind him. The other wolf was coming at him. He spun around and let another arrow fly. He missed completely, with the arrow going over the wolf's back. He dropped his bow and lunged with his spear instead. The wolf leapt at him and the spear took him in the chest. It wasn't dead, though, and snapped at the spear. Caes reached down and picked up the bow and his remaining few arrows. Then, he ran to the tree and climbed as quickly as he could.

He heard growling and snarling from the ground. He looked and saw that two other wolves had arrived, but were fighting the two injured ones. That was fine with him!

Safely high in the tree, he sat and watched the battle between wolves. It didn't take long. The new big red wolves made quick work of the two injured ones and in just a minute or two, were feeding. *I think I'll just stay in the tree tonight. I still have jerky to eat.*

Caes ate three pieces of jerky. By then, the battle and feeding was over. The victorious wolves were nowhere to be seen. Carrion birds were feeding on the carcasses.

After another half hour, Caes climbed back down from the tree and gathered his sticks and vines and climbed back up. He wove together a new bed and got it fastened in the tree, and then laid back in it and started chipping the obsidian.

He'd seen obsidian arrowheads before, but never made them himself. Catscratch had explained the basic steps, though. Caes hit the obsidian with a piece of sharp rock, and pieces of volcanic glass broke away. Several fell from the tree to the ground, and Caes was pretty sure he'd never find them. He took off his shirt and used it to cup the rocks. That worked better. He had to put the obsidian up against the tree trunk to hold it still enough while chipping it with the other rocks.

About two hours later, he had three very crude looking arrowheads. There was still quite a bit of volcanic rock left to work with. He took his three remaining arrows and used his knife to cut a slot in the pointed end. When he finished cutting them, he inserted his obsidian arrow heads into them and wrapped them with vines. The finished product looked very crude, but when he held them, the arrows seemed much better balanced than they'd been before.

The sun was still in the sky, although it was getting a bit lower. He guessed the people in Westvale were probably sitting down for dinner about now.

He climbed back out of the tree and nocked one of his new arrowhead-pointed arrows, and headed for the wolf carcasses. He really wanted to recover one or two arrows, and hopefully his spear, as well.

One of the arrows was broken, but the other seemed intact. He pulled it from the shoulder of the wolf. The spear seemed okay, so he pulled it free also. He looked around to make sure no animals were close, and went to the creek for another drink of water.

Caes looked into the sky and saw a couple different rocs flying around. Was one of them White Feather? He wasn't positive, but one of them looked smaller, and might have been him. He pulled his flute out and slid it into the shorter length – for calling rocs. He played, *"White Feather"*.

Of course, nothing happened. He didn't expect it to because the wild roc didn't understand the musical language. He focused on the small roc and whispered the Call Birds cantrip, releasing it towards the roc. Then, he played *"White Feather"* again.

The roc banked and came in his direction. When it was closer, he was almost certain it was the same bird. He played *"White Feather"* again as it flew over his head.

The bird circled his position, and then flew away.

Caes went back to his tree and climbed it again. He sat in the tree, working on a spear head until the sun went down, and then rolled over and fell asleep.

He awoke in the early morning. The sun was just peeking over the mountains to the east. Caes rubbed his eyes and stretched as best he could. *Oh, wouldn't it be nice to come across a ranger cabin?* His back was sore. He was glad he hadn't had a repeat of his dream from the night before. He reached into his pocket and took out two of the jerky pieces, eating them slowly. He wanted to climb down and get some water, but saw a cow elk wandering from the trees to the creek. She wasn't far from his tree – only 30 or 40 feet away.

Caes slowly grabbed his bow and the arrows. He nocked an arrow and watched the elk. He didn't see a predator stalking her.

The elk drank from the creek and then stook, looking around. She was a beautiful animal, but he planned to eat elk today. He drew the arrow and sighted along the arrow. He was in a tree, aiming down, which would make the arrow hit higher than normal. But the arrow was heavier than before, which would make it hit lower. He aimed right at the elk, and released. The arrow hit the elk perfectly – right through the heart. She took about three steps and fell dead.

Caes climbed out of the tree with his spear in his hand and ran to the elk.

The arrow wasn't broken, so he pushed it through the animal and set it beside his other two arrows. Then, he cut a the skin along its back and exposed the backstrap. He cut it free, setting it on some leaves. He started cutting one of the rear legs free when he saw a roc fly overhead. It was quite a ways up in the air, and Caes didn't feel immediately threatened, but it encourage him to cut quicker.

He'd just gotten the leg free when he saw another roc fly overhead. This one looked like White Feather. He wiped his bloody hands on some leaves and pulled his flute out. *"White Feather"* he played. The roc banked hard in the air and circled over him. *That's interesting!*

He played *"White Feather"* again, and the roc flew lower, swooping past him about 75 feet high.

Caes had an idea. He picked up the leg and backstraps, and backed away. When he was 20 yards away, he cast the Call Birds cantrip, and then played *"White Feather"*.

White Feather flew straight towards Caes, and then changed direction and landed on the elk carcass. Caes was entranced. Had he really called the roc to the ground? White Feather looked at the elk, then at Caes, and then grabbed the elk with his talons and leapt into the air. A minute later, and the bird and elk carcass were gone.

Caes retreated to his tree, and made a fire not far from the base of it. He skinned the leg, and then found some reeds near the creek. He poked the reeds through the meat and cooked it all over the fire.

He ate as much meat as he could, and put more in his pocket. His pants would be a mess, but it would be good to take some meat with him. The jerky was fine, but not as good as elk meat. After that, he spent some time fitting his new obsidian spear point to his spear, and then put out the fire. He started walking again, deciding to change his path more southerly in direction.

By midday, he reached the northern edge of a large lake. He wasn't positive, but guessed his was likely Lake of the Woods. If it was, he was about at the western edge of the Waha. That was good because he was tired of seeing phantom shadow cats every time he heard a noise.

He hadn't seen White Feather since giving him the elk that morning, but he had run across a couple of wolves. Birds flying in the air had given him sufficient warning to find a safe tree to climb. Once in the tree, he'd cast Animal Smell and confirmed the presence of wolves. With himself safely in the tree, it hadn't been necessary to do anything but wait.

Caes felt dirty, and the lake looked appealing. He wondered if he would be safe taking a quick swim to rinse off, but decided it probably wasn't a good idea.

He walked up to the lake and looked around. It was very pretty here.

The lake water looked clean, and Caes suspected there were a lot of fish in it. He started gathering some reeds to make a fish trap. Once he had enough reeds, he waded into the lake and started poking the reeds into the lake bottom to form a new fish trap. He'd just stuck the sixth reed when he had a bad feeling. He felt like something was watching him.

He looked left and right, and then behind him, but didn't see anything. He was just about to turn back to the lake when he saw a slight movement in the bushes. He looked to the right and saw his spear. He leaned over and grabbed it.

He watched the bushes, hoping to see what had made the movement. At first he couldn't tell, because the dark color of the animal blended into the shadows of the trees, but then a shape began to show itself. It was a shadow cat!

There was nowhere close for Caes to retreat to. He supposed he could back into the lake, but wasn't sure if shadow cats swam or not. The cat was about 15 feet away and right in front of him, looking right at Caes.

His blood ran cold, and he felt death might have finally caught
up to him. He had a tight grip on his spear. As far as he could
figure, he had two chances. He could back further into the lake
and hope the cat wouldn't swim, or he could throw the spear at
it. Neither of these sounded good to him.

The cat crept closer.

Caes backed up slightly. The water didn't seem to get deeper,
and that bothered Caes. He'd feel safer if he were swimming in
deep water.

The cat crept even closer, its eyes never leaving Caes.

Caes threw the spear as hard as he could at the cat. It was so
close he didn't see how he could possibly miss, but he did. One
instant, the cat was in front of him, and the next it wasn't there
at all. A wave of nausea hit Caes, and he vomited into the
water.

He looked to the right and saw the cat in the water, only about 6
feet away. It was about to leap on him! He had no weapons
except his belt knife, but no time to draw it.

As his hand moved to grab the knife, a dark shadow rushed
across the ground from behind the cat, and a roc grabbed it
from behind. It was White Feather!

The roc soared up into the air, carrying the cat with him, and
disappeared over the tops of the trees.

Caes couldn't believe his luck. If White Feather hadn't shown
up, there was nothing he could have done to save himself. He
was certain his knife wouldn't have saved him. He started
shaking, and he saw all the vomit in the water. He backed up
further and moved away from the shore. Finally, the water
started to get a little deeper. He rinsed himself off, and then
went back to shore – avoiding the vomit water.

He recovered his spear and went to a tree, climbing it a moment
later. For tonight, he intended to eat whatever was still edible
out of his pockets. There were still a few pieces of jerky and a
little of the elk meat left.

After eating, he felt brave enough to climb back down the tree
to see if he could find some berries or something to eat. As
much as he'd love to find some ripplefruit, he didn't find any.
He also didn't find any huckleberries. He did find some wild
vanilla and some thimbleberries. They weren't as tasty as
huckleberries or ripplefruit, but they were still good.

After eating the fruit, he returned to the lake and finished the
fish trap. By this time, the sun was starting to set. He got to
work building a bed in the tree. When the bed was finished, he
went back to the fish trap and looked inside. There were two
small fish in it. He stunned them, stuck them with his knife,
and then took them by the tree. He made a fire, gutted the fish,
and cooked them for dinner. By the time this was all done, the
sun was dropping behind the trees in the west.

Caes climbed up into the tree and laid down on the bed. He fell
asleep for his sixth night in the woods.

26
Bear Fight

Caes was dreaming again.

Jory, Jatt and Ronni were patting him on the back. He'd just finished the Rider Trials, and they were patting him on the back and telling him how great he'd done. Ronni gave him a big hug and a kiss on the cheek. He turned his head and kissed her on the mouth and she returned it eagerly. His roc – the one he'd just ridden – took off and flew over his head, screeching loudly. The crowd cheered and he kissed Ronni again. His roc screeched again. He looked and saw another roc – this one a wild roc – trying to snatch him from the platform. His roc – White Feather – attacked it, biting and clawing while flying over the attacking roc. The two rocs locked into each other and fell to the ground, rolling over the ground and biting each other. (Where did all the trees go?) *The attacking roc got free and flew away. White Feather was injured, limping on the ground with one bad leg. "White Feather!", Caes called to his roc.*

The roc looked up at him, from the ground, and limped through the trees. Okay, the trees are back. Where were they a minute ago? *White Feather tried to leap into the air, but his leg was giving out on him. Caes slid down a rope* (where did the rope come from?) *and ran to his roc. He picked up the roc's leg and checked it for injuries. There was a big gash. Caes held it closed and used a spell to heal it, and then looked up at the roc's eyes. He could tell the roc was grateful. He could almost see White Feather smiling at him. The roc lifted his face to the sky and screeched again, and...*

Caes woke up. He was completely disoriented. The sun was up
already. It was later than he normally slept. He blinked his
eyes to try and clear the sleep from them. His eyes came into
focus. As he started to look around, he heard a loud SCREECH.
Looking up, he saw a roc flying overhead – really close
overhead. The roc couldn't be more than 30 feet above him. It
was so close, he jumped in surprise.

Another roc appeared not far away. It was about the same size,
but a darker color than the first. The dark one looked like it was
heading right for him. *Oh crap!* Caes jumped out of the bed and
slid down the trunk of the tree, giving himself splinters, and
landing hard on the ground. As soon as his feet (and then butt)
hit the ground, the jumped to his feet and ran into the closest
cluster of trees. Another SCREECH came from above.

Caes looked at the birds, above. The dark one seemed to be
trying to reach him! Caes ducked behind a tree trunk, but kept
watching. White Feather was right behind the dark roc. He
wasn't positive, but it almost seemed like White Feather was
trying to protect him. He grabbed a rock and threw it at the
dark roc, and missed by a mile.

The dark roc circled above him, and White Feather clawed its
back and wings with his talons! The dark roc SCREECHED
again and tried to pivot to counterattack, but fell to the ground
instead, landing in the shallow water of the lake shore. White
Feather landed in the water next to the dark one and bit into the
dark roc's wing. The dark roc grabbed White Feather with a
talon and launched into the air.

White Feather was carried several feet into the air and finally
broke free – dropping into the lake.

The dark roc turned and dove at White Feather. Caes grabbed
his spear and ran towards the lake, throwing the spear as hard
as he could at the dark roc, screaming at the top of his voice.

The spear hit the roc in the bottom of its left wing, and flew out the top of the wing, bounced off the roc's back, and fell and into the lake. Caes continued running, screaming, at the bird. The roc veered away from White Feather, and came at Caes, but then beat its wings hard and lifted up into the air. It kept going until it disappeared over the treetops.

Caes turned and looked towards where White Feather had fallen into the lake. He'd fallen quite a ways off shore, and had disappeared completely under the water. Suddenly his head popped above the water, followed by his wing tips. Caes had no idea if rocs could swim.

"Come here, White Feather!", he called, and then reached into his pocket and took out the flute. *"Come here, White Feather"*, he played. Then, as the big bird struggled to swim, Caes cast the Call Birds cantrip, and released it towards the roc.

It took a couple minutes of wing flapping and struggling, but the bird made it into the shallow water, and then walked onto the shore, coming right towards Caes.

Caes continued to cheer the bird on with his flute. *"That's it. Come, White Feather!"*

White Feather walked to within ten feet of Caes and then shook his wings. The bird watched Caes, and then jumped into the air, flapping his wings hard. The bird took off, circled once, and disappeared over the trees.

Caes wandered back to his tree, struggling to understand what had happened. Why had the two birds been fighting? Was it a coincidence? Or, had White Feather been protecting Caes? It didn't make sense to him. White Feather was a wild wood roc. He shouldn't have any urge to protect Caes.

He sat down on a rock and took a piece of jerky from his pocket. He was nearly out. There were only a couple pieces left. *Did White Feather protect me because I've given him meat? I didn't exactly give it to him, but he did eat wolf and deer from my kills.*

He finished eating the piece of jerky. He was thirsty, but didn't exactly want lake water. Well, he needed water from somewhere and didn't see a stream anywhere close. *Oh no! My spear! I need to try and retrieve it.*

He looked out at the lake, and was pretty sure he knew where the spear had landed. Before he could change his mind, he stripped his boots and clothes and ran naked into the lake. It was chilly, but felt good. When he got to waist deep, he dove forward and swam out to about where the spear had landed. He dove down and looked around, but didn't see anything but mud and water plants. He surfaced again and took several deep breaths and dove again. Again, he came up empty.

He swam a little further out and dove again. This time he saw the spear laying on the bottom of the lake. It was deeper than he'd expected. The water was at least 15 feet deep here, and maybe even deeper. He went to the surface and took several deep breaths, held it, and dove down again. He went down and down and just got his fingers on the spear when he felt like he'd run out of air. He turned for the surface and pushed off the bottom, breaking the surface just as he felt like he was going to take a breath of lake water.

Caes rested a moment while treading water, and then swam for the shore with his spear. He carried the spear to the fish trap and looked inside. *Yes, there's a fish!* It was only one, but it was medium sized and would fill his stomach. He felt very self-conscious, with no clothes on. He looked around to verify there weren't people around, and then felt pretty silly. Why would there be people in the middle of the Waha?

He looked at the fish in the trap and whispered the Stun cantrip at the fish. When it rolled sideways, Caes stabbed it in the gills with the spear, and reached down to grab the fish. As he started back to his camp, he noticed some cattails he'd missed yesterday. They weren't far away. The idea of flatbread sounded great. He went to his camp and set the fish on the ground, and put on his boots. Then he grabbed his clothes and carried them back to the lake and rinsed them out. They'd been starting to stink, and it was good to at least rinse them out.

When he was finished with the clothes, he wrung them out and laid them on a log to dry in the sun, and then took his knife and spear to the cattails to harvest some of the heads. He cut several loose and carried them all back to his camp, and then went looking for some large leaves to use to hold some water while he mixed up cattail flour.

A little over an hour later, Caes sat eating roasted fish wrapped in cattail flatbread. It filled his stomach nicely! He went to his clothes and flipped them over to let the bottom side get some sun. The top side had dried pretty nicely. They were still damp, but not soaking wet. He retreated back to his tree and climbed the tree – carefully this time. Without clothes to protect his legs, chest, and private parts he took extra care as he made his way to the bed. He sat in the bed for about an hour. The temperature was getting hot and he was sure his clothes must be getting dry by now.

He thought about home and his family. Of course, Crislan wasn't there. It still hurt Caes' heart every time he thought of his brother. His mother and father must be worried sick about him. He'd been gone, what, six nights or was it seven? He wasn't sure. No one had been on the platform when he was taken. He wondered how long it had taken for someone to find his pack and pouch.

Were his friends worried about him, or had they just decided he'd been eaten by a roc? Was Ronni worried about him? He could almost feel her lips from his dream this morning. *Of course, that wasn't real. I was probably kissing my armpit or something gross like that.*

Why did he hear his mom's voice yesterday? Was that yesterday? *No, dummy, that was the day before.*

Oh man, time was messing with his head. It was hard to remember what happened on which day. He'd had so many encounters with animals. There were bear, shadow cats, wolves, deer, elk, rocs, and of course the small animals and fish. He was sitting there thinking about his adventures when he heard a flute, *"Caes, are you there?"* What?

Caes reached for his flute and realized he was still naked. The flute was down by his clothes somewhere. He raised his head and shouted, "I'm here. Rider! Do you hear me?"

He held still and listened. Further away this time, he heard, *"Caes, are you there?"*

Damn! He scooted down the tree as quickly as he could. He'd just gotten his feet on the ground when he heard the growl of a bear. He turned towards the noise and saw a huge bear looking at him. It stood on its hind legs and growled again. The bear was huge! He didn't have any weapons!

His spear was up in his bed, and his bow was hanging on a branch next to the bed. Even his knife was up there. The bear pawed the ground and dropped its head towards the ground. It was much larger than the bear he'd seen in the river. *Oh man, now what? Bears can climb, right?*

He reached down and picked up a fist-sized rock. He slipped
behind the tree and threw the rock behind the bear. It crashed
into some bushes and made a good noise. The bear turned its
head to look, and Caes climbed up the tree as quickly as he
could. He was eight or ten feet up when the tree started
shaking. He looked down and saw the bear was climbing it
also. *Oh no!*

Caes kept climbing, trying to get to the smaller branches where,
hopefully, the bear couldn't go. He got to his bed, and hooked
his arm through his bow and quickly grabbed his knife, which
he stuck in his teeth. He grabbed his last two arrows and the
spear and kept climbing. When he made it another 30 feet up,
the bear stopped but was still watching him.

Caes stopped also to catch his breath.

The bear started shaking the tree, and when Caes didn't fall out,
the bear started climbing again. Caes looked around to see if
another tree was close enough to jump to, but nothing was close
enough. *White Feather, I'd love for you to show up now!*

He was high enough now that the trunk was thin, and the
branches small enough he was worried about them breaking.
He looked up to the sky, but didn't see any rocs. He looked
down and saw the bear still climbing. *How is it not breaking
branches?*

Feeling panic, Caes decided he had to try and fight the giant
bear. He aimed his spear at the bear's head and pulled his arm
back to throw – while holding on tightly to the trunk with his
left hand.

The bear climbed five feet higher, and was now only about ten feet from Caes. It was now or never. He threw the spear at the bear and stuck it in the eye! The bear roared and started shaking its head. The tree shook all over, and felt like it was going to snap! Finally, the bear let go of the tree and fell to the ground, bouncing off three branches on the way, and landing hard on the ground.

It rolled around, but seemed injured. Caes slipped the bow from his shoulder and nocked an arrow, taking aim at the bear – now at least 40 feet below him. He released the arrow and hit the bear in the back. The bear roared again.

Caes nocked his last arrow and took aim again. This time he waited for the bear to move around and try to dislodge the spear from its eye, and he shot again. The arrow found its mark close to the heart. The bear ran headfirst into the tree and laid down.

Is it dead? I'm out of weapons. I sure hope it's dead!

All he had left was his knife. It was far too small to be a threat to a huge bear like that. Caes decided to sit in the tree for a while. He waited for what seemed like half an hour, but in hindsight was probably only 10 minutes. He slowly started making his way back down the tree.

When he made it where his bed had been, he saw it was gone now – destroyed by the bear's claws as it climbed. He stopped and watched the bear some more. He couldn't tell if it was still breathing, but thought it was probably dead. He decided to give it another ten minutes, and sat on a branch.

After sitting for a while, he continued to climb down. He dropped on the opposite side of the tree from the bear and ran quickly to his clothes, all the time watching the bear. He pulled his pants and shirt on, and then found a large rock. It was too large to hold in one hand, so he stuck the knife in his scabbard and held the rock with both hands. Caes walked up to the bear, which was still laying in the same position. *It's dead.* Caes held the rock up and threw it on the bear's head. It busted his spear, and the bear didn't move.

Finally, Caes was sure the bear was dead. He pulled his knife from the scabbard and went to the bear to start gutting it. Right as he poked the knife into the bear's stomach, it roared and swung a paw, hitting Caes right in the chest. Caes went tumbling, head over heels, backwards. He landed on his back and looked up to see the bear right over him, broken spear in its eye and all. The bear opened its mouth and bent down to bite him, and Caes did the only thing he could think of. He stuck his knife into the bear's mouth – right into the roof of the mouth.

The bear fell right on top of Caes. This time it really was dead.

Caes wiggled and scooted and pushed for a long time. Blood was flowing in his eyes and mouth. As much as he wanted the blood to be the bear's, he was sure it was his own. About the time he started to panic about being trapped, he managed to push himself out from under the huge bear.

My flute! The rider was calling me! He pulled his flute out of his pocket and inspected it. It didn't seem damaged. He hoped the rider was still within range to hear him as he played, *"Rider! Help! This is Caes!"*. He waited a minute to listen for a response, but didn't hear anything. He tried it three more times, each time waiting for response. Nothing.

He put his hand to his face and looked at his palm. Blood
covered it. He walked over to the lake and splashed water on
his face. It stung badly. He tried to look in the reflection of the
lake, but couldn't see how bad the wound was.

Caes knew head wounds bled quite a bit, and knew he had a
gash on his forehead. He must have hit his head on some rocks
when the bear hit him. He was starting to feel light-headed,
and he sat down for a bit. As he sat, he looked around and saw
peat moss growing in a bog off of the lake, not far from where
he'd found the cattails. Catscratch had said it could be used to
stop bleeding. He needed to get some.

After sitting for about ten minutes, Caes got up on shaky legs
and pulled his knife from the bear's mouth. It was harder to
pull out than he expected. Then, he went over to the peat moss
and pulled several handfuls. On the way back to his camp, he
watched for vines, and when he found some, cut several and
took them with him.

He wove the vines together into a sort of rope and then stuffed
peat moss into his wound and wrapped the viny rope around
his head, tying it in place. Caes was sure it looked silly, but he
hoped it would help. Then he sat and rested some more.

After he'd sat as long as he could manage, he went back to the
bear and tugged on the arrows. One was broken, but he was
able to pull the rest of the arrow and the arrowhead free. The
other was still intact, and he was able to pull it out. He was also
able to tug and use his knife to dig the spear point out of the
bear's eye. *I'm definitely going to need to make more arrows!*

With that done, he stacked his arrow and bow next to the bear, and started cutting through the skin. The bear was much too large to move. He cut backstrap from it. Then his eyes fell on the claws. They were so large! He went to work cutting one of the front paws off. When he had that done, he cut several strips of skin from the bear. One was a short strip – about 2 feet long and an inch wide - and the others were about 4 feet long. All were still covered with fur. When he was done, he gathered his things, and the meat, claw, and strips of skin, and moved away from the bear. He walked several hundred yards away, along the west side of the lake and looked for another good tree to climb. When he found it, he gathered sticks and made a fire. Once the fire was burning nicely, Caes found a cooking stick and poked it through the bear meat, and then hung it over the fire to cook. Then, while he waited, he started scraping meat off the inside of his bearskin straps. When he had them pretty clean, he carried them to the lake and rinsed them real good, and then wrapped them around sticks and twisted them tight to try and wring them out. Then, he repeated the scaping, rinsing, and wringing process several more times. Finally, he laid the leathery strips next to the fire to dry and smoke.

He took burning sticks and used them to sear the flesh on the claw, and took it to the lake to rinse as well.

When he was finally done with the skin and bear claw, his food was ready. It was only midday, but he felt like he'd been fighting for days. He was exhausted.

How am I ever going to make it back home?

He took his chunk of bear meat and climbed the tree he'd chosen. Once safely up at a good height, he sat on a branch and started eating the meat. When he finished eating it, he saw White Feather fly overhead. He fumbled in his pocket and pulled out the flute. It seemed to still be intact, so he played, *"White Feather!"*

The big bird circled overhead while Caes watched. It swooped down and flew over him, and then landed by where his previous camp – and the dead bear – was. *Well, hopefully that means the bear meat isn't going to waste.*

The sun was getting low in the sky. He'd wasted most of the day with all the excitement. He should try to replenish his arrows before morning. Caes looked around to make sure it was safe, and then climbed out of the tree and went to the brush along the lake, looking for sticks or bamboo. He walked several hundred feet along the lake before finding a small patch of bamboo. He took his knife and cut about a dozen of the smaller shafts and one large one and carried them back to his tree.

The rest of the evening was spent making arrows with bamboo and the rest of the obsidian. He ran out of obsidian after six arrowheads, but at least he now had seven in total. The larger shaft became a new spear, and he attached the spear point he'd made before. By the time he was done, it was starting to get dark.

He used the other half dozen bamboo shafts and some sticks from around the base of his tree and made a new bed. He laid down on it and tried to sleep, but sleep was slow to come.

He'd been gone for about a week. At least one Rider was still looking for him, but he was sure they were losing hope. How much longer would they look for him?

White Feather was a dilemma to him. The bird stayed close. He saw him several times a day – sometimes passing overhead and flying without apparently seeing him. Other times, the roc circled over him. Then, sometimes several hours would go by without a glimpse of the roc.

He was thinking about Ronni when he finally fell asleep.

27

Ella Returns

She was anxious to get back on the ground. Ella and Grayce had been flying for nearly two days. It was a long trip from Daener City to Westvale. They'd stayed just north of the Crags again on the return flight. As much as Ella wanted to press on, it simply wasn't safe to fly at night, especially over the Crags.

Ella saw the platform marking Westvale a few miles ahead. She tapped Grayce on the shoulder. "Grayce, should we call for Jerod to see where he is? I want to find him as soon as possible."

"Good idea, Ella. When we get a bit closer, I'll call for him. My guess is he's either at the platform or the aerie. We can land at either place."

In about another minute, the platform became easier to see, and Grayce played, *"Jerod!"* and waited a few seconds, then, *"Jerod where are you? I have Ella with me."*

They heard a response, *"This is Jerod. I'm at the aerie."*

Grayce played, *"We will meet you there."*, and turned to Ella. "I'm sure you understood that, right?"

Ella answered, "I did. Thanks!"

A minute or so later the roc with the two women landed at the aerie. Jerod was standing there with Brun and Tuck. Ella swung out of the saddle and jumped to the ground. Jerod went to her and gave her a big hug and then a kiss. He stepped back. "Ella, did you find the mage – Zoe? Did you learn anything?"

Ella could barely contain herself. "Yes, I did. She cast the spell and I talked to Caes for just a few seconds. He's alive! At least, he was alive two days ago."

"Where is he? I can go get him now.", Jerod said.

"We couldn't tell where he was. It was strange, but I called his name and he answered back. He sounded okay, but the spell ended before he could tell me where he was."

"What do you mean? Why didn't Zoe cast the spell again?", asked Jerod.

Ella said, "She couldn't. The spell destroyed his things when it was cast. All we know is he's alive."

"I wonder where he is. Yesterday several of us flew over the Waha and into the Crags again. We played his name, but never heard or saw anything. No fire. No flute. Nothing."

"Do you think we've been looking in the wrong direction? Could a roc have taken him east or west instead of north?", Ella asked.

"Unlikely", said Brun. "Most wild rocs nest in the Crags, but we've also had riders flying east and west. Jerod, the Trials are tomorrow. What do you want us to do?"

Tuck interjected, "We should keep looking for him today. Tomorrow, though, we should be here to watch the Trials. Unless, of course, you think we should delay them. I just think we should keep them as scheduled. Too many people have travelled from other villages. It wouldn't be right to send them home or have them stay longer."

"I don't like it, but I think you're right, Tuck", said Jerod. "Let's send more riders out today for another pass of the surrounding areas, then keep everyone here tomorrow. Ella, are you okay with that?"

She nodded her head. "I guess. He's been gone for a week already. I guess one more day will be okay. I just hope he isn't hurt."

"I know, honey. We all hope that", said Jerod. "Brun, Tuck, can you call a riders meeting for as soon as possible? I want to talk to all the riders and explain what's happening."

"Sure, Jerod", Brun said. "We'll do it right away."

"Thanks", Jerod said. "I'm going to walk with Ella back to our house. I'll come back shortly after. Maybe we can do the meeting in an hour? Maybe two?"

Brun nodded to him and turned to walk up the steps to the highest point in the aerie. When he got there, he took out his flute and played, *"Attention all riders. Rider meeting at the aerie in two hours. Attention all riders. Rider meeting at the aerie in two hours."*

Tuck had followed him up the steps. "Two hours?"

Brun answered, "Yes. Two hours. I thought about one hour, but a lot of riders are still quite a ways off. Would you put out more calls and ask riders to relay the message to anyone who didn't hear?"

"I will, Brun", answered Tuck. "I'll call again in 15 minutes, and then every 15 minutes after that."

"Perfect, Tuck. Thank you", said Brun.

Catscratch was walking with Hops in the forest north of Westvale when the call for a riders meeting went out. He held his hand up for Hops to stop and listen. "Interestin' don'cha think, Hoppy?"

Hops answered, "It sure is, Scratch. What do you think it means? Did they find something?"

"I dunno, but I'm thinkin' we should be there. Ya ready to walk fast? Let's head back."

They turned towards Westvale and started back. Both were well armed for any of the forest denizens, but it was looking like they wouldn't need their weapons today.

The walk back took a little over an hour. They'd walked fast, and both were out of breath when they came to the bottom of the steps leading up to the aerie.

They arrived at the aerie as dozens of riders were taking seats in the courtyard. Catscratch knew several of them, but not all. He walked around, shaking hands of the ones he knew. He saw Tuck sitting near the front of the crowd. "Tuck, how ya doin?".

Tuck looked up at Catscratch and said, "Hi Catscratch. I'm surprised to see you here."

"Surprised? Why that? Not invited, huh?" asked Catscratch.

"What, oh, no, that's not what I meant. I just didn't think you'd come to a riders meeting.", said Tuck.

Catscratch looked at him, and Tuck felt like the ranger was looking into his soul.

"Is this just a meetin' 'bout the Trials? Or's somethin' else goin' on?" asked Catscratch.

Tuck said, "Uh, there's several things to talk about. You know, the Trials are tomorrow, but Jerod wants to talk about Caes also."

"Fellas, how are you doing?", came a voice behind Catscratch. The ranger turned and saw Brun.

"Brun, how ya doing'? Hoppy and me welcome here? Sounds like somethin' might be happenin' I should know 'bout.", said Catscratch.

"Friend, you're always welcome here. Yeah, something's happening. There's some info on young Caes. Pull up a seat.", said Brun.

"Good news, Brun?", Catscratch asked.

"Pull up a seat", Brun repeated, and walked off.

Brun looked at Hops and his fingers were moving. *Something about Caes. Good news I hope.*

About ten minutes after Catscratch and Hops took their seats, Jerod came out of one of the buildings and walked to the center of the chairs and benches in the courtyard. The riders, who had all been talking among themselves, suddenly quieted and watched Jerod.

Jerod motioned to Brun, and he came to join Jerod in the center. Jerod cleared his throat, and then started talking, "Good afternoon riders". There were several voices saying, "Good afternoon" back to him.

Jerod looked around and saw Catscratch and Hops. "Catscratch. How are you and Hops doing? I should be surprised to see you here, but I guess nothing surprises me with you around." Several of the riders chuckled. Catscratch's reputation for always knowing what's happening was well-deserved.

"Hope ya don't mind us here, Jerod", Catscratch said.

"Not at all, my friend", Jerod responded. Then he continued, "Riders and rangers, thank you for joining me here. I want to start by thanking each and every one of you for the countless hours you've put in this past week, looking for my son, Caes. I owe you all my gratitude.

"You all know how Caes was taken from the platform by a roc. Well, at least that's what we think happened, and that's determined how we've been searching. All of us riders have been searching places a wild roc might have taken him. We've looked east and west, but mostly north along the Crags."

Jerod paused and watched the riders. Many were nodding their heads or whispering to their neighbors. They all looked back at him.

"Up until this afternoon, we were all feeling like it's been hopeless. No one has found signs of my son. Honestly, we've been close to calling off the search. That's been very hard on me and my wife, Ella.

"Now, you all know Ella and how strong she is. This whole thing has brought us to the breaking point. It's been very tough. Well, anyway, Ella and Grayce took a roc north of the Crags, all the way to Daener City. They left a few days ago and just got back this afternoon. Maeve – you all know her – she found a spell in one of her books that was supposed to tell whether or not Caes was alive, but she didn't have the right magic to cast it. So, Ella and Grayce went all the way to Daener City to meet with a mage.

"Well, they found the mage and she – her name is Zoe – she cast the spell." He paused and wiped tears from his eyes. He looked at them again, and continued, "She cast the spell and it worked. Ella was able to speak to Caes. He's alive!"

The riders all clamored loudly. Jerod stood patiently while the riders talked loudly among themselves. Brun whistled, and they looked at him. "Hey you all, be quiet! Jerod's not finished talking. Let him continue!"

One of the riders called out, "Where is he, Jerod?"

"We don't know, Cotty. The spell Zoe cast was a short duration, and before you ask, yes, they tried to cast it a second time but weren't able to.

"Ella talked to Caes. She knows he's alive and he sounded okay. Then, the spell ended. We don't know where he is or whether or not he's hurt.

"Now, this brings me to the Trials tomorrow. This thing has been scheduled for months. We've got guests here from other villages, and really can't reschedule it. So, we're going to have the Trials, as planned. I want each and every one of you here to cheer on our new riders. Got it?"

The riders responded with claps and cheers and some just holding thumbs up in the air.

"Okay", Jerod continued, "So, I want you all to get your rocs and keep looking this afternoon. I hope we find Caes sooner rather than later. He's been out there for a week now, and honestly I'm shocked he's still alive. Anyway, keep looking for him today. Watch for smoke from a cooking fire. Keep your ears open and listen for shouts. Caes doesn't have a flute. His picco was in the pouch we found on the platform. If you use your flutes to call him, he can understand – at least if he hears it – but won't be able to answer you. He'll be yelling and screaming instead. Listen for that."

Jerod looked at the group of riders and rangers. "Catscratch, thank you for being here. Do you have any wisdom for my riders?"

Catscratch stood and looked around. "Welp, guess I should. Caes is a good man. If'n anyone could s'vive out there it be him. He's a fast learner, he is. Guessin' he'd be in the trees and not the meadows. Ya know what I mean? Be hard to see 'im from the air. Just cuz ya can't see 'im don't mean he ain't there. I told 'im to stay 'way from the Waha, but if that's where the roc put 'im, then he's there. If anyone can s'vive there, Caes's the one. Jerod, I wish there's more I can say, but ya know, I just don't. He's a good kid. Let's find 'im."

The riders clapped for him.

Jerod started again, "Thanks, Catscratch. Okay, riders, here's the plan. This afternoon you'll keep looking for Caes. Be back by dark and ready to watch the Trials tomorrow. I want several safety riders in the air tomorrow. I think you all know who the safety riders are. Let's celebrate our new riders and have a great day tomorrow. The next day, I want each and every one of you back in the air and find my son!"

Jerod held his hand up and walked back to one of the buildings. Brun said, "Alright riders! There's still five hours or so of daylight. Get out there and find Caes!"

28

Flying

Caes awoke when the sun hit him in his face. He rolled over and realized he was about to fall, and repositioned himself instead. His body ached, especially his chest. He felt like a big bruise. He wondered if he'd broken some ribs when the bear swatted him. If he survived the forest and actually made it home, he was looking forward to a soft bed, good food, and safety until he was healed up. He put a hand to his forehead. The moss had fallen off, but the bleeding was stopped. He needed to clean it, but wanted to wait until he found a small creek or a spring instead of the lake.

He picked up the bear paw and looked at it. It was very large. The paw must have been at least 9 inches wide. Caes didn't want to lose it. If he survived his time in the woods, he wanted to keep this paw as proof of his experience. He took his knife, and the short strap he'd made from the bear skin, and fastened them together, and then hung it around his neck. It was heavy, but he thought he'd get used to it.

He looked around, but didn't see any animals, with the exception of small birds and squirrels. It was time to move away from the lake and get closer to home. He ate one of his last pieces of jerky and then climbed down the tree. Caes gathered his bow, arrows, and spear, and then checked the fish trap. It was empty, so he tore it down. It didn't make sense to trap a fish if no one was here to eat it.

Caes looked around on the ground and up in the sky to check for hazards and then started walking along the west side of the lake, heading south. He walked for about an hour and decided to take a break. His ribs were aching, and he had a headache from the cut on his forehead.

He saw some ripplefruit growing in a tree, and it didn't look too difficult to get to. Caes leaned his spear against the tree trunk and climbed up. The fruit was near the top of the tree, and it took a while to get there. When he did, he realized he was over 100 feet up. This was a big tree. He gathered as many of the tasty fruits as he could shove down his shirt, and when he was about to climb down, noticed White Feather flying overhead. He smiled to himself, and rested on a branch. He took out his flute and played, *"Good morning White Feather!"*.

The big bird didn't act as if he heard the tunes. Caes continued climbing down to the ground. When he reached the ground, Caes ate one of the ripplefruit, and left the rest in his shirt. He picked up his spear again, and continued his journey south.

An hour later, Caes came to a large meadow. It was at least a mile across, and maybe 2-3 miles wide. He was bothered by the idea of crossing the open space. He'd be a sitting duck to any passing wild roc. Of course, he's also be wide open to anyone searching for him, but had been feeling like everyone had given up on finding him. It had been over a week since he'd been taken. How long would they keep looking for him?

He knelt down by a tree and watched the meadow. It looked like he just needed to detour around it. That would add hours to his walk, but there didn't seem to be any way around it. His choices seemed to be either to walk along the shore of the lake – and jump in and swim if a roc or other predator came at him, or stay in the trees and walk around the western side of the meadow. He went to the lake and drank several swallows of water, and then started out, away from the lake, to go around the meadow to the west.

Ten or fifteen minutes later, he saw some elk feeding near the tree line, and dropped to a knee to watch. There were five of them. One was a bull and the other four were cows. His jerky was almost gone – one piece left – and fresh meat would be good.   He stayed low and crawled as close as he could get. When he was about 60 feet away, he stopped and nocked an arrow.

As he drew the string back to his ear, he saw a movement in the trees. He released the tension on the bowstring and watched the trees. Was it more wolves? He didn't want to fight more of them, and he was low on arrows. If it was wolves, he'd just back off and wait for different game to shoot.

The movement didn't happen again, so he drew the string back to his ear again and took aim on one of the cows. He was about to release it when the movement happened again in the trees. He twisted to get a good look at it when he saw a shadow cat stalking the elk. *Crap, just what I need. Another damn shadow cat!*

He was about to let the tension out of the bowstring again when the shadow cat took a step forward. It was crouched down, looking like it was about the pounce. The elk hadn't noticed it yet, so it must have been downwind from them. He aimed at the big cat and released the arrow. It flew true and struck the shadow cat right behind the front legs. The cat screamed and twisted, trying to get to the arrow. The elk all took off running away from the cat and right into the meadow.

The shadow cat disappeared right as Caes was watching it, and reappeared about twenty feet behind where it had been before. The arrow was no longer sticking from its side. The cat turned around to change directions, and Caes let fly with another arrow. This one struck the cat in the neck. It screamed again – and disappeared again. This time it reappeared just in front of Caes, but luckily facing away from him. He'd already nocked another arrow and drew back to shoot again, but this time the cat collapsed onto the ground – before he could shoot it again. Remembering what had happened when he approached the bear, Caes decided to stay where he was and watch. He kept his eyes on the shadow cat, but also looked out into the meadow to see what the elk were doing. They had gone out into the meadow about 100 yards and stopped. They seemed to be looking around for the predator that had been stalking them. After five minutes, the shadow cat still hadn't moved, and the elk had relaxed and gone to eating the grass in the meadow. Caes was pretty sure they'd make their way back to the trees once they were sure the cat was gone. He slipped the bow over his shoulder and took the spear and low crawled to the cat. He was surprised to see that both his arrows were gone, but the wounds were still there. He'd killed the shadow cat! He poked it with his spear, just to be sure.

Caes sat up on his knees and looked at the elk. They were starting to head for the tree line and would pass him less than 50 feet away. He had five arrows left, and hopefully he could take one of the elk.

He nocked an arrow and waited. When the elk was as close as it was going to get, he lifted up and let fly at the cow closest to him. It hit the elk and it started running away from him. The other elk followed the one he'd shot. They were in full run.

After less than 100 yards, the one he'd shot dropped to the ground. Suddenly after that, a large shape swooped down from the sky and grabbed the bull with its talons, and lifted it up in the air. It carried it up a couple hundred feet and dropped it. The bull elk fell to the ground and lay still.

The roc pivoted in the air and landed by the elk. It was White Feather! He bent his head down to the elk and started feeding. Caes took his flute and played, *"White Feather!"*, and stood up to walk towards his own elk. When he got there, the roc was still feeding several hundred feet away. Caes took his knife and started gutting the cow elk. When he was finished, he dragged the guts away from the elk carcass as far as he could without getting too tired. Then, he cut the backstrap from the elk and walked back to the trees just on the other side of the shadow cat. He looked around and then made a fire, carefully feeding sticks to it until the fire was burning enough to cook over. He found a sturdy stick and sharpened the end of it with his knife, and then stuck the backstrap on the stick and propped it over the fire to cook.

While it was cooking, he went to the dead shadow cat and gutted it, as well. He dragged the guts out by the elk guts. White Feather was finished eating by then, and watching Caes. Caes wiped his hands on his pants and pulled the flute from his pocket. *"White Feather. Feed."*, he played. The big bird just stayed where he was, watching Caes. Caes played it again, *"White Feather, Feed."*, and then cast the Call Birds cantrip, releasing it towards White Feather.

The big bird started walking towards Caes. When the roc got closer, Caes backed away from the guts by about 10 feet and waited. The roc continued to come closer, and stopped when he reached the pile of guts. He looked down at them, and then at Caes. Then, he dropped his head and started eating the guts.

Caes walked to the shadow cat carcass and started skinning it. He wasn't interested in eating the meat, especially with a big elk dead on the ground. However, he had plans for the skin, and wanted to keep it if he could. He cut off the head and finished skinning the cat. When he finished, he saw White Feather watching him again. The gut pile was gone.

Caes picked up the cat skin and carried it over to the elk and laid it down next to it. White Feather was still in the same place, watching him.

Caes walked over to the shadow cat carcass and played his flute again. *"White Feather. Feed."*, he played.

White Feather walked over to the cat and started eating it, as well.

He watched the bird eat for a minute, and then turned and went to the elk carcass. He knelt down and cut some more meat off, deciding to make more jerky. He cut a piece, and then looked at the roc, and then cut another piece, and then looked at the roc again. Then, he cut another piece, and looked at the roc, and… The roc wasn't at the cat carcass anymore. He was almost to Caes. *Uh oh! No, I'm not going to give you my elk also!*

He stood and held his hand out, willing the bird to stop. White Feather stopped only a couple feet from Caes. It watched him, but didn't seem like he was being aggressive.

Caes glanced down at the elk, and then back up at White Feather, and the sneaky bird was right next to Caes now. He did the only thing that felt right. He reached out and patted White Feather's neck. The bird jumped back and stared at Caes. Caes stared right back at him.

Caes' heart was beating rapidly. He was nervous but not scared, although he was pretty sure he should have been terrified. Caes held his hand out again, and took a couple slow steps towards White Feather. He whispered the Calm cantrip at the bird. White Feather dropped his head slightly, and Caes walked closer and patted him on the neck again. "Good boy, White Feather", Caes whispered, and he patted the bird some more.

He was forming an idea in his head, and he knew he was half crazy to be even thinking about it, but he'd ridden White Feather once. Could he do it again? Maybe White Feather could be his way home? It was nuts, but at the rate he was going, he'd be alone in the forest for another week or two, if he survived that long. He'd had too many encounters with shadow cats, bears, and wolves to be confident in his continued survival.

Caes backed away from the elk carcass – realizing the roc would most likely start eating it. White Feather just looked at him, so he bent down and grabbed the shadow cat skin and carried it back to the elk, and then he sat down next to the elk and started scraping meat off the inside of the skin. After he'd been scraping for a few minutes, White Feather leapt into the air and flew away.

Caes watched him fly away, and then started working on how to take the skin with him. He decided he'd cut holes in the skin and use them to tie some of his bear skin straps to it and hopefully wear it like a cape. It was going to be too long, but he figured he could double it over and have the fur facing out as well as in against his body.

He worked on it for at least an hour. Finally, he put it over his head and stood up. It was heavy, but he could carry it. He hoped it would dry and lighten somewhat as time went by.

Next, Caes took the other straps he'd cut and tied a couple of them together to make them longer. Lastly, he tied other straps around his right his left leg and used them to hold his remaining arrows in place.

It was after mid-day when he finally finished. The hunk of elk meat was cooked, and Caes savored the taste as he finished it up. The strips he'd cut to make jerky were cooked most of the way through. They weren't dry enough to last long, but he didn't want to spend the hours it would take smoking them right now. He shoved the pieces in his shirt, put out the fire, grabbed his weapons, and walked out into the meadow. It was time for him to try his plan.

Two hundred feet into the meadow, Caes knelt and looked around. There were rocs in the distance, but he didn't think any of them were White Feather. He took the flute out and played, *"White Feather. Come!"*

A few minutes later, he saw the roc circling overhead. He played it again, *"White Feather. Come!"*, and then cast Call Birds at him.

White Feather dropped quickly to land in the meadow right in front of Caes. Caes cast Calm at him, and waited for a minute to pass. Then, he stood and walked slowly to White Feather. When he got to him, he gently patted the bird's neck, whispering, "Good boy!"

While Caes was patting the bird's neck, he wrapped one hand to the back of the neck and gently pulled forward. White Feather let his neck be pulled forward. Caes continued to whisper gently, "Good! Good boy. Good boy!"

His heart was beating like crazy again. It was now or never!

He moved his hands down slightly and pulled himself up onto the bird's back. White Feather didn't know how to respond, and extended his wings, flapping some, and moving around in a sort of bird dance. Caes cast Calm one more time, and White Feather relaxed. His wings tucked back in.

Once Caes felt like he was positioned properly, he took the loop of bear skin he'd made and looped it over the bird's head. Finally, Caes tapped the bird's sides gently with his heels. White Feather leapt into the air and flew up. He circled the area twice, and then dove to the ground, talons extended. White Feather seized the elk carcass and swooped back into the air! Caes couldn't believe he was flying on the bird! The first time he'd been on White Feather had been a total accident. This time it was on purpose. He decided he'd probably be thrown off in just a few minutes, but in the meantime he felt victorious. He leaned forward and stroked the bird's neck, saying to him, "Good job, White Feather. Good job!"

They circled the meadow. It was larger than he'd thought. He probably would have spent all day walking around it. He and White Feather spent the next half hour getting used to each other. Only once did the bird act up. They were flying over the lake, and White Feather apparently decided he wasn't ready to have a rider. The bird suddenly shook and turned. If it hadn't been for the strap Caes had put around the roc's neck, he probably would have fallen. As it was, it scared him quite a bit, but he managed to keep a grip on the leather straps. Then, he guided the roc to the southern end of the meadow and used the leather straps to push the bird's head down. White Feather flew close to the ground and then dropped the elk in the meadow and landed just past the carcass. Caes patted White Feather's neck and whispered, "Good job, boy." He slipped off the bird and looked at the elk. Its body looked okay. The talons of the roc hadn't punctured it anywhere that he could see. Caes pointed his hand at the sky and White Feather launched into the air and flew high.

Caes found a fallen log in the trees to sit on. He pulled out some of the elk strips he'd cooked and ate them. Then, he wandered into the trees to look for berries or ripplefruit. He found a patch of thimbleberries and ate them. He walked back out into the meadow and looked up in the sky, trying to find White Feather. The roc wasn't there, so Caes played on his flute, *"White Feather. Come!"*

He stood watching the sky and the roc appeared over the trees. Caes felt excited. *He came when I called him!*

White Feather landed right in front of him. Caes petted his neck and pulled himself back up onto the bird's back, sitting just in front of the wings. He tapped his heels to the bird and White Feather launched into the sky again.

They flew around for another 10 minutes, and Caes landed him again, and slid off the roc onto the ground. He was starting to feel comfortable with the personality of the roc, but warned himself to be wary of little tricks the bird might play to get rid of his rider.

"Okay, White Feather. Are you ready for a longer flight?" Of course, the roc didn't say anything back. Caes gave the bird a pat and climbed back onto his back. "Okay, White Feather. Let's go for a longer flight." He turned the roc's head to look at the elk carcass and touched his heels to the bird. The roc took a couple steps forward and grabbed the elk carcass, and then launched into the air again. They flew high, circling the meadow and flying over the lake. *I think it's time to try to find home.*

He looked at the sky and around at the horizon in all directions. He had a pretty idea of where Westvale was from here. It should be due south-southwest. He pointed White Feather that direction and watched the trees and hills pass by under him.

Two hours later, he recognized the area round Westvale. Then, a few minutes later he saw the huge platform in the top of the trees. There were several rocs flying around with riders on them. *Are those people on top of the platform? It looks like it. Oh man, is today the Trials?*

He was flying higher than the other rocs, and two of the riders turned their birds and rose to meet him. *They probably can't see me from where they are. They probably just think this is a wild roc and they're going to chase it away.*

Caes took his flute and pulled it to the lower sound position – so the humans could hear it – and played, *"Riders! This is Caes Wind! Riders! This is Caes Wind! Permission to land requested!"*

The riders flew up to his level and turned to fly beside him. He recognized the one on his left. It was Ember. The one on the right was Bo. They were friends of his parents. Ember played, *"Is it really you, Caes?"*

Caes responded, *"Hi Ember! It's me. Can I land?"* He looked at Bo and waved. Bo waved back and had a huge smile on his face.

"I'll clear an area. Wait for my signal", Bo played, and he dove down toward the platform.

Jerod and Ella sat in the bleachers, watching the newly-arrived roc and rider flying high above them. Jerod had his hands shielding his eyes from the sun, looking up at the rider. "Ella, that's weird. That roc is smaller than most others, and it's carrying an animal in its talons. It looks like a big deer or elk."

"Who is it? Can you tell?", asked Ella. She turned to the woman sitting beside her, "Bay, can you see who that rider is?"

"No, I can't. Just a minute. Let me look again", and she started muttering. Whiskers appeared on her cheeks and her eyes changed so the pupils looked like vertical slits. "It's a man. Wrapped in fur. He's injured. I don't know who it is."

They heard flutes playing. Jerod looked at Ella. "Ella, did they just say Caes?"

"I'm not sure. It sounded like it, but I don't know", she said.

Bo landed his roc on the platform and called out, "Clear some room. A rider needs to land. Clear some room!"

Jerod got up to walk to Bo.

Bo held his hand, palm out, facing Jerod. "Jerod, just sit for a minute. Let him land." He took his flute and played, *"Platform is clear. Land your roc."*

The new rider on the small roc circled down over the platform, and then turned and flew over the Scar. They could see the rider looking down over the bare spot in the forest. Then, he turned back towards the platform, and glided in. When it was just over the platform, the roc released the animal from its talons and landed gently. The rider, covered in a charcoal grey animal hide, slid from the roc onto the platform. Then, turned to the roc and patted the bird on the neck and pointed his hand up to the sky. The roc leapt into the air and flew away.

The rider turned and faced the crowd. His face was swollen from some kind of trauma. He had animal skin draped over his shoulders, and had arrows tied to his left leg. A bow was over his back and he had a crude-looking spear in his hand.

He looked at the bleachers and his eyes settled on Ella and Jerod. He smiled wide and everyone could see tears running down his face.

When he smiled, Ella's heart clenched. *Was it Caes?* She stood next to Jerod.

"Mom! Dad!", yelled Caes, as he ran across the platform and grabbed his mother in an embrace. He turned and embraced his father next. The three of them cried, and they heard cheers and applause from all over the platform.

"Caes. Caes. Where have you been?", his mom was saying.

"You wouldn't believe it, mom. It's been crazy out there", Caes said, and then he hugged her again.

They heard a girl screaming, and suddenly more arms were around him. He spun around and saw Ronni embracing him. "Caes, I thought you were dead! I can't believe you're back!" Behind her was Jatt, Jory, and Pi. All were smiling, and all had tears running down their faces.

He went from person to person, hugging everyone. Finally, he turned and saw Catscratch. The old ranger was smiling. "I knew ya had it in ya! I never thought ya was lost!", and he grabbed Caes in a hug and lifted his feet off the ground. "Now what do we do with ya?" and he laughed for a long time.

Ella took Caes' arm and tried to take Caes down to their house, but he resisted. "Are the Trials over, mom?"

"No, they're still going on. Ronni, Pi, and Jory all passed. Jatt was about to start when you showed up", she said.

Caes looked around and noticed a few of guys picking up the elk carcass and trying to get it off the platform. Catscratch pointed at the stairs and yelled, "Take that thing downstairs. Hoppy, show 'em where to take it."

"Well, we should stay and watch the rest of the students then", said Caes.

"Are you sure, Caes? Your head needs attention, and that fur you're wearing kind of stinks. And what is this claw thing hanging around your neck?"

Caes laughed. He was so happy to be back in Westvale. "I can take these off and put them somewhere. I don't want to lose them, though."

Catscratch laughed. "I 'spose there's a story around 'em. Can't wait to hear it! Here, hand 'em to me. I'll keep 'em safe."

Caes pulled the shadow cat hide over his head, and then took off the bear paw, and handed them to Scratch. He sat down on the bleachers next to his parents, and Catscratch took the hide and paw somewhere.

"The roc you were riding... Where did you get it, son?" asked Jerod.

"White Feather? He… uh… well, he was supposed to be my dinner, dad. I had a sharp stick, and well… Let me back up a minute. It was my first day out there. It was by Hidden Falls Lake, in the Crags. I was trying to find a way down off the cliff and looked down on a roc nest." Caes chuckled. "You know, I thought he was a baby great roc. I decided to jump on him with my spear and kill him. Oh man… I jumped and landed on his back, and missed with my spear. He took off flying and I held on as hard as I could. He tried to throw me off. He dove and spun and climbed and tried to bite me. And… I don't know. I finally got him to land down by the river at the bottom of the cliffs. I jumped off and ran to get away from him. After that… well… I kept seeing him, and I started talking to him and playing my flute." He took out his flute and showed his dad.

"That's a Rider's flute. Where did you get that?" asked Jerod.

"Um… I guess this is why I was taken in the first place. It was on the platform that night when I was guarding it. When it started to get light I saw it over there", and pointed his hand across the platform. "I ran over to see what it was, and when I started back, some big roc snatched me up and flew away."

"Was that your roc? White Feather, I think you called it?" asked Jerod.

"Oh no. That one was a lot bigger. It had me really hard. It knocked me out when it took me, and when I woke up, we were way up in the air and my arms were trapped in its talons."

"How'd you get away?", asked Ella.

"Uh, well, I used a Stun cantrip on it. That let me get my arms free. Then I stabbed it in the leg with my knife. It dropped me then and… I landed in the lake – Hidden Falls Lake – I mean. And then…"

Brun had walked up while Caes was talking. "Hey folks, we
need to get the Trials going again. Only a couple more students
and we'll be done. Caes, I'm happy to see you back."

"Let's sit down, mom, dad. I'll tell you the rest later."

They all sat down to watch the rest of the Trials. Brun walked
to the center of the platform and whistled to get everyone's
attention. "Well, folks, that was a bit of unexpected excitement!
Caes is home safe, and we're all thankful for that. Now let's get
back to the Trials. Our next number today is four. Jatt, come on
up and introduce yourself."

Jatt stood and walked to the center of the platform and turned
to face the audience. "Hello, my name is Jatt, and I'm from
Westvale. This is my second attempt at the Trials."

Jatt turned and looked at the three rocs remaining on the
platform. After a moment of studying them, he reached down
and took a harness from the platform and slowly walked
towards the largest roc there – a huge brown bird. He got close
to it, whispering soothing words as he got close. The bird
started to get agitated so he whispered the Calm cantrip – this
was a standard cantrip all rider students learned – and threw
the harness over the bird's head.

Fifteen minutes later, Jatt glided his roc back to the platform for
a gentle landing. As a rider came up and took the lead rope
from it, Jatt slid off the side and stood, beaming, at the audience.
Brun walked up to him and announced, "Rider Jatt,
congratulations on successfully completing the Trials! Folks,
please give our newest rider a hand of applause!"

The audience clapped. Some people whistled and cheered.

Brun held up his hand and the crowd quieted. "Rider Jatt, as you're well aware, it's time for you to select your rider name. What will it be? Don't give me any crap about not knowing what you're going to pick, either. You've been training for this for a long time!"

Jatt smiled and chuckled. "Rider Brun, I would like to be known as Jatt Tornado. If I'd failed today, I was going to throw myself into a funnel cloud if I could find one."

Brun had been taking a drink from his water skin. He coughed and spit water, and then looked at Jatt. "Did you wait for me to take a drink of water just so you could do that? Now, what's your real rider name going to be?"

Jatt was laughing. "Sorry, Brun. I couldn't resist! I would like to be known as Jatt Cirrus. Is that one okay?"

Brun smiled. "That would be perfect, Jatt. You can be Tornado if you really want it, but I think Cirrus is a great name."

"Okay, then Cirrus it is", Jatt said.

"Ladies and Gentlemen of Westvale and guests, let me be the first to introduce Jatt Cirrus, our newest rider!"

When Jatt was finished, one last student – number five – finished her Trials. She was from Red Cliff Village, and named Keri. Her flight was uneventful. When she landed, and announced her rider name, her family cheered loudly, as did the others on the platform. Her rider name was Keri Hail, which was the same as the rest of her family. Her father, Aaron, was senior rider at Red Cliff.

The Trials were over. Caes went to Jatt and congratulated him on completing the Trials. "Thanks, Caes. You know, I'm a little surprised Brun didn't ask YOU for your Rider name."

"Huh? I'm not a rider student, Jatt. I'm a ranger apprentice", responded Caes.

"I don't know, buddy. I saw you take a wild roc – a wood roc – and teach him to carry you, and you flew here and landed on the platform in the middle of the Trials. I think you're a rider now", said Jatt.

Jerod was standing behind Caes, and said, "Interesting thought, Rider Jatt. I hadn't thought of that." He scratched his short beard.

"What's an interestin' thought, Jerod?", Catscratch walked up and asked.

"Well, Jatt just said he thought Caes is a rider now. There might be something to it.", said Jerod.

"Ah bear shit! Caes is a ranger, not a rider. I was thinkin' he just 'pleted the ranger Ordeal. He spent more'n a week in the woods by himself with no help from no one and no weapons at that!", Catscratch demanded.

Caes' head was spinning. Was he done with training? What was he? A ranger or a rider?

Jerod said, "We need a meeting to discuss this, Catscratch. I'll have the rider leadership meet tomorrow in the aerie. Who do you want there from the rangers?"

"We don't need a meetin'. Caes is a ranger and that's that", Catscratch said. "I been trainin' 'im for the last two years and I ain't givin' up on 'im."

"Why don't you come to the meeting tomorrow morning, Scratch. We can think about it tonight and discuss it tomorrow", Jerod said.

"It's Catscratch to you if your gonna push me. Fine. I'll be there. I guess Bonk'll join me. I don't 'spose the other rangers are back from lookin' for Caes. If Hops is here, he can come too", said Catscratch. "Oh, and we're meetin' at Rangers Cottage not the aerie. He's a ranger student. We'll meet at a ranger buildin'."

Jerod rolled his eyes and shook his head. "Fine, Scratch. We'll meet at Rangers Cottage. I'll see you there in the morning. Are you going to the dance tonight?"

"Well, o' course I am! There's free beer an' wine ain't there?" said Catscratch. He smiled and punched Jerod in the arm, and then turned away and went down the stairs.

The dance was held at the aerie, and all the town people where there. Every time there was a Rider Trials, there was a party and dance afterwards. The whole town looked forward to it. More than a few couples had become couples at the dance over the years.

Caes walked into the courtyard of the aerie. He was clean, and wearing nice clothes. His head looked much better, thanks to some attention from Camron. He'd cleaned and closed the wound, and enchanted some sort of healing spell. In the mirror, it still looked sore, but it was no longer open. His mother had taken all his clothes and sent them to be cleaned – including his boots. He'd apparently lost a little bit of weight over the last seven or eight days, as his clothes were a little loose, but he was sure he'd put the weight back on in no time.

When he'd arrived at the dance, he was surrounded by his friends. They all wanted to know details of where he'd been and what had happened to him. Jatt, Jory, Pi, and Ronni gathered by him and peppered him with questions.

"Were you really all by yourself in the Waha?", asked Jory.

"Yeah, I was. I mean, I didn't realize it was the Waha at first. I knew I was close to the Crags and was just trying to get home", answered Caes.

"Was that really a shadow cat skin you were wearing?", asked Pi.

"Yes. I wanted to keep it after I killed the cat", said Caes. "It was trying to kill the elk I was hunting."

"How far did you drop when you escaped the roc?", asked Jatt.

"I'm not sure, Jatt. I think it was, like, maybe 40 or 50 feet. It was a long way to fall", said Caes.

"How many shadow cats did you see?", asked Jory.

"Uh… I'm not sure. Three, I think. Maybe four", said Caes.

"All you had was your knife, right? How did you kill animals?", asked Jatt.

"I had to make my own weapons, Jatt. I cut reeds, bamboo, and stuff, and found some obsidian – you know, it's the volcanic glass we find sometimes. I used rocks to chip them into arrowheads and tied them onto the arrows I made", said Caes.

"How did you know how to do all that? How did you know how to catch fish, and which plants and berries you could eat?", asked Ronni.

"Scratch - I mean Catscratch - showed me how to do it. That's
the kind of thing you learn in ranger training", answered Caes.

"I'm really glad you made it back, Caes", Ronni said. It meant
more coming from her than it did the rest of his friends.

Jatt said, "What about…", and Caes interrupted him.

"Can we talk more about it tomorrow? I'm hungry. Let's go get
some food and something to drink."

"Okay. Enough questions for tonight, huh?" said Jatt.

"Yeah, it's been a lot. I just want to enjoy being home and not
talk about what happened anymore tonight", said Caes.

"Fair 'nuff", Jatt said.

Caes laughed. "Are you trying to sound like Catscratch?"

"Maybe!", Jatt laughed.

The four friends went to the buffet line and filled their plates
with food and grabbed glasses of beer and wine and carried
them to an empty table.

The music started as the sun started dropping below the trees,
and people started moving to the dance floor. Jory grabbed Pi's
hand and whispered in her ear. She smiled and walked to the
dance floor with him. Jatt looked at them and said, "I think I'm
going to look for someone to dance with", and took off. Caes
and Ronni were alone at the table.

"Do you know where your roc is now?", asked Ronni.

"No, not really. I guess he's somewhere not too far away. But maybe he went home. I'm not really sure", said Caes.

"How did you get him to land again once you got away from him the first time?", she asked.

"Well, basically I just played my flute and called him. You know, 'White Feather. Come!", and he chuckled. "I usually followed that up with a Call Birds cantrip once I saw him in the air."

"I haven't learned that one", she said. "Would you teach me?"

"I can, but Maeve would probably do it better", answered Caes.

"Maybe I'd rather you teach me", she said.

"Oh. Okay. I can do that. Maybe tomorrow?", he asked.

"Sure. I'd like that", Ronni said.

"Um… This is kind of embarrassing, but, you know, I dreamed about you a couple times when I was out there", he pointed his finger north. "I didn't think I'd see you again. I guess you kept me motivated to keep trying to make it."

"Ah, that's sweet. Were they naughty dreams?", she said, and took his hand in her lap. Caes felt himself getting blushing, and was glad it was getting dark. "Why do you call your roc White Feather? He's not white."

"Oh, one time when he landed, he dropped a white feather on the ground when he took off again. I was planning to use it as fletching for arrows – you know the feathers on arrows – but I never got around to using it. Here, I wanted to give this to you", and he pulled a big white feather out of the inside of his shirt. "I've been carrying this with me for the past four or five days. See how white it is?" He handed the feather to her.

"Wow, it really is white. Thank you!", and she gave him a hug.

"Um… Uh… Do you want to… I don't know… Do you want to maybe dance with me?", he asked her.

"Of course I do!", she said. She stood and took his hand, dragging him to the dance floor.

The rest of the evening went great. He danced with Ronni, and spent most of the evening with her by his side, talking and holding hands.

29

Home

The morning after the dance – and Caes' return to Westvale – Caes woke early and went into the kitchen. His parents were sitting at the table, drinking coffee and eating breakfast. Ella looked up and saw Caes. "Good morning, Caes. Would you like some breakfast?"

"I'd love some!", he answered, and filled a coffee cup. Ella scooped breakfast onto a plate and handed it to him. She'd made scrambled eggs, sliced fruit, and fresh bread. It smelled fantastic! He sat down and started eating. The breakfast tasted even better than it smelled.

"I was just telling your mom I'm about to head to the meeting at Ranger Cottage in a few minutes. Is there anything you want me to keep in mind when I'm there?", his dad asked.

"What do you mean, dad? You mean like the roc and stuff?"

"I mean your career, son. I think we're going to argue about your future. Some people are arguing you're a ranger – that's Catscratch saying that. Others – like me – are saying you're a rider now. What do YOU want?"

"Um, I don't know. I didn't really consider that", Caes said. "I figured I was training to be a ranger, so that's probably what I'll be."

"Well, you trained a roc and rode him, and even landed during the Trials. Maybe that makes you a rider?", his dad said.

"Oh, yeah, that makes sense, I guess", he said.

"Let me ask you a different question, Caes. If you wanted
White Feather to come get you, do you think he'd do it?", asked
Jerod.

"Yes. He would. I'm pretty sure he would. He came whenever
I called him yesterday and before."

"How did you train him to do that? You haven't been taught
it.", asked his dad.

"Well, I use this", and he pulled the flute from his pocket. I
play his name and say 'come'. He flies over me and circles
shortly after. Then I call him again, but sometimes use a Call
Birds cantrip. He lands right in front of me then."

"Interesting. Where'd you learn that cantrip?", his dad asked.

"Maeve taught it to me one day. We practiced calling small
birds over, and they landed on my arm. I just thought I'd try it
on White Feather one day."

"I'm kind of surprised a cantrip had any effect on him, at all,
especially when he's in the air flying 50 or 60 feet above you",
said his dad.

"I don't know, dad. I was surprised too, but maybe it doesn't
really compel him to land, but just kind of, you know,
encourages him instead."

"Maybe", said Jerod. "Or, maybe you're better at magic than
you've been letting on. Okay, I'm going to head to the meeting.
Are you going to be upset if they say you're going to be a ranger
or a rider?"

"No, dad. I won't be upset. I'd like to think about it for a while,
though. Is that okay?"

"Why don't you think about it while I'm gone. We can talk when I get back." Jerod stood and patted Caes on the shoulder. "I'm glad you're home, son", and he kissed Ella and walked out the door.

Jerod walked into the Ranger Cottage. Several people were already there. Catscratch sat in a chair by the window, watching people arrive. Bonk stood in the corner. Hops stood next to him, talking quietly in Bonk's ear. Brun was in the kitchen, pouring some coffee. He looked at Jerod and held his cup up. Jerod nodded at him and said, "Sure, Brun. I'd love a cup."

He walked over to Catscratch. "How are you doing, old friend?"

"Morn'n Jerod", said Catscratch.

Brun walked over and handed a cup of coffee to Jerod. "Thanks, Brun", Jerod told him.

"How are you today, Jerod? Hung over?", Brun asked.

"Heh, no", Jerod chuckled. "I left that habit behind a long time ago. Now I focus on moderation."

"Well, I haven't learned that yet. My head is a tad bit sore today."

"Yeah, well, stop trying to keep up with the young riders. You're an old man now, you know", said Jerod.

The door opened and Tuck walked in with Ronni beside him. That surprised Jerod. This was a leadership meeting, for the most part. Everyone except Hops was in a leadership role.

Jerod waved his hand at them and said, "Good morning Tuck, Ronni. Is anyone else coming?"

"I don't think so, boss", answered Tuck. "I think this is it."

"Okay. Catscratch, this is your house. Do you want to get things started?", said Jerod.

"Yup. I'll do that", and Catscratch stood up to address the room. "Riders, rangers, welcome. We're here to talk 'bout Caes and what to do 'bout 'im. You all's seen 'im when he got back last night, right?"

There were mumblings of agreement and heads nodding. "'kay. How's I see it is young Caes 'complished the Ordeal this week. Unofficially-like, ya know. I means we dint take 'im out and drop 'im somewhere, but a wild roc did it for us, ya know.

"So, I think we otta call 'im a ranger and give 'im a name t'day. I mean, he kilt a shadow cat. He kilt a bear – didja see that big ole paw on 'is chest? Anyways, he s'vived in the wild without a soul helpin' 'im. He even hadta make 'is own bow and arrows. I'm real impressed, misself. I don't know many could do the same. I guess that's what I gotta say 'bout it. Rangers, whatcha think?"

Hops and Bonk nodded. "I agree, Catscratch", Bonk answered. "He did more than I think any ranger student has for as long as I can remember."

"I say yes, also", said Hops. "I mean, I'm not a leader or nothing, but since I'm here, I think I have a say, right? I'd be proud to call Caes a ranger."

"Thanks, boys. Riders, what say you?", asked Catscratch.

"Well, I'll go first", said Brun. "As I see it, Caes jumped on a wild roc and broke it. He spent not just ten or fifteen minutes on it, but rode him off and on over several days. When he was on the ground, he played a Rider's Flute and called the roc, and the roc responded and landed. Caes climbed on the bird and rode him for over a hundred miles. That's more than we ask the students during Trials. I say we name him a rider and get it over with. Damn, man, it wasn't even a great roc. It was a wild woody. Who do you know that's ever broken one of those? Name him a rider."

Jerod nodded and looked at Tuck. "Tuck, what do you think?" Tuck answered, "Caes is a rider, whether we call him one or not. Even if you say he's a ranger, there's nothing to stop him from climbing up on the platform and calling his bird. If the roc lands and Caes climbs on, then what? He's a rider even if we don't call him one. So, I guess what I'm trying to say is make it official."

"Okay", said Jerod. "I think the riders all feel the same way, Catscratch. How do we resolve this?"

"Well...", started Catscratch, and he was interrupted by Ronni.

"I have something to say before you all make your decision", she said.

"Oh, sorry", said Jerod. "I didn't mean to exclude you. Go ahead."

"Thank you, Jerod." She cleared her throat. "I'm not used to talking to the leadership, but I know Caes pretty good and I talked to him all evening at the dance. I have an idea for you to think about.

"I agree with you, Jerod, and with Brun and Tuck. Caes should be a rider. But, at the same time, I agree with you, Catscratch. And you, Hops and Bonk. This idea is unconventional, but I think it works.

"I think we ought to, as a group – rangers and riders alike – call Caes a rider ranger. Or a ranger rider. I don't think it matters what we call it. Maybe we give him a different title, altogether. If you think about it, he did the final test of both careers at the same time. He survived in the forest for a week – more than a week, actually – and he broke and rode a wild roc while he was out there.

"Catscratch, you ought to be very proud. Caes never would have survived without all you taught him. I don't think it would be right to not call him a ranger. It would be unfair to him, and it would be unfair to you after all you did to teach him.

"Jerod and Brun, Caes spent his whole life, up until now, watching you two, and learning as if he was in your classes. Um… I think I'm done. What do you all think of this idea?"

Catscratch was smiling. "Girl, I'd be mighty pleased if ya'd call me Scratch. All my friends call me that!"

Jerod was laughing, as was everyone else in the room. "I think I can probably speak for my riders in agreeing with you, Ronni. Tuck, Brun, any disagreement from you two?"

Both riders muttered "no", and were smiling.

Jerod continued, "Bonk? Tuck? What do you rangers think of Ronni's proposal?"

Brun said, "Oh hell yeah, I like that idea."

Tuck said, "Yes, Jerod. I think the riders all agree with the idea."

"Okay", said Jerod. "I don't know why I didn't think of that idea last night. It's a great idea. Do we need to vote on this?"

Catscratch said, "Why don'cha just ask if anyone disagrees. No one will, and I'll bash anyone's head who does, but we should make it 'ficial. Once y'all vote, we can d'cide how to tell the young man."

"Sounds good", said Jerod. "Does anyone here disagree with naming Caes a rider/ranger or ranger/rider? We can come up with a formal title later. Who doesn't want to name him as both a rider and a ranger?"

No one said a word, and no hands were raised.

"Okay, then it's official. The leadership councils of the riders and rangers have unanimously named Caes Wind a rider and a ranger. Catscratch, what now?"

Catscratch smiled. "Well, now we hafta have another party. We gotta give 'im a ranger name, and we gotta eat the elk our new ranger brought us!"

The whole room clapped and laughed.

"Alright, meeting adjourned", Jerod said. "Catscratch, you and I need to stay and talk about how the party is going to go. Do we do it tonight or tomorrow?"

"Well, we gotta do it t'night. It's tradition. I'll have the rangers prepare the elk. Can we use the courtyard at the aerie again?", asked Catscratch.

"We can, my friend. Brun, would you go make arrangements for that?", Jerod said.

"I'm on it, Jerod", answered Brun.

Word was passed throughout Westvale that morning and into the afternoon. There was to be a town meeting at the aerie in the courtyard. Everyone was invited, but all rangers and riders were expected to attend, if possible. The meeting would be held early evening, and dinner would be served afterwards.

Caes and his friends were sitting in the secret hideout he shared with his friends. It was mid-morning. They'd been hanging out since just after breakfast.

"What's going on this evening, Caes? Someone came to the aerie this morning and told us all we had to be there for a big meeting this evening, like before dinner", Jory said.

Caes answered, "I don't have any idea. Mom and dad told me the same thing. They said everyone has to be there this evening. I asked them what it was about, but they said I have to wait and hear just like everyone else."

Ronni was sitting right next to him, and had a hand tickling his back. "Oh look, a cat!", she said. A small black cat was walking along a tree limb towards them. That was odd. Not many people in Westvale kept pets. Their life expectancy wasn't long here, especially if they got loose and made it to the ground.

"I haven't ever seen a cat here", said Jatt. "Come here, kitty!"

The cat ignored him and continued along the tree branch. It stepped on Ronni's lap and looked at her. She petted it for a minute, and then the cat continued over to Caes and laid on his lap, purring. He looked at his friends and laughed. "Okay, I think the cat likes me!", and he started petting the cat. "I wonder who it belongs to?"

Pi asked, "So you really don't have any idea what's happening tonight?"

"No, Pi, I don't. My parents didn't tell me anything at all. Just that it's some kind of village meeting. Everyone is invited, but all rangers and riders are expected to attend", said Caes.

"That's weird", said Jory. "I don't remember anything happening like this since the big storm a few years ago. Do you think another storm is coming?"

"The sky looks good to me. I think it's something else, but I don't know", said Caes.

"So, Caes", Pi said, "Ronni said you used a cantrip – Call Birds – when you were in the Waha. And, she said you were going to teach it to her."

Caes looked at Ronni. It bugged him that she'd shared that with Pi – but then, Pi was her best friend. Still, it bugged him.

"Yes, I did use that cantrip", he said. "Why?"

"Well, did you use any other ones? It sounds like Call Birds was really helpful. Did any other ones help a lot?", Pi asked.

"Um… Let's see. Yes. Another one was interesting. I only used it once or twice, but it helped me a lot. It was called Animal Smell. It was strange! When I cast it, I tried to smell like a squirrel, and I could all of a sudden smell so much clearer than normal. I actually smelled… I don't know… I guess I have to say I smelled danger. Once I realized something was dangerous, I was able to avoid it. It was a shadow cat up ahead, and I climbed a tree to get away from it."

"Animal Smell? I've never heard of that one. How hard was it to cast?", Pi asked.

"It wasn't hard, but Maeve told me it was a brown spell, I mean cantrip. Do you have brown gifts, Pi?", asked Caes.

"That's what I was told. Do you think you could teach us how to use some of the cantrips you learned?", she asked.

"It would be better to get Maeve to teach you. I barely know what I'm doing. If she doesn't want to teach you, I'd be happy to try, though. I'm just not that good at magic, though", said Caes.

"I think most riders take it for granted that their job is to ride, you know", said Jory. "They don't think about trying to learn more magic. I think one of the reasons you survived in the Waha was because you knew more magic than most people. I think the rest of the riders should try to learn more. What do you think, Caes?"

"Maybe...", said Caes. "I think the older someone gets, and the more they get comfortable in their job, the less they think about making themselves better. If any of you get in a leadership position, you should make people learn more all the time. I mean, not just their job, but like, other things. You know... like magic and stuff. Or... I don't know... I learned a lot about what plants are safe to eat from Catscratch. Why doesn't everyone learn that kind of stuff? Or, like, how to shoot a bow and arrow. Rangers know that, but most riders never learn it because they don't need to. But, if everything goes wrong, you know, like if you get dropped into the Crags all by yourself, you'll die if you don't know how to find food and water. And... I'm rambling. I'm sorry."

"Don't apologize, Caes", said Ronni. "All of that makes sense!"

"Well, maybe this new generation of riders will make all other riders learn survival skills", said Caes.

"I think that's a great idea", said Pi.

The cat stood up on Caes' lap and walked over to a branch, and sat down again.

"If I make into leadership, Caes, I promise I'll make the riders learn survival skills", said Ronni.

He took her hand and held it. "Thank you, Ronni. I'm sure you will – both things – I'm sure you'll make it into leadership, and I'm sure you'll make the riders learn new things."

Jatt smiled. "So are you two, like, a couple now?"

"What? No... I mean... uh... I... uh...", stammered Caes.

"I think he's trying to say 'yes'", said Ronni. She smiled and leaned over and gave Caes a little kiss. "I think Caes is embarrassed. Look at him blushing!"

"Um... I... Well, yes. I guess we're a couple". He smiled broadly, and squeezed Ronni's hand.

"He doesn't know it yet, but I think we'll probably get married in the next year or two", said Ronni.

"Ronni!", Caes exclaimed.

All of the friends laughed.

"You are all good friends, aren't you?", said a strange female voice. Sitting where the cat had been was a pretty young lady with blonde hair.

"Who are you?!", said Caes. "How'd you get here?"

"Hi Caes. I'm Bay. I was sitting with your mother last night", she said.

"Hi Bay. How'd you get here without us seeing you? How'd you know where we were? How did you get past me? You couldn't get to where you are without stepping over me?", said Caes.

"I've been here for quite a while, Caes. Like I said, my name is Bay. I'm a mage, and I shape shift. Usually, I take the shape of a cat. Thank you for petting me. It was very nice."

"That was you?!", asked Caes. He was feeling a bit panicky. He'd been touching her!

"That was me, Caes. Are you going to faint on me or anything?
I'm not a healer, you know. If you fall out of the tree, you'll
probably die. I wanted to talk to you, and I wanted to learn
what you're like. I've never heard of someone taming – or
breaking – a wood roc before. When I heard you'd used Call
Birds and actually reached a roc with it, I began wondering if
you have stronger gifts or talents than Maeve was able to detect.
Maybe tomorrow – after tonight's activities – you and I can talk
for a while. I'd like to test you to see if you have more than just
gifts. I kind of suspect you have talents instead. Maybe even
more than that."

"Do you know what's happening tonight, Bay?", asked Caes.

"Of course I do. People talk freely around cats. You'd be
surprised what I learn regularly just by walking around", said
Bay.

"Well, what is it?", asked Caes.

"I'm not going to tell you that. You'll have to learn with
everyone else – well, except me, of course. I already know."
She seemed smug, kind of like a cat.

"Okay, yeah, I can meet with you tomorrow. Where can I find
you?", asked Caes.

"I'll be at your house. Just sit somewhere. It can be here or
anywhere else. I'll come find you and sit next to you", said Bay.

"Okay. I'll see you tomorrow then?", said Caes. He was feeling
uncomfortable with this.

"I'll see you tomorrow." She stood up and grabbed a branch
above her head, and stepped over his legs to get back to the
walkway. A minute later and she was gone.

"That was weird", said Jory.

"No kidding", said Jatt.

Caes walked up the stairs to the aerie with his mother and Ronni. His father was already at the aerie, preparing for the meeting.

People were filling the courtyard. He saw rangers, riders, and many of the other people from the village. He even saw some people from Red Cliff Village, which was about an hour's walk from Westvale. Chairs and benches were sitting around in a semi-circular shape, and people were taking their places in or around them. They saw Jory carrying a serving plate full of fruit into a side building and ran over to him.

"Hey Jory, do you know what's going on?", Caes asked.

"Just a minute. Let me set this thing down", Jory responded. He walked into a room and set the plate down on a table that was getting full as more riders came in carrying more food.

"So, what's going on?", Caes asked again.

"I don't know any more than you do, Caes. Your dad and Catscratch put out the word that there's a meeting. That's all anyone knows. I guess it's going to start in a few minutes. There's dinner after, and Brun's got us all putting the food out."

"Okay. I guess we'll go sit down and wait for the meeting." Caes and Ronni went back into the courtyard and took seats near where Ella was sitting.

Fifteen minutes later, Jerod walked into the courtyard with Catscratch. They both stood in the center of the semi-circle of chairs and looked around at the crowd. Brun walked over to them. "You ready to get this thing started, Jerod?", Brun asked. "I think everyone's here. You want to grab their attention?", Jerod asked.

Brun whistled and waved his arm around. "Listen up everyone!", Brun shouted. Maeve got out of her seat and walked over.

"Are you ready for me to give you more volume?" she asked.

"Yes, please, Maeve", said Jerod.

Maeve cast a volume spell on Jerod and Catscratch and then went back to take her seat.

"Can you all hear me?", Jerod asked. His voice boomed throughout the courtyard.

"We hear you, Jerod", said several people in the audience.

"Okay, good. Thank you for that spell, Maeve." Jerod said. "It seems like just yesterday, we were together on the platform – many of us anyway. You witnessed some of our rider students pass the Trials, and while you were there, you saw my missing son, Caes, make his way back home on the backs of a wood roc. That was shocking, because wood rocs are very difficult to tame and ride. In fact, the riders stopped trying to tame them generations ago. They're just too difficult to work with.

"We often try to breed a wood roc with a blood line of great roc. That combination produces very good, spirited, rocs that are great to ride – even if they are a bit more work to train.

"Anyway, the reason we called this meeting is to talk about Caes and announce his role in our community from this day on. Catscratch, as you all know, is the leader of our rangers in Westvale. Standing beside him is Jumper. For any of you who don't know Jumper, he's Catscratch's counterpart in Red Cliff. He runs the rangers there. Catscratch and Jumper, do you want to talk about what we're doing?"

"Hi folks!", Jumper yelled, and he waved at the crowd. "Yup, Jerod. Thanks!", Catscratch's voice boomed into the crowd. "Well, we all been talkin' since Caes come home. Ya know, he threw us for a loop when 'e came in on a roc, bein' a ranger student and all. I guess Ridin' is in 'is blood, ya know. Makes sense with 'is dad and such." The crowd laughed.

Catscratch continued, "So we had ta get creative with Caes. He was a good 'prentice. I've taught a good number of rangers o'er the years. Caes is a fast learner. He soaks in the knowledge. Anyways, ya'll know 'bout the Ranger Ordeal. When a ranger 'prentice is good 'nough, we take 'im out in the woods and leave 'im 'lone, ya know. He gets a knife and a bow and arrows. If he don't want the bow 'e can have a spear. In the Ordeal, the 'prentice has ta s'vive for a week by himself. He has ta feed hisself and stay 'live. And at the end of the week, 'e gotta kill a game animal and bring it back here to feed the village.

"Now that kinda sounds like what Caes done, ain't it? He came back lookin' kinda strange. The Ordeal does that to a ranger. Caes was wearin' a shadow cat skin. That's cuz Caes killed a shadow cat. He had a bear claw – a big-ass bear claw – hangin' on 'is neck. That's cuz Caes killed a big-ass bear. And 'e done it all with no weapons. All 'e had was 'is knife. He made 'is own bow and arrow and spear." He paused and looked at Jumper. "With that, we rangers of Westvale and Red Cliff 'ave d'cided Caes finished the Ordeal and is 'titled to be called a ranger."

The crowd started clapping.

"Now jus' wait a minute. I ain't done yet", Catscratch said. "Like Jerod said, this is a special situation. Jerod, ya wanna say more?"

"Thanks, Catscratch", said Jerod. "So, we know Caes is entitled to be called a ranger now. That's great, but… and this is where this is going to get weird for you all. The riders have a test too, as you all know. A rider student has to break a roc during the Trials, and take the roc through a series of maneuvers given to him or her, and then land safely again on the platform. Caes broke a roc – a wood roc at that – and rode the bird over 100 miles from the Waha to here. The riders have decided that Caes has successfully completed the Trials and is entitled to be called a rider.

"So, for the first time in our history, we have a new rider ranger. Caes, please come up here and face the audience."

Caes felt shocked. He stood up and walked to his dad – standing in between his dad and Catscratch. It felt unreal. He was just trying to survive and get home yesterday and the last week or so.

"Maeve, would you please come back up here and cast your volume spell on Brun also? I'd like to have him speak", Jerod said.

She got out of her seat and walked up to Brun. A minute later, she waved at the crowd, smiled, and returned to her seat.

"Thank you, Maeve", Brun's voice boomed. "You all know me here. I'm the main teacher of new riders. Caes, new riders have the choice of a rider name. In your case, you already have one. Do you want to continue to use Wind, or is there a different name you'd like to have?"

"Uh, this is a surprise to me, Brun. I've always been a Wind and I want to keep that name if I can", Caes said.

"Good! I was hoping you were going to say that", Brun said. "Catscratch? You want to take over?"

"Yup! Caes, we 'sign new rangers a ranger name. You gave us a lotta stuff ta go on. Shadow cat skin 'round your shoulders anna bear paw 'round yer neck. So we 'cided your new ranger name is Bearpaw. From this day on rangers will know ya as Bearpaw. Got it?"

"Okay, yeah, I get it – I think. I'm still kind of confused Catscratch", Caes said.

"I figgered you was. Caes 'Bearpaw' Wind is your new name. Yer a ranger rider now. Ya gotta special name."

Jerod called out, "Caes Bearpaw Wind, do you accept your new role as rider ranger?"

"Yes! I do accept it. Thank you!", Caes said. He had a huge smile on his face, and he hugged his father, and then gave a bearhug to Catscratch.

"Easy, Bearpaw! I'm an ole man. Ya gonna break my ribs!", Catscratch laughed.

Ronni and Ella joined them. Ella gave Caes a hug, and then Ronni embraced him and gave him a kiss on the lips. The whole crowd laughed and cheered.

When the noise quieted a bit, Brun whistled again, and the
crowd quieted. "Alright you all. Caes brought us a big elk
yesterday. It's all cooked and ready to eat. We also have
venison and boar, and a shitload of fruit and vegetables and
bread and things. We have wine and beer. We're going to
party tonight. If you didn't have a hangover this morning, I
expect you to have one tomorrow! Let's eat and drink and
party to celebrate our newest rider ranger!"

The End (for now)

Names and People of the Cragwoods

You have surely noticed some of the ways people are named in the Cragwoods. Two of the most exciting occupations are the people who ride rocs (Riders) and the rangers.

Everyone is given a first name at birth, and these are almost always chosen by the parents. For most people, the surname is also given at birth and is the surname of the parents. As time goes by, and the person leaves adolescence and becomes an adult, their surname often changes according to the career field they've chosen or had chosen for them. For example, if John Doe becomes a blacksmith, he usually becomes known as John Smith. If John Smith has children, those children also have Smith as a surname until such time as they take a different career, or are married and assume their spouse's surname.

Riders are allowed to choose a surname when they successfully complete the Riders Trials. At this point, they normally choose a name associated with weather, air, or something along that line. Short names tend to already be taken, and so a new Rider may have to come up with a longer name or even a combination name. If a new Rider comes from a family of Riders, he or she will typically keep their family name. For example, Jerod Wind's parents and grandparents were all Riders. They had already selected Wind as their surname. All children of their family can also use the same name. If a family ceases to have Riders in it, all members of the family revert to their original surname.

Rangers have their own naming tradition that occurs after successful completion of the Ranger Ordeal. When a ranger apprentice returns from the Ordeal, they are given a name by the other rangers present, and always with their ranger master having final word on their new name. This name can be almost anything. Some of the names poke fun at the ranger for their personality. Some are related to something that happened during the Ordeal. Either way, when the new name is given, that is the ranger's full name for the rest of their lives. Catscratch was born as Jon Walker. During the Ordeal, he tangled with a mountain lion and received a big scar on his face afterwards. His ranger master named him Catscratch, and he's had that name ever since.

Caes Wind - Pronounced like "kay ess". Son of Jerod and Ella Wind, of Westvale. Brown talents.

Crislan Wind – Son of Jerod and Ella Wind. Green and brown gifts.

Jerod Wind – Senior Rider of Westvale.

Ella Wind – Wife of Jerod. Gardener and tree tender. Talented in green magic.

Jatt – Best friend of Crislan, and later good friend of Caes. Rider student.

Jory – Best friend of Caes. Rider student.

Brun Updraft – Rider from Westvale. Second to Jerod in seniority.

Catscratch "Scratch" – Ranger from Westvale. Originally from Northridge. Caes' ranger teacher.

Pienna "Pi" Halvorson – Daughter of Ryan and Melony Halvorson, of Roc Harbor. Rider student.

Ryan Halvorson – Mayor of Roc Harbor.

Melony Halvorson – Ryan's wife, of Roc Harbor.

Saffron "Ronni" Seller – Best friend of Pienna Halvorson. Rider student.

Hops – Ranger from Westvale. Formerly known as Ben. Friend of Caes.

Corwin Stormcloud – Leatherworker and store owner in Roc Harbor. Former Rider and good friend of Jerod Wind.

Maeve – Red adept (magician), of Westvale. Also talented in brown magic.

Camron – White adept (healer), of Westvale.

Antony – White adept (healer), of Sea View Village.

Bonk – (M) Ranger from Westvale.

Lucky – (F) Ranger from Westvale.

Evvik – (M) Household manager for Ryan Halvorson. From Roc Harbor.

Random – Tavern owner in Roc Harbor. Retired ranger from Westvale and good friend of Jerod Wind.

Jordyn Redsky – (F) Rider from Westvale.

Rylee – Brown adept (magician) from Sea View Village.

Jack – Trader.

Ash – (F) Trader.

Bay – Purple mage from Roc Harbor. Shape shifter with ability to take form of a cat.

Pepper – Trader.

Doug – Trader.

Fang – (M) Ranger.

Chucker – (M) Ranger.

Masen – Construction worker from Westvale.

Tuck – Rider from Westvale.

Grayce – Rider from Westvale.

Ember – Rider from Westvale.

Bo - Rider from Westvale.

Zoe – Brown mage from Daener City.

Chrystin – Brown apprentice studying under Zoe.

Lee – Wagoneer in Daener City. Originally from Northridge.

Jumper – Ranger from Red Cliff Village.

Quain – Yellow adept (Tinker) from Roc Harbor.

Shon – Great Roc from Westvale.

Tosh – Great Roc from Westvale.

White Feather – Wood Roc from Westvale.